"The man's an amnesiac!"

Andi's sister looked at her in horror. "What if he suddenly remembers he's a serial killer? How can we let our great-aunt travel alone with him?"

Andi chuckled. She was no great judge of men—as her choice of boyfriends over the years had proven— but she'd bet anything that Harley Forester was a decent human being with a past no more nefarious than Andi's...or her sister's.

"Well, it wasn't my idea to have Harley drive Ida Jane home, but it's a done deal. They'll be here any minute." Unable to resist teasing her sister, Andi added, "Unless he's dissecting her body as we speak."

Andi was still smiling when she entered the kitchen. She tried to shake off her sense of anticipation at the thought of seeing Harley Forester, as he called himself. A man who—while probably not a murderer—was definitely no cowboy.

He was an enigmatic stranger playing at being a ranch hand, when anyone could tell he knew nothing about the business. Andi's attraction to him was just a silly diversion.

"I need to get out more," she muttered as she dashed to the p̶o̶r̶c̶h̶. S̶h̶e̶ d̶i̶d̶n̶'t̶ w̶a̶n̶t̶ t̶o̶ m̶i̶s̶s̶ her chance to watch H̶

He mig̶h̶t̶ ooked good in Wran̶

Dear Reader,

The idea of a trilogy based on three sisters appealed to me on many levels, but largely because I have two sisters. And, like the Sullivan sisters, my siblings and I are as different as sisters can be. Yet, like the triplets, we love each other and our family wholeheartedly.

This book is Andi's story. Andi was the most difficult of the three heroines to pin down. Outwardly she was the most self-sufficient, but inwardly the most fragile. As a child, she searched for the perfect man to fill the role of father for her and her siblings. As an adult, she joined the marines to broaden her search, but when called home, she gives up that quest to take on another—saving her great-aunt's business and protecting her town from the threat of change. And though her life is jam-packed, she can't resist the opportunity to help a stranger without a past. Harley— or should I say Jonathan—is full of complexities as well. Leave it to Andi to fall in love with one man when he's really another. I hope you enjoy her story!

And for those of you who've come to expect a dog in my books, I hope you'll like Sarge—a hound with the wisdom and patience to help my hero heal a gaping hole in his heart.

Your correspondence is always welcome. Write to me at P.O. Box 322, Cathey's Valley, CA 95306 or contact me through my Web site at www.debrasalonen.com. Also, I drop in often at the "Let's Talk Superromance" bulletin board at eHarlequin.com. Come by and say hello.

Debra

Books by Debra Salonen

HARLEQUIN SUPERROMANCE

986—BACK IN KANSAS
1003—SOMETHING ABOUT EVE
1061—WONDERS NEVER CEASE
1098—MY HUSBAND, MY BABIES

And coming next month:
1110—THE COMEBACK GIRL

Without a Past
Debra Salonen

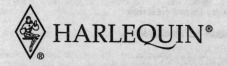

TORONTO • NEW YORK • LONDON
AMSTERDAM • PARIS • SYDNEY • HAMBURG
STOCKHOLM • ATHENS • TOKYO • MILAN • MADRID
PRAGUE • WARSAW • BUDAPEST • AUCKLAND

ISBN 0-373-71104-2

WITHOUT A PAST

This edition published by arrangement with Harlequin Books S.A.

® and TM are trademarks of the publisher. Trademarks indicated with
® are registered in the United States Patent and Trademark Office, the
Canadian Trade Marks Office and in other countries.

Visit us at www.eHarlequin.com

Printed in U.S.A.

To my sisters in life: Jan O'Brien and Jeanne Harming.
And to my sisters in writing: Alisa, Jen, Sus, Mel, Anna and Ro.

CHAPTER ONE

ANDREA SULLIVAN HOISTED herself to the top plank of the roofing contractor's scaffolding and looked around. Heights didn't bother her, but she hated the slight tremble in her biceps after the minuscule workout.

"Deskitus flabosis," she muttered, bending over to touch her toes. Her calves—exposed by the black crop pants she wore—quivered from the climb. Scaling what amounted to a three-story-tall ladder shouldn't pose a problem for a former marine.

She let out a long hiss of disgust and shook her head. The upside-down perspective made her a little dizzy. Slowly returning to an upright position, she moved closer to the roof to see for herself just how bad it was.

Using the toe of her running shoe, she nudged the blunt edge of a moss-covered shake. The thing practically disintegrated. The up-close inspection also revealed a buildup of petrified acorns beneath certain shingles—deposits left by generations of woodpeckers planning for that rainy day.

Andi grimly scanned the length of the roof. The fascia around the building's tower was as pockmarked as some of the road signs in the county. In this case, a product of red-headed birds not kids with birdshot in their guns.

"Your aunt should have replaced the roof ten years ago." Bart McCloskey, Gold Creek's only roofing contractor, had delivered the bad news yesterday. "I told my mother to warn Ida Jane. But once those garden club ladies get together, all they do is gossip.''

Bart's mother, Linda McCloskey, was a retired nurse who never hesitated to remind Andi and her sisters about the role she'd played in their births. Andrea, Jennifer and Kristin Sullivan had come into the world twenty-nine years ago on the heels of tragedy. Their parents' Volkswagen bus went off the road in a snowstorm, and only through the courageous efforts of the Gold Creek rescue team and hospital staff were the triplets saved. Since neither of their parents survived the ordeal, the triplets became the wards of their great-aunt Ida Jane Montgomery, a fifty-three-year-old spinster and town icon. Residents of Gold Creek pitched in to help raise the triplets, and many were still inclined to give the girls motherly or fatherly guidance at will.

Especially generous with unsolicited advice were the ladies of the Gold Creek Garden Club. Bart's mother was the current president.

Ida Jane Montgomery was still a member, although her attendance had dropped off since her broken hip and convalescence at the Rocking M ranch. But Ida was scheduled to return home to what was fondly—or not so fondly in some cases—referred to as the old bordello. A two-story, turn-of-the-century, poor-man's Victorian, the modern white elephant had once been the town's house of ill repute.

By the time Ida's father bought the building, which sat on a quarter-acre lot near what was then the edge of town, the ladies of the evening were long gone. The house had been converted to a boardinghouse for a few years then had sat empty until Ida Jane's father—Andi's grandfather—restored it to a residence. He'd filled the front parlors with the furniture his wife had inherited. Ida Jane had capitalized on her family's pack-rat tendencies and had opened the Old Bordello Antique Shop fifty-five years ago.

At one time a successful endeavor, the shop had fallen on hard times. Andi was still trying to figure out what had happened.

Andi had fond memories of the old place, but she'd left Gold Creek to join the marines after two years of junior college. She'd had no intention of making a life for herself in the small town located in the heart of the Gold Rush corridor.

But Jenny, the oldest of the triplets and an accomplished arm-twister, had had something else in mind. "When your hitch is up, would it kill you to come home for a few months? Ida Jane would do it for you."

Jenny knew just how to work the guilt angle.

"We both need you, Andi," Jenny had begged a year and a half ago, when Andi had returned home for Thanksgiving. "Ida Jane won't consider selling out, and I simply don't have the time or energy to help her. And in nine months, I'll have the baby to consider."

Andi had vacillated until a sonogram showed two babies, then not long after that, Jenny's husband, Josh, started having health problems.

By the time Andi completed her discharge from the marines, Josh had discovered that what he thought was a lingering bout of allergies was something much more serious. Cancer.

Sadly, her brother-in-law had passed away last August, mere hours after Jenny gave birth to Tucker and Lara. Even seven months later, on a bright spring morning like this, Andi felt a pang of sadness for her family's loss.

But life went on. The twins were growing like weeds, and Jenny would soon wed Josh's brother, Sam, in what some people were calling a marriage of convenience. Andi knew otherwise.

Sam and Jenny loved each other. And the twins—while

conceived in spirit by Josh—were actually Sam's geneti-
cally. Josh's childhood bout with cancer had left him sterile,
and Josh had asked Sam to donate his sperm. Tucker and
Lara were not only miracles of science, but also true gifts
of the heart.

And while her sister had agonized over her speedy second
marriage, Andi knew that Josh was undoubtedly smiling
down on them.

The portable phone that she'd clipped to the waistband
of her pants chirped like a strangled bird. Andi hooked one
knee over the cross-support rail and balanced her butt cheek
on the sun-warmed metal. Flab there, too, she thought.

"Yeah," she snarled.

"Oh, that's a pleasant greeting," her sister complained.
"What happened to, 'Good morning, the Old Bordello Antique Shop and Coffee Parlor?'"

"I reserve that for customers."

"I could have been a customer," Jenny argued.

Andi looked toward Main Street. Only three cars traveled
the thoroughfare. Sunday mornings were slow and peaceful.
That was why, historically, Ida Jane had never opened the
shop before one o'clock on Sundays. When the triplets were
little, she'd dress them up in matching outfits and take them
to the Methodist church for Sunday school, and then the
four of them would walk to the Golden Corral for brunch.

"I know your ring. It's bossy. Like you."

Her sister made a huffing sound. "That's not true. You
and Kristin always claimed I was bossy, but somebody had
to keep you two flakes in line."

"Flakes?" Andi cleared her throat. "Kris was the
dreamer, not me. Ask anybody. Ask Gloria. In fact, I'll have
you know I received an almost-favorable mention in her
"Glory's World" column last week. Did you see it?"

Jenny's hoot of amusement produced a funny twinge in

Andi's chest. After all the grief and pain Jenny, Josh and Sam had suffered, it was good to hear her sister laugh. "What planet are you living on? I happen to have the *Ledger* right here. Should I read it aloud in case those years in the military compromised your ability to interpret a slam?"

Andi rubbed her knuckle against the sudden pain in the center of her forehead. "No, that's okay—"

But her sister plunged ahead, "'In other news, or should I say *old* news, Ida Jane Montgomery's great-niece Andrea is at it again. It's been four months since she introduced her ambitious espresso bar, and while some locals seem to find it as addictive as Starbucks, the tourist trade seems to have forgotten that the old bordello exists.'"

Andi made a face. She didn't know how the bigmouthed gossip hit the nail on the head every time, but Gloria Harrison Hughes was more observant than Andi would have guessed.

Jenny went on. "She also says that a face-lift at the bordello's age is like removing a section of barnacles from the *Titanic*. Why bother?"

"And we thought she didn't have a sense of humor," Andi said dryly.

The Sullivan triplets' war of wills with the acid-tongued Gold Creek *Ledger* gossip columnist had begun in 1991— the year Andi, Jenny and Kristin turned eighteen. Gloria's son, Tyler, was a classmate. Unfortunately, he was part of an ugly scandal involving Kristin and her old boyfriend, Donnie Grimaldo. As a result Tyler had dropped out of school and left town. Gloria held the triplets responsible, and the girls had paid the price in bad press ever since.

Andi turned her chin to locate the roof of the *Ledger's* office a few blocks away on Second Street. Two overgrown bushes bearing early-spring plumage bracketed the building's entrance. "So, why'd you call? I told you I wasn't doing brunch this morning."

Ever since Jenny and Sam had announced their engagement at Christmas, Andi and, occasionally, Kristin, who lived in Oregon but came to visit at least twice a month, would get together on Sunday morning to catch up on the week's business and plan the wedding. The nuptials were scheduled to coincide with the annual St. Patrick's Day celebration this coming Saturday. Although Andi knew Jenny could use her help this morning, she'd needed the time to prepare, mentally and physically, for Ida Jane's return.

Their beloved aunt had served notice of her intention to move home. "I'm going back to the bordello once you get married," she'd informed them months earlier. "A newly married couple doesn't need an old woman hanging around. Besides, now that I'm up and around, Andi can use my help."

That would have been the truth ten years ago, Andi thought. But Ida Jane had changed recently. Almost anything—especially anything Andi said—could send Ida Jane on an emotional roller-coaster ride. Gaps in memory, sudden bursts of anger and bouts of depression were new and unwelcome aspects of their aunt's personality.

"All part of the aging process," Ida's doctor insisted.

And Ida had shown improvement while living with Jenny, but Andi wasn't Jenny. Jenny was patient, understanding. She could bite her tongue or look the other way when Ida said something outrageous. Andi tried, but much as she loved her great-aunt, she wasn't looking forward to Ida's homecoming.

"I didn't call about brunch. Or the wedding," Jenny said, pulling Andi back into the present. "Actually…"

Her sister was obviously stalling.

"Just tell me." Andi felt off balance. She gripped the

rusty metal. Its heat reminded her that she had to make a decision about the roof soon. *Maybe I could borrow on my insurance.*

"Ida Jane's coming home," Jenny said.

"Yeah, I know. Next Sunday."

"Today."

"What!" Andi's stomach almost ejected the orange juice she'd chugged for breakfast. "No, Jen. Not today."

"I'm afraid so."

"Who's bringing her?" Their aunt no longer drove, and Jenny wouldn't have been talking this freely if Ida were in the car with her. Just to reassure herself, Andi stood on tiptoe to check on Rosemarie, Ida's 1972 pink Cadillac. In the parking lot. Right where Andi had left it. The triplets had convinced Ida Jane that she'd arrived at a time in her life when she deserved to be chauffeured from place to place rather than risk life and limb behind the wheel.

"She got a ride," Jenny said. "She arranged it herself. When the twins and I came downstairs for breakfast, we found her bed stripped, bags packed and Harley Forester waiting to carry her stuff to the truck."

Andi let out a small squawk—partly because of her aunt's premature move and partly because the name Harley brought to mind the image of a lanky, too-handsome-for-his-own-good cowboy, who was, in Andi's opinion, absolutely, positively *not* a cowboy.

She forced her mind away from the memory of his trim behind in faded jeans, and the dish-shaped scar on his high, well-sculpted forehead. Why did she care if he was content to hide out from society on Sam's ranch when it was patently obvious to everyone who met him that Harley Forester was an impostor?

"He...I mean, she..." Andi started over. "Does she know I'm not ready for her?"

"I begged her to stay, Andi. The wedding's not until Saturday. She's our chaperon."

Andi laughed at her sister's wail. Nobody in town believed that Jenny and Sam hadn't consummated their relationship.

"I know what you're thinking and you're wrong," Jenny vowed, her voice low and angry.

Andi would have rolled her eyes but the ache building behind her eyes changed her mind. "I was thinking I really wanted to have the new roof on before she came home. She wouldn't have even known the difference, but now the place is surrounded by scaffolding, and the guys are bringing in a fleet of Dumpsters to catch the rotting shingles."

For reasons Andi couldn't fathom, Ida had turned a blind eye to the house's steady decline since before her nieces headed off in their own directions. Neither Andi nor her sisters had paid much attention to the old bordello's state of disrepair in high school. They were far too absorbed in the high drama of tragic relationships and unrequited love. Then right after graduation, Kristin went to Ireland to live with their father's sister and her family, where she worked as a caregiver; Jenny moved to Fresno to attend college, and Andi had done her thing—two years of junior college with summers spent in Yosemite's high country, then the marines.

Ida had stayed in Gold Creek and peddled antiques from the front half of the old bordello, but she hadn't spent a dime on upkeep. Now, Andi was working against the clock—and a dwindling checkbook—to save the building.

She plopped down on her bottom, letting her legs hang over the edge of the thick plank. She hadn't been rock climbing in years and had forgotten how much she loved the feeling of being above the rest of the world.

"Are you sure you can't talk her into staying a little longer?" Andi asked. "Maybe if Kristin called her…"

"I stalled for as long as I could. I offered to feed them breakfast, but she couldn't sit still. You know what Ida Jane is like when she gets a bee in her bonnet."

Andi smiled at the Ida Jane–ism.

"Where is she now?" Andi asked.

"They just pulled out of the driveway."

The Rocking M was thirty minutes north of town. *Too late to hide and nowhere to run. Might as well go move the boxes of coffee and paper cups.*

"What about her furniture?"

"Harley managed to load the bed and dresser with Hank's help," Jenny said, referring to the foreman at the Rocking M. "But Hank and Greta were just leaving for their nephew's son's christening. Ida told Harley you would help him unload. I believe her exact words were, 'Andrea has better muscles than most men. She can lift anything.'"

Andi would have groaned but she didn't want her sister to get the wrong idea. Jenny had been known to play match-maker a time or two—usually with disastrous consequences. "Great. Maybe I can challenge Harley to a bench-press competition."

"My money's on you, sis," Jenny said, her tone ripe with humor.

"Gee, thanks." Andi sighed. "Well, I'd better go air out her room. I've been storing coffee-shop supplies in there. She won't be happy. She's gotten a little irritable lately." *At least where I'm concerned.*

"Make sure you place her bed by the window. She insists she can't sleep without fresh air," Jenny advised.

Andi wedged the phone under one ear and started to climb down the skinny rungs of metal tubing. "Whatever."

"Oh, wait," Jenny cried with such volume Andi almost lost her footing.

"What?" Her knuckles whitened as she regained her balance.

"I wanted to ask your advice about birth control," Jenny said with a hushed whisper.

Andi looped her arm under the rung for better leverage then moved the phone to the opposite ear. "It's not a problem for me. I don't have a sex life. And anyway, Jen, aren't you getting into the birth control game a little late?"

"I told you, Andi, Sam and I decided not to make love before the wedding. He's got it in his head that he wants to be able to tell the kids that we didn't sleep together before we were married."

The only reason Andi believed that was because she knew Sam O'Neal. He was truly an honorable man.

"Whatever," Andi returned. "I just meant that you should have started on the Pill a month ago to be safe."

Jenny groaned. "I don't like taking anything when I'm nursing."

"So, stop nursing. The twins are six months old. You did good, Jenny Perfect." Jenny hated her childhood nickname. "By the way, why are you whispering?"

"The twins are watching me. Tucker can almost pull himself up. He's going to be walking long before his first birthday."

Andi grinned for real. She loved her niece and nephew. But they made her all too aware of what she lacked in her own life—a husband, children and a home with her name on the deed. Andi felt as though her whole life had been spent in transition, but transition to what? She didn't have a clue.

"Gotta run, sis. Thanks for the heads-up. Maybe if I'm lucky, she won't notice the scaffolding."

"The roof *has* to be replaced, Andi. We've all tried to

explain that to her. Nothing stays the same, even though she wants to believe otherwise.''

Andi dropped to the ground and let out a deep sigh. *Too true, sister dear. Change is coming.*

Andi had been selected to fill Ida's seat on the Chamber of Commerce Board, and rumors were flying about big development companies with big plans for her little town. Who knew what kind of changes were coming to Gold Creek?

"LET'S TAKE the long way back to town,'' the woman to Harley's right suggested.

He might have taken the hint to mean something else if his passenger wasn't in her eighties. He cranked the steering wheel of the rattletrap flatbed to the left. ''Sure thing, Miss Ida. My pleasure.''

Harley was happy at the chance to escort Ida Jane Montgomery back to the town of Gold Creek. He liked spending time with the talkative old woman. Of all the people he'd met, Ida Jane seemed to understand him best. Of course, her forgetfulness was a result of age and very different from the huge gap in his memory caused by the accident. Still, Harley felt very comfortable around her.

''Tell me more about the triplets when they were growing up,'' he said as the truck started to climb. At the summit, a turnout provided a vista of the Rocking M, the ranch where he worked and where Ida Jane had been living with her great-niece, Jenny Sullivan O'Neal for the past six months.

Ida shifted on the dusty bench seat. The morning sun streaming through the window made her thin bonnet of silver hair glow like a halo. ''Believe you me, there's nothing easy about triplets, but my three were treasures. Each one an individual from the very beginning.'' Her smile was poignantly sweet, and Harley felt nostalgic for something he didn't understand. Did he have family somewhere thinking kind thoughts about him?

He brushed aside the disturbing thought as the old woman continued. "Jenny was the little mother. People called her Jenny Perfect growing up. Andi was the worrier. And Kristin…" Her look turned wistful. "She used to be happy-go-lucky and carefree, but she isn't anymore. People change, you know."

Harley tried to imagine what it must have been like for a single woman in her fifties to take on three orphaned infants. "You must have had your hands full," he said.

She shrugged elaborately. "Everybody in Gold Creek pitched in, from the minister to the school-bus driver. It wasn't so bad. For the first few months, we worked in shifts."

The rutted pavement, which had returned to gravel in some spots, meandered around Carson Peak, a minor pinnacle in the Central Sierras. The Rocking M occupied six hundred acres of scrub bush, bull pines and grassy meadows on the mountain's shoulder. Harley couldn't say for certain whether or not he'd ever seen a more peaceful setting, but the foothills in spring were something to behold. The lush green that covered the hillsides was dotted with patches of a tiny white wildflower the locals called popcorn. California poppies and blue dicks swayed in the morning breeze.

He eased the creaky old truck to the side of the road. "Isn't this view something? I can't imagine wanting to live anyplace else."

Ida Jane's fluttery sigh sounded sad. "I grew up here, you know. Too many years ago to count."

"On the Rocking M?" Harley asked, wondering for a second if she was confused about the facts.

"Where do you suppose the M came from?" she asked with a gamine wink. "My daddy. Penrod Montgomery."

Harley had heard a slew of family sagas since arriving at the ranch. Cowboys were great storytellers, but he had no way of discerning truth from fabrication.

"I must have missed that tale. Wanna tell me about it while we drive?"

Ida Jane folded her hands in her lap. "My mother and father took over the ranch after her folks passed in a bad flu epidemic. Daddy wasn't much of a rancher. When he knew he was going to come up short paying the taxes, he threw the deed on the line in a game of poker. And lost."

Harley couldn't help but flinch. That sounded like a pretty risky proposition. Would he be that adventurous? He doubted it. Maybe before he lost his memory. Now, he was content to follow Hank's directives and collect a regular paycheck.

Occasionally he questioned this lack of ambition, but not often. Questions brought worries, worries brought dreams. Bad dreams.

"Daddy never forgave the fella who won it. A neighbor named Bill Scott." She made a soft snickering sound. "Made things pretty uncomfortable when my younger sister, Suzy, married the man."

The connection didn't surprise Harley. After listening to bunkhouse gossip, he decided everyone in Gold Creek was either related to or had close ties with nearly everyone else in town. Except him.

"One night the house burned down with Bill in it. Just an awful tragedy. Suzy sold the place pretty soon after that. She took Lorena—her little girl— and went traveling." Ida sighed. "I didn't see either one for nearly ten years. When they finally came back, my sister was sick. She died just after Lori graduated from high school. Tragedy seems overly fond of my family, I fear. You heard about Lori's accident, right?"

Harley nodded. The first night he'd spent in the bunk-house, in fact. He'd casually asked about Andi Sullivan, the pretty girl he'd met when Lars Gunderson, the old miner who'd saved Harley's life, dropped him off at the ranch. Petey, a sixtyish ranch hand, had related the tragic tale of the Sullivan triplets' birth.

A monumental blizzard combined with a car accident, heroic rescue and the sad deaths of two young parents was dramatic enough even without adding the miraculous birth of three tiny baby girls. As far as Harley could tell, Jenny, Andi and Kristin Sullivan had been the center of talk around Gold Creek for every one of their twenty-nine years.

And they still are. He glanced at the newspaper on the seat beside him. Under a column labeled "Glory's World" was the headline: Sullivan Triplet At It Again.

For some reason, Harley was tempted to snatch it up and read the story. Instead, he made himself ask, "So who owned the ranch before Sam bought it?"

Ida hoisted a fabric carryall to her lap and started digging in it. "A couple from back East. Reno, I believe. They were going to raise those funny-looking sheep with long hair. Can't remember what they're called."

"Alpaca?"

She looked at him sharply, her eyes narrowing. "Sounds right." Her thin lips pursed. "You don't talk like any cow-boy I ever knew."

Feeling uncomfortable under her scrutiny, Harley stepped on the gas. The old truck sputtered for a second then surged forward.

"How come Jenny didn't give you a ride into town this morning?" he asked, to change the subject.

"Oh…she has her hands full taking care of Josh."

Josh? Although Harley hadn't been living at the ranch at the time, he'd heard the whole sad story of Josh O'Neal's death. Josh, Sam's younger brother and Jenny's husband, had died of cancer the day after Jenny gave birth to the twins. "You mean she's busy with Tucker and Lara, right?"

Ida Jane looked momentarily baffled then frowned. "That's what I said."

Harley let it go. He knew how unnerving it was when your memory betrayed you. "How are the wedding plans coming?" he asked, more to be polite than out of curiosity.

Of the seven-member crew that shared Sam's bunkhouse, two felt it was wrong for Sam to marry his deceased brother's wife. Three thought it was noble of Sam to want to provide for Jenny and the twins. One—an itinerant rodeo hound looking for a stake—didn't give a damn one way or the other. And Harley had no opinion.

The trouble with amnesia, he thought, is that you have no history upon which to base an opinion. From his observations, he believed that Sam and Jenny were genuinely kind to each other and seemed happiest when they were together. Was that enough to make a good marriage? Something told him not to bet on it.

"Oh, fine. I think. They don't tell me much."

Harley found that odd. Jenny didn't seem the type to exclude her aunt. "Why is that?" he asked.

She shrugged. "Because my mind is going to hell in a handbasket."

Harley had overheard Sam and Jenny discussing Ida's increasing forgetfulness, but she seemed pretty sharp to him most of the time.

"Maybe they don't want you to overdo," he suggested. "Is that why you're moving back to town? To rest up for the festivities?"

"Maybe."

Her answer—instead of coming off coy—sounded confused. Harley's heart went out to her. He didn't always understand why he did certain things, either. Starting with why he'd been on a remote mountain road in the middle of a storm. All he knew for sure was that he'd woken up in a miner's shack with a raging headache. His only possession—a scuffed leather Harley-Davidson jacket. He'd taken the name Harley from that emblem. But not a single memory of his life before that moment survived what both Lars, the miner who'd found him, and Donnie Grimaldo, the sheriff's deputy who'd filed the report, figured had been a motorcycle accident.

The bike he'd presumably been riding had disappeared, perhaps into one of the many steeply walled ravines near Lars's Blue Lupine mine.

"The twins are getting big," Ida said, apropos of nothing. She opened her canvas bag and poked around a minute. "I have the article. About the birth. Quite an event, you know." She pulled a crinkled clipping from the bag. "See here? 'Jenny Sullivan O'Neal won't be returning to town anytime soon. Caring for twin babies and an aging aunt—'" Ida Jane snorted indignantly. "Big Mouth Gloria Hughes. Who's she calling aged? She's no spring chicken herself."

Harley bit down on a smile.

She cleared her throat and started reading again. "'...aging aunt must be a handful. But Glory's pleased to see a smile on sweet Jenny's face the past couple of months, and we hope she's found a bit of happiness after her grievous loss. We know she misses Josh—just like the rest of us, but life does march on.'"

"*Grievous,*" Ida muttered. "Pretentious old biddy."

Harley swallowed his chuckle. "Jenny and Sam do seem to get along well," he said sincerely. "What does Andi think about the wedding?"

Harley didn't doubt for a minute that the real reason he'd volunteered to give Ida Jane a ride home was the likelihood of seeing feisty Andi Sullivan. Which was both a good thing and bad.

Good because a little verbal sparring stimulated his mind; bad because stimulation of any kind kept him awake at night with a sickening headache caused by dreams he couldn't remember in the morning.

He'd bumped into Andi the night before last when he'd joined two of the younger ranch hands in town for a beer. Andi had been at the Slowpoke Saloon with a group of friends when Harley arrived. To his surprise, she'd asked him to dance when the jukebox played a mellow tune. He'd enjoyed every moment of holding her in his arms, but later—alone in his bunk—he'd had to claw his way past blistering pain. He'd awoken in a pool of sweat and had barely made it to the bathroom before losing the contents of his stomach.

Do all amnesiacs have bad dreams? Or just me? Maybe my past is so bad that I'm afraid to remember it. Unconsciously, Harley reached up to run his fingers over the irregular scar at his temple.

"That still bothering you?" Ida Jane asked.

He glanced sideways. Ida Jane appeared the quintessential grandmother—silver hair cut short and functional, her glossy skin marred with irregular brown age spots. Harley wondered, not for the first time, whether or not he might have a grandmother somewhere in the world. He hoped not. He didn't want to think he might be worrying an old lady by having dropped out of her life so suddenly.

"No, ma'am. Itched like heck for a while. Now I rub it out of habit."

"I've always felt a scar lends a person character. It seems to say you weren't afraid to take risks." He could feel her staring at his profile. "You have a nice, handsome face, but that scar will keep it from being too...perfect."

Harley had spent a good deal of time the past three months staring at his face in the mirror trying to find some clue to who he was, and although he was satisfied that his looks weren't going to frighten young children, he wouldn't classify himself as handsome. His nose was…pugnacious, and the line of his jaw was too short. His eyes were blue, and his hair—probably his best feature—was thick and wavy. A medium brown now laced with gold—thanks to his recent stint at mending fences in the California sunshine.

"No worry there, Miss Ida. I'm a long way from perfect. Especially when it comes to fixing fences. Look at these cuts." He held up his right hand to prove it. Three bandage strips adorned his thumb and index finger; two more were on the heel of his hand.

"Could be you're in the wrong trade. You have a fine way with words. Maybe you were a teacher," she suggested.

Ida Jane wasn't the first person to comment on his less-than-impressive performance as a cowboy. At his doctor's suggestion, Harley had pored over lists of other professions to see if anything jumped out at him. So far, nothing had.

"I don't think I have the patience to work with kids," Harley told her. "But I do like to write. The doctor I saw at the Gold Creek Clinic when Lars first brought me into town suggested I keep a journal. She said sometimes the mind heals so slowly we can overlook signs because we become comfortable with the way our lives *are*—not what they could be."

"My, my," Ida Jane said. "A local doctor told you that? Most of the ones I've known couldn't prescribe their way out of a paper bag without directions."

Harley chuckled. Dr. Franklin had been gentle and kind, but in the end there wasn't much she could do. She was a general practitioner who said her lone brush with amnesia had come on a psych rotation in medical school some twenty years earlier. Although curious and concerned, the best she could say was that he was in overall good health, and there was a chance his memory would return.

"Dr. Franklin wanted to run some tests and consult a specialist, but I don't have the cash," Harley admitted.

"Doesn't Sam give you health insurance?"

He nodded. "It works if you break a leg. But the lady at the clinic said most plans would consider this a preexisting condition and would probably deny coverage."

Ida Jane was silent for a few miles then said, "Like I said, you don't talk like any cowboy I've ever known."

Harley remembered that her grandniece had expressed the same opinion the day they met.

"He's no cowboy," Andi had said moments after being introduced to him. She'd looked at Jenny and Sam as if waiting for the punch line to a joke.

When Sam confirmed that Harley was indeed his newest employee, Andi had remained unconvinced. "No offense, Harley, but you walk like an accountant, talk like a politician and smell like a pothead," she'd told him.

Harley had been offended. At first. But then he realized her observation was amazingly accurate. He hadn't taken the job at the Rocking M out of any sense of familiarity. He didn't know a halter from a heifer, but he'd felt even less affinity with mining. Closed spaces made him uncomfortable, and he'd been almost sick to his stomach the first time Lars tried to get him to climb down a twenty-foot ladder.

When the old miner suggested ranch work as a possible source of employment, Harley had jumped at the chance.

His peculiar body odor could be attributed to his recuperation period in a tiny cabin shared with the pot-smoking loner named Lars Gunderson. Brusque. Isolationist. A ren-

egade from society, Lars smoked ten to twelve joints a day
and still managed to work his gold mine by hand.

"Well, you may be right," Harley had told Andi, impressed by her shoot-from-the-hip manner. She didn't cut
him any slack, but she didn't treat him like an invalid, either. "My past is a closed door, the future a blank slate and
I've chosen to be a cowboy. Do you have a problem with
that?"

Harley couldn't say how much of his macho swagger
came from leftover personality traits and how much came
from listening to Lars's nonstop antiestablishment ranting,
but his lack of memory made one thing clear—the only
person Harley could depend on was himself.

She'd met his challenge with a grin that seemed to call
his bluff. The tilt of her lips had sent a tangible jolt of
awareness right through the center of him. Harley would
have sworn nothing like that had ever happened to him before, but he had no way of knowing for certain.

"There's home," Ida Jane said, cutting into his reverie.

The road curved tightly to the right in preparation for a
downward switchback. From this point, one could take in
the whole town—from the copper-shingled steeple of the
Catholic church to the rounded dome of the courthouse with
its distinctive bell tower. Businesses lined both sides of
Main Street for four blocks, giving way to a natural gap
where two seasonal tributaries drained into Gold Creek.
Several gas stations, motels and a couple of fast-food shops
were grouped at a fork in the road where travelers could
choose to go downhill into the Central Valley or uphill toward Yosemite National Park.

"Gold Creek's a nice little town," Harley said.

"It's a good place to raise a family, but the young people
don't stay. My girls left home as soon as they could. Jenny

went to college. Andi went to junior college, then joined the marines. And Kristin went off to Europe to be a nanny.''

Harley had only met the elusive Kristin once. Sam had mentioned that she lived in Oregon. Harley had gotten the feeling she was slightly estranged from her sisters and aunt.

"I miss those girls," Ida Jane said with a heavy sigh.

A shiver of disquiet passed through him. *Miss? Or missed?*

"Andi's going to be at the old bordello when we get there, isn't she?"

Ida looked as puzzled by his question as Harley felt. One of the problems with amnesia, Harley decided, was not being able to decipher social nuances. Was Ida Jane's apparent forgetfulness something he should mention to her nieces?

He'd found it odd that Ida Jane had suddenly moved up the date of her return to the bordello from next Sunday to today. Jenny hadn't seemed overly perturbed by her aunt's change of plan, but Harley doubted Andi would be quite as calm.

Andi's fiery temperament was just one of the things he liked about her. Which, he thought again, was why he'd jumped at the chance to play taxi driver.

ANDI STOWED the last of the boxes in the basement storage room then brushed off her hands and looked around. She'd forgotten about the spacious area. As children, Andi and her sisters had avoided the cellar because of the threat of spiders, but now she evaluated it through the eyes of a businesswoman.

"If we made that window into an egress…" She peered out the cloudy glass. By investing a few bucks, she could probably rent out the space for seven hundred dollars a month. Maybe more.

A few bucks. A hurdle taller than the surrounding mountain peaks, she thought grimly. She'd invested nearly all the money she'd saved while in the military, but no amount of venture capital seemed enough to stem the steady drain on their resources. Sooner or later, she'd have to admit that the old bordello was a losing proposition.

So why am I fighting so hard to save it? She didn't know the answer.

She was about to head back upstairs, when the phone at her waist rang. *Jenny again, no doubt.*

"What now?"

"Andi? Why are you always so grumpy?"

Wrong sister. This was Kristin. "I thought you were Jenny. Again. I'm busy getting ready for Ida Jane. A week ahead of schedule."

Instead of walking up the open wooden steps, Andi sat down, plopping her elbows on her knees. She wanted to whine to somebody. Why not Kristin?

"I just heard," Kris said. "Why the change? Can you believe Jenny sent our eighty-two-year-old aunt off with a stranger?"

Andi smiled to herself. Kristin's take on any given subject was usually a hundred and eighty degrees opposite of Andi's. Always had been.

"Harley Forester isn't exactly a stranger. He's been working at the Rocking M for three months."

"Am I supposed to find comfort in that?" Kristin asked facetiously. "The man is an amnesiac. What if he suddenly remembers he's a serial killer?"

Andi chuckled. She couldn't help herself. She was no great judge of men—as evidenced by some of her boy-friends over the years, but she'd bet the deed to the old bordello that Harley Forester was a decent human being with a past no darker than Andi's or her sister's.

"Hey, this wasn't my idea, but it's a done deal. They'll

be here any minute." Unable to resist teasing her sister, Andi added, "Unless he's dissecting Ida's body as we speak."

Kristin hissed with outrage. "You're impossible. I only called because Jenny told me to tell you that we need to be especially gentle with Ida. Apparently she's been restless and unhappy all week. Jen said she found her crying a couple of times."

Andi closed her eyes and frowned. Gentle was Kris's thing. Understanding was Jenny's thing. Andi was pretty sure none of her *things*—whatever they were—would prove beneficial to Ida Jane's emotional well-being.

"Could be she's homesick," Kristin suggested.

Andi wished it were that simple, but she'd witnessed a steady decline in her aunt's mental acuity over the past year. Neither of her sisters believed it was serious, but Andi feared otherwise.

"I'd better go," Andi said. "If Ida's feeling depressed, she'll really flip out when she sees the For Rent signs. We'd planned to talk to her about that when you got here, remember?"

Kristin, who was due back in town Friday to participate in Jenny's wedding, said, "You're right. Sorry. I can't talk to her right now. I was just leaving the house. I have to go to a...I'll call later. As soon as I get back."

Typical, Andi thought sourly. Kris always seemed to be gone when there was an emotional confrontation of any kind. She'd been running since high school and hadn't stopped. "Don't worry. I'll handle it, provided Harley gets her home in one piece."

"You like him, don't you?"

Andi jumped to her feet. "No."

"Yes, you do. I could always tell when you liked a boy."

Andi made a rude sound and started up the stairs. "Nu-uh,'' she returned, purposely trying to sound like one of the teenage girls who frequented the old bordello's coffee parlor. Double mocha freezes were all the rage at the moment.

Kristin snickered. ''You're attracted to him. But who wouldn't be? He looks like that actor from *Ever After* with Drew Barrymore. Do you know who I mean?''

Just as she reached the basement door, Andi heard the sound of a truck engine turn into the parking lot. Her heart rate went up a notch.

''Never saw it,'' Andi lied. She'd rented it twice—for that very reason. And it irritated her to no end that her sister— her beautiful sister—saw Harley as an attractive, sexy man.

''You should. He's a cutie. Wish I could remember his name. Oh, well. Gotta go. Good luck with Ida Jane. Tell her I love her, and I'll call later.''

Andi quickly entered the kitchen, closing the door securely behind her. She tried to shake off the sense of anticipation at the thought of seeing Harley Forester, as he called himself. A man who—while not a serial killer—was no cowboy, either.

He was an enigmatic stranger playing at being a ranch hand. Her attraction to him was just a silly diversion, probably the result of too much worry and not enough of a social life.

''I need to get out more,'' she muttered as she dashed to the porch. She didn't want to miss her chance to watch Harley getting out of the truck. He might not *be* a cowboy, but, damn, he looked good in Wranglers.

CHAPTER TWO

"YOU SHOULD HAVE BEEN here when Andi announced she was joining the marines," Ida Jane told her dining companion a short while later. "The town was up in arms. You would have thought she'd said she was running off with the circus."

Andi, in an effort to distract her aunt's attention from the roofing paraphernalia—there'd be time for that talk later—had hustled Ida inside with an offer of breakfast. Harley had begged off, but Ida Jane had insisted he join them.

Unfortunately, the invitation included a recap of Andi's life story.

"Why did the people of Gold Creek care what Andi chose to do with her life?" Harley asked. His tone seemed to express true curiosity rather than polite chitchat. She'd noticed that inquisitiveness about him before, too. He delved into the story beneath the superficial.

"Well, you see, the town had set up scholarships for my girls when they were just tiny babies," Ida said. "Jenny used the money to go to college, but Kristin left home right out of high school. Never asked for a dime. Andi went to junior college for two years, but instead of finishing up her degree, like the town expected, she joined the army."

"Marines," Andi amended before she could stop herself.

"Whatever," Ida returned testily.

To hide her blush, Andi fetched a loaf of bread from the olive-green painted bread box. She *had* to stop correcting

Ida Jane. It did no good, and only served to increase the friction between them.

Ida continued, "The thing is, everyone in Gold Creek thinks they had a hand in raising the triplets, so they're quick to add their two cents' whenever they see the need."

Isn't that the truth? Andi thought, stifling a sigh. She withdrew a carton of eggs from the ancient slope-shouldered refrigerator and carried it to the gas range. As she passed by the CD player on the counter, she turned down the volume. Paula Cole's "Where Have All The Cowboys Gone?" was one of Andi's favorite tunes, but it didn't seem appropriate with Harley Forester sitting in her kitchen. He might not *be* a cowboy, but he sure looked like one.

She added a lump of butter to the cast-iron skillet then looked at their guest. His presence seemed to fill the dining nook across the room from her. He sat casually, one elbow resting on the table while he drank his coffee. His straw hat occupied the empty space to his left. Backlit by the morning light from the bay window, his long-sleeved cotton shirt revealed a glimpse of undershirt at the neck and a line across the middle of his upper arms.

A flutter kicked in below her ribs. *Why am I such a sucker for a man in an undershirt?* she wondered crossly.

"But why the marines?" he asked, as if Andi weren't present. "That seems like an extreme choice."

For a woman, Andi mentally added.

She'd answered the question at least a thousand times, but before she could open her mouth, Ida Jane said, "For the men, of course."

The two, extra-large white eggs Andi had been preparing to crack into the skillet nearly wound up on the floor. She hastily added them to the sizzling butter then put the lid on the pan. She wiped her hands on a towel as she turned to face them. "Auntie," she scolded. "That was *not* the reason."

"But, dear, you've been looking for a man for this family ever since you were old enough to walk."

Andi almost groaned with horror. *Not* that story.

Ida launched into the tale before Andi could think of a diversionary tactic. "It's understandable, of course," she told her audience. "All of her friends had fathers. So, Andi figured our family wasn't complete without one."

"Ida, that's not true. We had…we *have* a great family."

Her aunt ignored her. "Andi was always bringing home one prospect after another." She snickered softly. "Some cases were rather humorous—like that fellow who worked at the hotel. What was his name?" She looked at Andi for help, but Andi was too mortified to answer.

Ida made a swishing motion with her hand. "The man was a little light in the briefs if you get my drift, but Andi couldn't have known that. She was only ten at the time."

Andi closed her eyes, but not before she spotted Harley's amused grin. Dang, the man was even cuter when he smiled. *Sometimes a girl just can't catch a break.*

"You weren't interested, I take it?" he prompted.

"I had my hands full with three little girls and a business. What would I want with another set of socks to wash? But I couldn't tell that to Andi. She was so determined."

Andi tried to catch Harley's attention to signal him not to believe a word her aunt was saying, but he leaned forward as if fascinated by what he was hearing.

"She made this elaborate list," Ida said, using her hands to illustrate. "On tablet paper. We called it the Daddy List."

Too embarrassed to look at their guest, Andi crammed two slices of bread in the toaster—itself an antique, but one that worked better than any of the newer models Andi had tried over the years.

"Auntie, please. I'm sure Harley's not interested."

Naturally, Ida Jane ignored her niece.

"Everybody knew about it. She kept it in a ringed binder under her mattress." Ida lowered her voice theatrically. "Most men considered it an honor to be on the list, and those who didn't make the cut had their noses a bit out of joint."

Andi groaned. She could imagine what Harley was thinking: *Poor little orphan girl on her self-imposed mission to find a father for her and her sisters.*

"Finally, she gave up on getting a man for me and decided she'd have to find one for herself. So she joined the marines."

Desperate for a distraction, Andi grabbed the glass carafe from the coffeemaker and trotted to the table. "More coffee, Auntie?"

"No, thank you." Ida covered her cup with her napkin, so Andi moved to the second cup on the table. "Kristin told me I should limit how much caffeine I drink," her aunt explained. "Says it's bad for you. She's a doctor, you know."

A doctor? When did Ida decide Kris was a doctor? Andi's hand wobbled and the stream of black liquid that had been heading for Harley's cup sloshed over the rim and splashed on his wrist. He jerked his arm, sending drops of coffee in every direction.

"Oh, damn, I'm sorry. Quick…" She dashed to the sink to run cold water. "Come here."

He followed, but hesitated as if uncertain whether or not to stick his hand under the faucet. Andi grabbed his arm and pulled him closer to the wide, old-fashioned basin. Beneath her fingers, she felt his muscles react to her touch. Sinew, strength and heat.

She let go, and almost dropped the coffeepot she was

carrying in her other hand. Flustered and embarrassed, she rushed to the opposite counter. It took two tries to return the pot to its slot. "Keep your hand under the water a full minute," she told him.

"Put butter on it," Ida Jane said.

Andi shook her head. "No. That's an old wives' tale. Cold water and aloe vera work best."

Andi winced at the sour look Ida gave her. "I'll run out to the porch and snip a stem."

"You aren't burning his eggs, are you?" Ida asked.

"Oh, nuts. They're probably harder than rocks," she muttered.

Before she could move, Harley beat her to the stove. With a grace she'd witnessed before—the man seemed naturally good at everything he tried—he smoothly slid the rubber-looking eggs to the plate Andi had left on the counter. "Just the way I like them," he said, giving her a wink Ida Jane couldn't see.

Feeling more than a little flustered, Andi said the first thing that popped into her head. "You seem pretty comfortable in a kitchen. Maybe you were a chef."

"Or a short-order cook," Harley said, taking the toast she offered then carrying his plate to the table.

Andi wondered at the way he downgraded her suggestion as if trying to minimize her opinion of him.

"Or he could be a confirmed bachelor," Ida Jane speculated. "That's what everyone said about Bill until he married Suzy. Goes to show you can't tell about a person just by his past alone."

Andi felt a momentary sense of relief. Now, *that* was the sharp-witted Ida Jane from her childhood.

She walked across the kitchen and put her arms around Ida's thin shoulders. "I love you, Auntie. Don't ever forget that."

Ida patted Andi's hand then tilted her head and said, "Forget what?" Fortunately, Andi caught the mischievous glint in her aunt's eye before her heart shriveled up completely. When she glanced at Harley, she knew that he'd sensed her fear. She could tell by the sympathy in his mesmerizing blue eyes.

Unnerved, Andi pushed a sweating, ruby-colored jar of preserves across the blue gingham tablecloth. "Look what I found in the fridge. The last of Ida Jane's famous cactus jelly." She patted her aunt's shoulder and said with pride, "How many women in their eighties do you know who can wrangle jelly from a cactus?"

"Even if I could remember, I doubt I knew any," Harley said agreeably.

Andi cringed. It was probably in poor taste to say things that reminded someone of his handicap. "I'd better get that aloe before your burn blisters. Excuse me a minute. Ida, love, I'll do your eggs next."

She closed the door to the screened porch behind her and took a deep breath. Her aunt's discourse on Andi's Daddy List wasn't anything new. Ida had told the story many times. And maybe, at a subconscious level, the absence of a father figure in her life had influenced Andi's decision to join the marines. But if that were the case, her choice had been a mistake. None of Andi's superior officers had been the least bit paternal, and her connection with the men in her unit had been either confrontational or platonic. Her lone romantic affair had been a one-sided, short-lived liaison that had gone nowhere fast.

Andi sighed. *Maybe Kris was right. Maybe I'm jinxed when it comes to men.*

Her sister's declaration—made in a moment of duress on their eighteenth birthday—had stuck with Andi, haunting her. Although she'd dated some in college, Andi doubted she'd know love if it walked up and introduced itself.

As for the attraction she felt toward Harley—who in her right mind would fall for a guy without a past?

"Idiot," she muttered as she snipped a stalk from the robust aloe plant in the clay pot sitting on a rusted metal plant stand. Two other succulents, a couple of leggy geraniums and a withered-looking spider plant in need of repotting were practically the sole survivors of her brown thumb.

Beyond the cluttered little porch, a whole jungle of living things cried out for attention. The lawn needed mowing, the fruit trees hadn't been pruned in years and the rose garden was on the verge of being overtaken by weeds.

Andi closed her eyes and ordered herself to take a deep breath. *Prioritize,* she told herself. Why was she thinking about men? She barely had time to shower, let alone worry about love and romance.

"Here you go," she said, returning to the kitchen a few seconds later.

To her surprise, Harley was standing at the stove, buttering two slices of toast. "I cooked three eggs," he told her. "Ida only wants one, so you'll have to eat the other two."

After cutting the bread diagonally, he arranged the halves on two plates, neatly framing the perfectly cooked eggs. He delivered the plates to the table then pulled a chair out for her.

Andi wasn't used to being waited on, and was oddly touched by the simple gesture. Since she was good at following orders, she sat. True, she'd already had juice and a doughnut, but unlike her sisters, who fretted and stewed about their weight, Andi had the kind of metabolism that processed anything she fed it—and in any quantity. A fact that annoyed her sisters to no end.

Once seated, she handed him the aloe. "Cut a line down the middle of the stalk, then smear it on your burns," she instructed. She reached for the salt and pepper before noticing that he'd already seasoned the food—just the way she would have.

Although the eggs were cooked to perfection—medium gooey just the way she liked them—Andi ate without tasting anything. She drank her coffee forgetting to add cream and sugar. She heard Harley and Ida Jane chatting, but would have been hard-pressed to recall a word of their conversation because the longer she sat there, the more she felt like dropping her head in the middle of her plate and weeping.

As long as she kept busy, Andi could ignore the growing sense of futility. She'd tried her damnedest to whip the antique business back into shape, but so far none of her schemes had worked. The store was hovering on the brink of bankruptcy, and the old bordello—Ida Jane's beloved home—needed more work than Bill Gates, let alone Andi Sullivan, could afford.

As long as Ida Jane was living at the Rocking M with Jenny, Andi could pretend things were improving. But now, her aunt would see, firsthand, how badly Andi had failed.

She took a deep breath and looked up. Too bad she wasn't the type to cry on the closest available shoulder. Harley's looked broad enough to handle all her tears.

As HARLEY SMEARED the sticky gelatin-like goo of the plant on the red spots just below his thumb, he studied Ida's greatniece. She was more dressed up than he'd ever seen her. A sleeveless white blouse topped snug black slacks that stopped midcalf. Her rubber-soled white sneakers were low cut, and the absence of socks displayed her shapely ankles. No makeup—as usual—save for a rosy lip gloss that made her lips look moist and kissable. Her watch was her only jewelry, but its rugged, molded rubber design seemed at odds with her feminine attire.

Artless. Unaffected. The adjectives might have been ones he would use to describe her—if he didn't know what lurked beneath that unpretentious surface. The heart of a lion.

That's how Ida Jane had characterized her niece when they were pulling into the parking lot half an hour earlier. "The triplets were born February twenty-sixth," she'd said. "I don't know much about the zodiac, but I do know that Andi is a Leo. My mother was a Leo and they're just alike. Strong-willed, proud, always wanted the best for her family."

Harley had been tempted to correct her. Leo represented August birthdays, not February—he had no way of explaining how he remembered this—but he'd kept his mouth shut. Partly because he'd spotted Andi prowling the length of the bordello's wraparound porch. She moved with feline grace, and the look in her eyes held an edgy, sort of Dirty Harry squint—as if she suspected Harley of something.

"Do either of you ladies know when Clint Eastwood's birthday is?" he asked without thinking.

Ida seemed to ponder the question a moment then shook her head. Andi, who a minute earlier had seemed miles away, looked truly baffled. "Should we?" she asked.

Harley wondered if aloe worked on red cheeks. "Sorry. Weird things pop into my head from time to time."

"Memories?"

Andi's tone sounded hopeful.

"Not exactly. I don't think so."

"Too bad. Have you had any breakthroughs?" she asked.

Harley couldn't help but resent the question. He knew people were curious—perhaps even skeptical—about his amnesia, but Harley didn't like to talk about it. This was simply who he was now, and it bothered him that people couldn't accept that.

Every morning, his bunkmate, Petey, would ask, "Remember anything new?" As if the sleep fairy might have miraculously filled in all the missing pieces of Harley's past while his eyes were closed.

He told Andi the same thing he told Petey. "Not that I know of."

He braced for some kind of platitude, but instead she looked at her watch and let out a small yelp.

"Dang. We have to hurry."

She grabbed all three plates and unceremoniously dumped them in the sink. After turning off the CD player and the coffeemaker, she paused, hands on hips. Harley could almost see her brain designing the most efficient plan of attack. *She'd have made a great general.*

"I'll brew the coffee while you move the truck. Pull up close to the porch," she told him. "That bed is a heavy sucker.

"Auntie, you can watch the shop while Harley and I move your stuff inside, okay? Once we get your dresser set up, you'll be able to unpack, then take a nap, if you want."

She didn't wait to see if her two subordinates would follow her directives. Instead, she dashed down the hallway that connected the family quarters with the retail space.

Harley, although anxious to keep Andi in sight, offered his arm to Ida Jane. "Always in a rush, that one," the old woman said. "She's a take-charge kind of girl. Always has been." She made a face. "And people said Jenny was bossy."

Harley chuckled under his breath. He spotted Andi in the foyer, apparently searching for a hidden key. The shape of her trim derriere and tanned calves was one of the prettiest sights he could remember. Which, in his case, might not be saying a lot, but Harley was certain the memory would hold up even for a man suffering from amnesia.

She produced the key from beneath a brass urn, looked over her shoulder and smiled—as if she'd guessed his thoughts.

"She never found one, you know," Ida Jane said, squeezing his arm to get his attention.

"I beg your pardon?"

"She went looking for a man, but never found one. Not the right one, anyway."

The innuendo couldn't be missed, but Harley pretended not to understand. "Too bad," he said. "She's a nice girl."

And people say I have a way with words?

Ida's laugh made him smile, too. She patted his arm as if to forgive him for being obtuse. "I want to show you something," she said, leading him to a group of photos on the wall. "That's Andi's award from the governor."

He scanned the framed certificate—recognition for her role in locating a lost family of hikers.

"She belonged to the Search and Rescue squad all through high school, then worked in Yosemite for two summers, rescuing stranded climbers."

His gaze drifted over the collage of photos, zeroing in on one of Andi in full climbing regalia dangling by a thread with nothing but blue sky below and sheer precipice above.

He muttered a low epithet.

"Used to scare the hell out of me, too, but when you get to my age, you realize life is too short to play it safe."

While Harley pondered the message behind her words, she added, "A man could get killed falling off a horse just as easy as a motorcycle, you know."

Harley automatically reached up to touch his scar. He didn't know what Ida Jane expected of him. Since that first morning when he'd opened his eyes in Lars's cabin, Harley had been re-creating himself—his understanding of the world and his place in it. Maybe his past was waiting for him to discover it, but Harley wasn't in a big hurry, because for some reason, he wasn't sure that reconnecting with his past was something he was ready to do...yet.

"YOUR AUNT THINKS I should hire you to find my bike."

Andi, who was trying very hard not to read anything into the fact that Harley had stuck by her side like glue since breakfast, almost dropped the dresser drawer she was carrying. "Are you sure about that? Ida told me the other day she thought you were dropped off on the mountain by aliens."

His bark of laughter held a masculine ring that reached something deep inside her. He followed at her heels carrying two drawers to her one. The crowded hallway didn't leave much space for maneuvering, but she turned around anyway.

God, he's built. Not for the first time, she wondered about his past. What did he do for a living before his accident? Before he decided to become a cowboy.

"I could probably find your bike, but I get the impression you don't really care one way or the other if it ever gets found."

He lowered his load, but looked out the window instead of at her. In profile he was even more handsome. *Down, girl. You aren't going to get involved with him.*

"Lars took me to the sheriff's office to report my...uh, accident. At least, we presume it was an accident. Lars said there was a bad storm that night, and I probably got turned around. But what I was doing out there in the first place is anybody's guess. Sam called everybody who lives on that road, but nobody knew me."

Andi remembered hearing about Sam's efforts to help his

new employee figure out what happened. But they'd had practically nothing to go on. No ID. No bike. No license plate.

"After we reported it, the sheriff—Donnie…"

"Grimaldo," she supplied. Donnie was an old friend. They'd been in Search and Rescue together, and he'd dated Kristin for two years before their big blowup.

Harley nudged her to keep walking then followed her through the door, which they'd propped open with an anvil. "Right. Donnie took me for a drive to see if anything rang a bell. He said locating a motorcycle in that part of the mountains would be a long shot. And recovering it would be very expensive."

Andi hurried. She didn't like leaving her aunt alone in the store for long. Partly because Ida complained about every change Andi had made and partly because the octogenarian had an almost childlike fascination with the espresso machine.

"Donnie's probably right about the cost, but I know a few guys who would do it for the challenge—and a case of Bud Light. Provided, of course, we find the bike."

"Would it be worth a try?"

Andi made a who-knows gesture. "The salvage value on a wrecked Harley—if that's what you were driving—definitely would be worth a few bucks. Unless it got burnt up or was too badly mangled in the crash."

He didn't say anything. Andi wasn't sure why he'd brought up the possibility. Whenever she'd mentioned his accident or his amnesia, he'd shut her down. She fitted the drawer she was carrying into the dresser, then turned to relieve Harley of his burden.

"Thanks," she said when the last drawer was in place. "You've been a lifesaver. No way could I have set up that bed by myself. Now, if I can talk Ida into a nap, I might be able to catch up on some paperwork." *While I figure out how to explain the For Rent signs on the front lawn.*

Renting out the rooms on the upper floor was Andi's attempt to increase the cash flow of the antique business. Unfortunately, the first potential renter—an accountant from the valley—had changed his mind because the rooms lacked a dedicated fax line and a separate computer telephone line.

Andi was meeting with an electrician next week. Hopefully he wouldn't tell her the whole building needed to be rewired. She hated to think what that might cost.

She smoothed her hand over the lace coverlet on Ida's bed. "I don't know if it means anything to you, but I'd bet dollars to doughnuts you were never a marine."

He gave her a questioning glance. "You don't fold tight corners. With the sheets. You'd have had that ingrained if you'd been in the military."

She couldn't tell by his look whether or not she'd offended him. He seemed a bit sensitive about his amnesia. She shouldn't have been surprised. Ida Jane didn't like to talk about her lapses in memory, either.

Everyone blamed Ida's problems on old age, but Andi remained skeptical. During the six months that Andi had lived with Ida Jane prior to Ida's hip injury, Andi had witnessed spats of temper and emotional outbursts that seemed completely unlike the aunt she'd known growing up. When Andi had mentioned her concern to Ida's doctor, the man—a new, young practitioner—had suggested prescribing an antidepressant. Ida Jane had refused to discuss it. "My sister took every pill under the sun, and none of them helped," she'd said. "In fact, I think they did more harm than good."

The sound of voices coming from the front parlor shook Andi out of her reverie. "Uh-oh. It's showtime," she said. As she turned away, she caught the look in Harley's eyes. A man's admiring look. She was both flattered and annoyed.

Her ego definitely needed the boost, but she didn't have time for a casual affair.

Andi's hitch in the marines had taught her certain fundamental lessons, including K.I.S.S. *Keep it simple, stupid,* she silently muttered. She had enough on her plate at the moment. Only a moron would get involved with a guy who had no past—no matter how cute he was.

HARLEY BACKED UP a step. *Time to go.* He didn't want to leave, but it was the polite thing to do. He might not be able to remember his name or date of birth, but he seemed to have an inherent knowledge of customs, language, mores and morals. Dr. Franklin had explained that such dichotomies were typical of his kind of amnesia.

"May I use the rest room before I leave?" he asked.

Her expression changed from serious to relieved. "Sure. First door on your left."

Harley wasn't surprised that she was anxious to get rid of him. He recognized the attraction between them, even though he couldn't give it any true perspective. Mild flirtation? Serious infatuation? Purely sexual? Maybe Andi— who'd probably known more boyfriends than Harley wanted to think about—could define it. But she was obviously doing her best to ignore it.

And why wouldn't she? No woman with any sense would get involved with a guy in his predicament. Just because Harley couldn't remember whether or not he had a wife and kids somewhere didn't mean they didn't exist.

"It used to be the butler's pantry," she said, leading the way to the hall. "It's just a sink and toilet. The only bath with a shower is upstairs, which is one reason I wasn't in a hurry to move Ida Jane home. She gets around pretty well now, but those stairs are tricky."

Harley wanted to tell Andi that in his opinion she was

doing right by her aunt—putting her life on hold to make sure Ida Jane didn't lose the home she loved and the business she'd built. Sam had mentioned a few of the hurdles Andi had tackled since her return, and Harley was impressed by her selflessness. But what good was his opinion? His views were less substantial than those flaunted by the gossip columnist in the local newspaper. At least that *Glory* woman had history and experience to back up her convictions.

He nodded and turned away.

The rest room was small and windowless, but it had been painted a cheerful yellow with a chain of white flowers stenciled beneath the crown molding. Like the rest of the house, every square inch of space was filled with antiques as well as personal treasures. On the wall to the left of the old-fashioned commode was a mosaic of yellowed macaroni that spelled ANDI in block print.

As he turned to leave the room, he felt a slight give beneath the toe of his boot. *Dry rot,* he guessed.

How do I know that? Was I a carpenter? Harley looked at his hands and pictured how pale and soft they'd been when he first started working at the ranch. No, he wasn't a man who made his living by working with wood and a hammer.

Which makes me what? A lawyer? A politician? A spoiled rich boy? He'd spent that whole first month playing the guess-my-past game. All it had ever gotten him was a headache.

Harley carried a small tin of extra-strength aspirin to help relieve the blinding headaches that could suddenly strike, making him want to crawl into a black hole and die. Dr. Franklin had predicted that the headaches would increase in frequency as his memory returned.

Which, Harley figured, was one reason he hadn't put more effort into finding out about his past. Not only were his dreams enough to turn his stomach, but the headaches left him weak and nauseous.

As he headed toward the shop to tell Ida Jane and Andi goodbye, he passed by an open door. Glancing in, he spotted an oil painting above the ornate fireplace and made a detour.

The room was filled with antiques like the rest of the bordello, but this room had a homey, lived-in feel to it. He ambled past the vintage sofa, running his fingers over the dusty keys of a player piano topped with knickknacks and photos in mismatched frames.

But it was the painting that drew his attention. Somewhat stylized, it was a bucolic portrait of the fraternal triplets at age twelve or so. The artist had managed to depict each child's individual essence. Harley had no trouble picking out Andi—the rebel. Her cap of red hair fell across her eyes like that of the huge Old English sheepdog she embraced. Her sisters stood on either side of her—prim ladylike Jenny on the left. Wistful, angelic Kristin to the right.

He didn't hear Andi approach until she said, "That's Daisy. We got her the first day of kindergarten. She'd be waiting for us every single day after school. A big doggy grin on her face."

Harley studied the animal for a moment. A sliver of pain made his eyelid flicker. He blinked and rubbed the spot. "You're sure it's not a hairy cow?" he asked disconcerted by his odd reaction. "That's the biggest dog I've ever seen."

"How can you be sure? You've lost your memory, re-member?"

Her question wasn't too different from the razzing he got from some of his fellow cowboys, but her smile made it more palatable. "How long ago did she die?"

"The summer after we graduated from high school. Kris was in Ireland living with our aunt and uncle. I was working in Tuolumne Meadows, and Jen was hiking with Josh before starting summer-school classes at Fresno State. I told Daisy we were coming back, but I guess she didn't believe me.''

Harley could tell that even now, all these years later, Andi was moved by the memory. ''You found her, didn't you?''

She turned away, as if his observation bothered her. ''I came home one afternoon, and she wasn't at the gate to meet me.'' She tried to shrug her shoulders, but the blasé motion fell short. ''She lived a good, long life.''

''That didn't make it hurt any less, I bet.''

Her eyes narrowed. ''That's a pretty empathetic observation for a guy with no past. How do you explain that?''

Harley might have been put off by her contentious tone if he didn't understand the feelings behind it. Andi kept her attitude front and center for protection, like a porcupine.

''I don't. I just tried to imagine how I'd feel if someone I cared about died. And I could tell by the look in your eyes, you really loved your dog.''

She lifted her gaze to the portrait. ''Daisy was special. I could tell her anything, and she seemed to understand. Not too many people are like that. Not around here, anyway.''

''You have two sisters. And Ida Jane. And from what I hear, a town that follows your every move.''

''A dog doesn't judge you.''

Oh. The sentence told him more than she probably intended. As if conscious of the slip, she added, ''Daisy was just part of a whole menagerie. Rabbits, goldfish, six, no…seven cats, a parrot, chickens, ducks, two turtles, peacocks and a bad-tempered Shetland pony named Homer.''

Harley pictured the cow dogs at the Rocking M, and his slight aversion to them. He'd wondered why he felt no affinity toward animals. Andi's pet history made him a little uncomfortable. ''That either sounds like a Disney movie or a horror story. I can't decide which.''

His observation seemed to startle her. "How come you know movies but not...? Never mind. I need to get to work before Ida decides she *can* make a cappuccino without help."

Harley took the hint. She was obviously reluctant to leave him wandering around her home alone. But Harley was just as reluctant to give up this connection he felt with her. And her life. Maybe this documented record of Andi's childhood filled a void he hadn't wanted to admit existed.

He pointed to a framed snapshot of a man and woman riding a merry-go-round. The woman resembled Jenny, although her waist-length red tresses were the color of Andi's. The man had Andi's serious gray-green eyes and Kristin's charismatic smile.

"Are those your parents?"

"Yes. They were honest-to-goodness hippies." Her sudden grin made his breath catch in his throat. *She doesn't smile enough.* "They lived on a commune near Shasta until our mother got pregnant. Ida Jane told us that a psychic had predicted a multiple birth but had seen tragedy associated with it."

Harley interpreted her slight shudder as skepticism. "Ida said they were afraid something bad might happen to us, so they moved in with her to be closer to a hospital. But because Mother wanted a natural birth, she saw a midwife, too.

"They were on their way back to town when a storm blew in. Their Volkswagen bus hit a patch of black ice and slid off the road. Our dad was killed on impact, but Mom hung on long enough to deliver us."

Harley had heard the story before, but listening to Andi tell it touched him differently. The repressed questions he struggled to keep at bay suddenly bombarded him. *What if my parents are alive? Are they worried about me? Have they been searching? What if I have a wife and family? Has my disappearance left them shattered? Destitute?*

Along with the questions came a blinding headache.

Harley squeezed his eyes closed and groped for the medication in his breast pocket. With his other hand he reached out for something to hold on to. His balance was the first thing to go. Whatever was in his stomach usually followed.

A strong, solid arm took his. "What's going on? You're white as a sheet. Come and sit down."

Her words sounded far away but overly loud. They competed with the ringing hiss that increased the level of pain. "Headache," he said. The words came off mumbled and slurred.

Andi helped him to the sofa and gently pushed him backward so he was slightly reclined. She disappeared for a moment, returning with a cold cloth that she pressed to his eyes. "My roommate used to get migraines. She thought they were caused by a food allergy. I hope it wasn't the cactus jelly I fed you."

Harley would have smiled if he could have felt his lips.

"I brought you some water," she said, wrapping his fingers around a glass. "Let me help with your pills."

She took the tiny container from him and a second later he tasted the bitterness of the tablets. "Thanks," he mumbled, right before he washed them down with a gulp of water. "They help. They just take a few minutes."

"Good. I know this isn't what you want to hear, but you look awful." Squinting against the pain, he saw her close the drapes. In the shadowy dimness, she returned to his side. "Just rest," she whispered. "Ida will be by to check on you in a minute. She'll love having someone new to play nurse with."

Her words were a blur. And he probably imagined the

kiss on his cheek. Then he was alone with his pain. Harley might have focused on the odd, disparate images that bombarded him in the blackness behind his eyes, but he was too busy concentrating on keeping his breakfast in his stomach.

CHAPTER THREE

ANDI GLANCED at her watch to double-check the progress of the grandfather clock across from her desk. Both timepieces said the same thing. Time was crawling this afternoon.

Of course, it didn't help that in the two hours since Harley Forester had nearly collapsed in her parlor, Andi hadn't been able to take even a five-minute break to check on him. First, a busload of retirees who were walking off the pancakes they'd eaten at the Golden Corral showed up to browse. Andi's total sales amounted to thirteen dollars, but she had a feeling she might have sold a few big-ticket items if she'd had a Web site to send them to when they returned to Illinois.

Not long after the customers left, Beulah Jensen and Mary Needham walked in, having just heard through the grapevine that Ida Jane was home. Both were Ida's cronies from the Garden Club, and the three old friends put away two caramel rolls, four biscotti and three extra-large mochas before Ida announced that she had a man in her room and she needed to check on him.

Andi would have explained to the dumbfounded women, but she was sidetracked by a phone call. A customer wanted to know if she had the written operating instructions to go with a circa 1950s slide projector that he'd bought from Ida Jane two years earlier. And if not, could she please talk him through the steps to replace the bulb.

It's been two hours. How long should I leave him there? What if he has a broken blood vessel in his head? He could be in a coma. Or—worse—Ida Jane could be showing him all my baby pictures. That would bore him to death. Maybe I should put the Back in Ten Minutes sign on the door and go check on him myself.

She straightened the basket of pink and blue sugar packages at the table where Ida and her friends had been sitting, and cleaned up the napkins and stir sticks. Andi didn't mind giving free coffee to Ida's friends, but the chocolate-drizzled biscotti and walnut-pecan caramel rolls were purchased from the bakery. Andi usually broke even on baked goods, but she couldn't do that if Ida gave them away. And these days every nickel mattered. Unfortunately, she didn't know how to explain that to a woman as generous as Ida Jane without sounding miserly.

"Ahem."

Andi spun around, nearly upending the molded plastic chair she'd been wiping down.

"Oh, hi. I was just coming to check on you. You look much better," she said, pleased to see Harley standing, hat in hand, in the doorway. He still seemed a little pale, but he didn't have that pinched look about his lips and eyes. "Are you okay?"

One shoulder moved incrementally.

She motioned him in. "Can I get you a cup of coffee? Caramel roll? Biscotti?"

He shook his head faintly—as if the pain still lingered. "No, thank you. I should be going. But I wanted to thank you for helping when that headache hit."

She was disappointed. Even though she knew it wasn't a good idea to get involved with the guy, she wasn't ready to let him leave. The afternoon loomed ahead, long and boring.

Maybe she was a little lonely. And she definitely wasn't looking forward to talking business with Ida Jane.

"Are you sure I can't bribe you into sticking around?" she asked. "I could use your help."

Instead of leaving through the back door, which was just behind him, he walked toward her.

"The pay isn't great—food and caffeine—but the work isn't overly difficult. Honest."

He stopped about an arm's length away, shifted feet as if uncomfortable with his choices and took a long, deep breath. "I owe you a favor. What can I do?"

Andi smiled at his serious tone. "Sit out front in the rocking chair and read the paper."

He blinked. "Excuse me?"

She turned away and finished wiping the table so he wouldn't see her blush. Her sisters would have been able to see right through her ploy. "You've heard of priming the pump, right? Well, I don't know for sure if this will work, but I thought that having a man sitting on the porch, looking relaxed and reading the paper—while his wife was inside spending money with carefree abandon—might draw in customers. And your presence—a big, masculine cowboy—would make other husbands less intimidated about going antique shopping with their wives. What do you think?"

When she looked his way, his smile started out slow then grew to a grin that made her knees tremble. "I think it's a brilliant idea. Very astute. I'm pretty sure I can be a dummy without any problem."

Dummy. The word made her flinch. "Shh…" she warned. "Not the D-word. Ida Jane would wash your mouth out with soap if she heard you say that."

His look of confusion made her explain. "Kristin had a few problems in school. One or two of her teachers suggested she was slow." Andi whispered the word. "So, we were never allowed to use derogatory words about each other's mental acuity.''

"Was the problem a learning disability?" he asked.

"Possibly," Andi said, motioning for him to follow her to the wicker rocker on the covered porch. "From what I've read, it sounds like attention deficit disorder. But whatever the problem, it was never formally diagnosed. Ida Jane tried taking Kris to some kind of psychologist for special tests, but Kristin refused to cooperate. She insisted she could do the work if it weren't so boring."

Andi remembered the running arguments between Ida and Kristin, who was as easygoing and malleable as a puppy except when it came to doctors and taking pills. It was no surprise to Andi that Kris had gravitated toward holistic healing in her adult life. "Kris kept her grades in the C's and D's range. But in subjects she liked, she could get A's."

"Then she must have been right," he said in that slow, thoughtful way of his. As if any statement he made was subject to change by the *real* Harley Forester—whoever he was.

"Have a seat," Andi said as she dashed inside to grab a newspaper from the pile beside her desk. When she returned, Harley was gingerly lowering his excellent derriere into the rocker. "I know the chair looks rickety, but it will support you. I promise. My friend Pascal—he's a teacher at the high school—comes by on weekday mornings before school, and always eats his roll and drinks his triple espresso in that chair. And he's a big guy. Three-fifty, at least."

Once seated, Harley tossed his hat on a nearby bench. "Is he a boyfriend?" he asked, not making eye contact.

Andi stifled a giggle. "He was my teacher when I was in school, and he was one of the names on my Daddy List, if that gives you an idea of his age."

"Oh." He held out his hand for the paper but didn't look up at her.

Andi felt compelled to add, "Poor Pascal. He's a sweetheart of a man, but he must have been mortified to find out I'd paired him with Ida Jane. He's at least twenty-five years her junior. But when you're a kid, *old* is anything over thirty."

As Harley rocked back, the chair runners made a soft creaking sound against the planking. "Then I must be old," he said, his voice heavy with a sigh.

Andi moved to the railing across from him and leaned against it, crossing her ankles. "How old do you think you are? Thirty? Thirty-one?"

"Older."

"What makes you say that? Did the doctor guess your age? You know, when she examined you?"

His laugh curled around the eaves like a warm echo. "You mean they way do a horse? By checking its teeth?"

Her cheeks grew hot. "Well, maybe. I don't know. I was just curious…"

"Don't get all defensive. I was only teasing." His tone let her off the hook. She really liked him way too much considering she knew absolutely nothing about him.

He rested his left ankle on his right knee and brushed at a scuff on his worn boots with the pad of his thumb. Andi knew he shopped at the local thrift store, because Jenny had been the one to take him there with an advance on his first paycheck.

"In all honesty, I don't have a clue how old I am. But after a headache like that one—" He nodded as if he'd left the pain behind him in the house. "I feel ancient."

Andi's impulse was to feed him. "Listen, caffeine might not be good for a headache, but a fruit smoothie could help.

You know…something cold. Let me get you one. On the house. For giving Ida Jane a ride home this morning.''

She started away, but he put his arm out to block her. "You don't owe me anything, Andi. I like Ida. I volunteered when Hank asked for someone to help out. Sundays can get a little long when you don't know many people and you don't have much money."

Since Andi's only day off was Monday—the day she ran nonstop errands—she hadn't really given that any thought. "So, what do you do with your downtime?"

"Read. Write in my journal, like Dr. Franklin suggested. Last Sunday, I visited Lars at the mine, but it's not always easy to catch a ride. The Blue Lupine isn't exactly on the beaten path."

Which made it all that much odder that someone would be riding a motorcycle in that vicinity, she thought. "I haven't been to the mine in years," Andi said. "When I was a senior, my science class had a botany project that required us to collect wildflowers from all over the county. I asked Lars for permission to pick flowers from his property."

"And he said yes?" Harley asked, his surprise obvious. Lars Gunderson's cantankerous personality hadn't won him too many friends over the years. Sam O'Neal was one of the few people who always kept an open door to the old miner.

"Actually, he was real nice once we got past the shouting," she said with a wink. "I once dated an army drill sergeant like him—all hot air and paranoia."

She might have elaborated, but the ringing of the telephone made her rush indoors. She snatched the portable from its cradle then walked into the "Coffee Parlor" to mix up a smoothie. "Hello," she said, adding as an afterthought, "the Old Bordello Antique Shop and Coffee Parlor."

"Nicely done," Jenny praised. "Almost made me want to rush over and buy something."

Andi chuckled. "Cool. That would make my third sale of the day. If you pick something big, I might even break twenty bucks gross."

Jenny groaned. "Bummer. I'm sorry business has been slow. How's Ida Jane doing? She got there okay, didn't she? Harley isn't back, and I'm starting to get worried."

Andi dropped a prepackaged frozen plug of concentrated puree of bananas and mangoes into the blender, along with additional ice. Before adding the milk, she ripped open an envelope with her teeth and dumped a grayish-looking powder on top of the pink-orange cube. When she'd first considered selling coffee as a sideline, she hadn't planned to make frozen drinks, too. But Kristin had pointed out that in the long hot days of summer, a chilled selection would be more appealing than hot coffee. Regardless of her performance in school, Andi thought, Kristin was no dummy.

After locking the lid in place, Andi hit the button on the mixer then moved around the corner so she could hear over the noise. "Ida's unpacking. Or resting. I'm not sure. And Harley is still here. He's my live bait. I've got him sitting on the porch to lure customers in."

"*Live bait?*" Jenny repeated, as if slightly repelled by the concept. "I'm not sure how his presence will help unless you're trying to get young girls to come in, but, hey, whatever works. As long as he's okay, and the truck is safe. Sam might call off the engagement if I lost one of his employees and his beloved flatbed truck while he was away on business."

Andi sincerely doubted that. Sam adored Jenny and doted on the twins. She peeked out the window. The cowboy in question was rocking lazily. He seemed to be engrossed in an article on the front page of the *Ledger*.

"Oh, damn," she groaned, catching a view of the headline. "What?"

"I gave him the wrong paper. This one's got the nasty article Gloria wrote about why I shouldn't take over Ida Jane's seat on the chamber of commerce."

Jenny's sigh said she understood. "I really don't like what I've been reading lately. It's so one-sided in favor of big business. I'm not surprised Gloria is trying to use her influence to get someone more in favor of growth onto the committee. I heard her son is now a hotshot developer in Seattle or Portland."

"Ty's into building things?" Andi croaked. "Somehow I pictured him more the plastic-explosives-under-a-bridge type. Go figure."

When she'd dated him—nearly a dozen years earlier— Tyler Harrison had been the town bad boy. His role in a three-way skirmish with Kristin and Donnie had resulted in Ty's premature departure from school. Andi couldn't picture him as a successful businessman.

"People change, Andrea," Jenny said with authority.

"True, Jen, but that doesn't mean we have to roll over and play dead because big business wants to change Gold Creek into some slick tourist trap with a casino right outside of town," she said, repeating one of the rumors that was circulating. When Andi returned to Gold Creek the previous April, she'd learned all too quickly that certain factions— like the owner of the newspaper, Gloria's brother, and his friends—were willing to do almost anything to bring new enterprises into town. Even at the expense of old, established businesses—like the Old Bordello Antique Shop.

Andi had heard the Growth versus No Growth controversy a dozen times in the past year. In all honesty, she was sick of talking about it. Before Jenny could reply, Andi cut her off. "I gotta finish making a smoothie for a customer, sis," Andi said, returning to the mixer. Best not to mention her *customer* by name. Jenny was something of a match-maker. "I'll have Ida Jane call you later."

After exchanging quick goodbyes, Andi set the phone down. She transferred the frothy mixture to a large opaque plastic cup and grabbed a paper-wrapped straw from the box stashed under the counter.

"Here you go," she said a minute later, presenting the mixture to her guest. "I added a shot of protein mix. You still look a little shaky. I've heard migraines can be very debilitating."

He took the glass with a smile of gratitude. "Thanks." He put the tip of the straw in his mouth and ripped open the paper wrapping. "But what happened to me wasn't a true migraine."

Andi leaned against the column supporting the roof of the porch and looked at him. "Really? It gave a good imitation of one."

Puffing lightly, Harley blew the paper off the straw, catching it in his free hand. "My doctor said the headaches are a result of the increased blood to the brain. They're usually triggered by a resurgence of memory."

"Seriously? Did our conversation about my family make you recall something from your past?" She tried to keep her tone as flat and disinterested sounding as possible, but the idea of his regaining his memory intrigued her.

She didn't want him to think she had some vested interest in having him reconnect with his past. *Although it would be nice to know whether he had a wife and six kids somewhere in the world.*

"I don't know," he answered. "The pain was blinding. None of the images in my head made sense or stayed with me. It's like waking from a nightmare. There are lingering impressions, but nothing feels real or solid. Do you know what I mean?"

Andi wondered if he was working to keep his tone flat, too. How could anyone be so indifferent about something so vital?

Just then, a Ford Taurus pulled into the parking lot and stopped in a spot beside the newly designated handicap parking space. "Uh-oh," Andi said under her breath.

Harley rocked forward and sat up to see over the railing. "Who is it?"

"Two older ladies from Coulterville. Sisters. They make the rounds from antique store to antique store every Sunday. They're like a tag team with the World Wrestling Federation. Just watch. They never agree on anything," she said in a low voice to keep her words from reaching her customers. "I live in fear that this might be Kristin and me in a few years."

The two women—probably both in their seventies—climbed the steps. "When are you going to get a ramp, Andrea?" the matron with salt-and-pepper hair asked. "We're not getting any younger, you know."

"Speak for yourself, Joan," her white-blond partner snapped. "A little exercise never hurt."

"Sorry, ladies," Andi said. "It's on my to-do list."

Andi made eye contact with Harley as the women—in their haste to be the first one inside—barely gave him a second glance. His lips puckered around the straw, but Andi had no trouble reading the humor in his eyes. Her throat closed, and she suddenly felt a little too warm.

"I think I'll see if I can break my record and actually sell them something today." She nodded briefly then hurried inside.

Think K.I.S.S., she told herself. Not *kiss.*

"WHY DON'T YOU TAKE a saucer home and see if it matches your set? Consider it a loaner."

Harley could hear every word through the open window behind his rocker. Andi's tone was still patient. Even after forty minutes of hand-holding and answering questions, Andi appeared no closer to a sale. The two old ladies, whom Harley had nicknamed the Bicker Sisters, could not make up their minds. Or, rather, their tastes were so disparate it would take an act of Congress to get them to agree on anything.

"But what if it doesn't match, Muriel? Then we have to drive all the way back to Gold Creek to return it," Joan Bicker said.

"We're here nearly every week, anyway. What does that matter?" Muriel Bicker answered. "I say we box up Mama's china and use something new for a change."

Blasphemy, Muriel.

"Don't be ridiculous," her sister snapped. "Only a fool would waste money on new china when Mama's Fosteria is as good as new."

"Except there's no sugar bowl or creamer and all the saucers are chipped," Muriel countered.

So there, Joan.

Andi suddenly appeared at his side. "Was I right?"

"On the nose. How do you stand it?"

She shrugged. "Actually, I've learned a lot from them. Joan and Muriel both know their antiques, and if I run across something that doesn't have a price tag and I can't find it in any of Ida's catalogs, I can ask them what it's worth."

"How can you trust them not to tell you a lower figure so they can buy it more cheaply?"

She brushed her fingers across the top of his arm and laughed lightly, "They don't come to buy. They come here to argue, and one-up each other. My sisters and I used to be the same way. I guess it's called sibling rivalry."

"Andi," Joan said, appearing suddenly in the doorway with a plate in each hand. "Muriel insists we take this one home." She waved the plate in her right hand. "But I'm positive Mama's pattern has more blue in it, so I'd like to take this one." The left one made a circle. "If you don't mind."

Andi smiled broadly. "No problem, ladies. Let me wrap those up for you."

Harley was still chuckling as he finished the last of his smoothie. Somehow Andi had guessed that he was in need of sustenance after his headache. The cool, frothy fruit drink had helped on several levels, but so had Andi's concern. He realized now how much he missed a woman's comforting touch.

Harley liked working at the Rocking M, but he had to admit his connection to his fellow employees was superficial at best. Understandable since he couldn't add anything when the guys started talking about their families, their ex-wives or girlfriends. And he couldn't contribute to the general conversation. Since many of the cowboys were itinerant rodeo hounds, three-quarters of the discussions centered around which bull bucked the hardest or twisted to the left when it started right.

With no memories of interesting exploits, no broken bones to compare or ex-wife to bitch about, Harley could only listen. While the men were aware of his amnesia, Harley had the impression they thought he was holding out on them. Listening but never sharing.

And, although it made no sense, Harley had to admit he felt more comfortable in Sam's company than with Petey and the other cowboys. He didn't understand why.

Sam was older than Harley. He was a businessman—a

successful rancher with responsibilities, a fiancée and two children. Harley had eighty-three dollars in his pocket, and barely enough clothes to fill a grocery bag. He was the only employee in the bunkhouse without his own vehicle. In fact, Harley was no more than a paycheck away from being homeless.

Which was another reason to stay away from Andi Sullivan. He had absolutely nothing to offer a woman, so why pretend otherwise? He'd leave as soon as he put in adequate "rocker" time to repay her for the fruit drink. He set his plastic cup on the porch and opened the newspaper.

The first thing to catch his eye was a full-page advertisement for an upcoming seminar on investment strategies for Gold Creek property owners. The ad itself didn't surprise him, but the fact that its tone and description matched the rhetoric in a *news* story on the front page did. The article, which lacked a byline, he noticed, criticized certain businesses, such as the Old Bordello Antique Shop, for failing to update their buildings with adequate handicapped access and a neater, more modern appearance.

Something in the piece made Harley uneasy. He couldn't claim to be a critical judge of writing, but the author's coverage seemed one-sided. Harley thumbed through the pages to the gossip column, "Glory's World" by Gloria Hughes, that Ida Jane had quoted that morning.

He read:

Glory was disturbed to learn that Gold Creek native Ida Jane Montgomery will not be returning to her position on the Gold Creek Chamber of Commerce's omnibus committee. Ida Jane cited her decreased mobility since her broken hip and too many family obligations as reasons for her resignation. She has asked that her grandniece Andi Sullivan take her place. Glory asks:

Is this former marine here for the long haul or is Gold Creek just a bivouac?

The implication was obvious. Gloria didn't expect Andi to stick around. Why? he wondered. Surely a great many people who left home to join the military eventually returned. Didn't they?

A small flicker of pain behind his left eye made him put the newspaper aside. This inability to make informed judgments really bothered him. While the average person could read an article and decide on the spot whether or not the opinions stated made sense, Harley had very little practical life experience upon which to draw. No family history. No faith. What sounded reasonable and rational could, in fact, be balderdash and hogwash. How would he know?

The sound of footsteps made him rock forward. He rose to his feet just as the Bicker Sisters walked through the doorway. They froze momentarily as if shocked to see him.

He tipped an imaginary hat, as he'd seen the older cowboys do. He liked the politeness of the gesture.

The ladies looked at him then glanced over their shoulders at Andi. The look they exchanged seemed to say they finally agreed on something. "Good afternoon, Andrea," the lady on the left said. "Don't work too hard."

Her girlish snicker earned her a frown from her sister. "Oh, for heaven's sake, Muriel, give the girl a break."

When Harley looked at Andi, she was shaking her head, a wry smile on her lips. He'd been amazed by the patience and genuine interest with which she'd helped the women. He also realized that he liked her. A lot. And that it wasn't fair to her—or to him—to continue their friendship unless he made every attempt to put them on a level playing field.

He motioned her closer. "Can we talk a minute?"

"Sure. There doesn't appear to be a line of customers, although maybe my ghost will show up."

He'd heard about her failed ploy to attract customers by circulating a rumor that the old bordello was haunted. According to Sam, the "Haunted Bordello" campaign drew some initial response, but interest waned when no ghost appeared.

"Well, poltergeists notwithstanding, pull up a chair. I want to run something by you."

Andi wasn't sure she was ready for a heart-to-heart talk with Harley Forester. She didn't even know for sure how he'd come by that surname. The *Harley* was obvious. She'd seen him wearing his scuffed Harley-Davidson jacket once or twice in January. But his choice of last name was a mystery.

"Before you say anything, can I ask you a question?"

He sat back down in the rocking chair. "Okay."

"Why Forester? Why not Smith? Or O'Leery? Or Rumpelstiltskin?"

His smile let her off the hook.

"You know Hank Willits, right? Sam's foreman?"

"Of course. I don't know him well, but his wife has been a lifesaver to Jenny. Greta's fantastic with the twins, and Ida Jane adores her."

He nodded. "Hank's a great guy, too, and he's been extremely kind to me. He took me to the motor vehicle department to see about getting a driver's license not long after Lars dropped me off at the ranch. DMV couldn't do anything for me until I produced a birth certificate—or my old driver's license. And in order to apply for a new birth certificate, I needed a name. So, he gave me his mother's maiden name. Forester."

"That was nice of him. It's a good name."

Harley nodded. "Hank's mother passed away a few

months before Sam's brother, I think. I got the impression Hank was too busy helping at the ranch to get to her in time to say goodbye."

"Oh," Andi said. Guilt could be a very compelling force.

"Hank said this would be a way of honoring her memory. Apparently, she was a generous person," he added. "The kind of woman who was always giving things away. Never turned down someone in need."

"Ida's mother was the same way. Ida used to tell us stories of the Great Depression when men were out of work and they'd come to the ranch looking for food. She said no one went away hungry from her mother's door." The thought made her feel a bit cheap for contemplating charging the Garden Club ladies that morning. "If you'd have mentioned it, I'm sure Ida would have let you use the Montgomery name. She always wanted a son."

He cleared his throat, then linked his hands in front of him and took a deep breath. "What I wanted to say was I'd like to hire you."

A skitter of excitement raced down her spine. Although Andi was pretty certain she knew what he meant, her impulse was to deflect the serious topic with humor. Was she ready to help him track down his past? "I beg your pardon, sir, but just because the sign says bordello doesn't mean I can be bought," she said in a pretty awful southern accent.

He looked confused—and she wanted to kick herself. She'd kidded her way out of any number of awkward situations in the military, and her flippancy had become a habit. "Sorry," Andi said, "I was joking."

He nodded. "Most people would have caught that right away. It takes me a little longer. And, frankly, I'm tired of being the last person to get the punch line. I want to do whatever it takes to get my memory back. Starting with recovering my motorcycle." He made a gesture of hope-lessness. "If there *is* a motorcycle."

Andi held her breath, acknowledging the two opposing reactions vying within her. The hint of action made her want to pump her arm in triumph. Sitting around waiting for the termites to take over the old bordello was not her idea of fun. But a heavy sense of responsibility shadowed her initial joy.

Climbing up and down the steep gullies and sheer-walled canyons along the road leading to the Blue Lupine mine wasn't exactly a walk in the park. It could very well turn out to be a time-consuming exercise in frustration.

Think with your head, not your quickly diminishing muscles, she cautioned.

But the prospect of action prevailed.

"Cool," she told him. "When do we start?"

He swallowed nervously. "When's a good time for you?"

"The store is closed on Mondays, and Jenny is taking Ida Jane shopping in Fresno for a dress to wear to the wedding. Knowing Auntie, that will take all day. Do you want to do an initial scope of terrain tomorrow?"

"Tomorrow," he repeated. The look in his eyes read: OhmygodwhathaveIdone? But Andi ignored it—along with all the reasons she should stay at her desk crunching numbers and comparing bids for the many assorted repairs on the bordello. She was going on a scavenger hunt. With Harley.

Under her breath she murmured a familiar marine cry of triumph. "Hoowah."

CHAPTER FOUR

AT SOME LEVEL, Andi heard the familiar early-morning sounds—the meadowlark's repetitive trill, the clock in the tower of the courthouse announcing the hour, her great-aunt's voice on the telephone. But at another level, frustration—and fear—twisted every ounce of pleasure out of her.

I can't believe I just spent twenty minutes arguing with Ida over whether or not today is Monday, she thought, running a hand through her short, time-saving hairdo.

Ida Jane replaced the phone's receiver on its cradle with a telling *thwack*. She gave Andi a petulant look. "Beulah agrees with you. It *is* Monday." Under her breath she added something that sounded like, "But it feels like Tuesday."

Andi's first inclination was to cry. A feeling alien to her nature. Her sisters would both vouch for the fact that the only time Andi Sullivan cried was in animal movies. Reading the young-adult novel *Julie of the Wolves* had reduced her to a blubbering idiot. Fortunately, she'd been in her sleeping bag with a flashlight at the time, so no one knew.

But this crisis with her aunt was having the same effect. As a see-a-problem-then-fix-it kind of person, Andi couldn't sit back and watch the only mother she'd ever known slowly deteriorate. Unfortunately, she didn't seem to have a choice.

"I'm sorry I upset you, Auntie," Andi said, trying for a conciliatory tone. Surely, she could muster enough patience to avoid arguing with a person who didn't know what day of the week it was.

Jenny would have cajoled Ida into dropping the subject; Kristin would have helped Ida work through her confusion. Unfortunately, neither of her sisters was handy. But Jenny was coming. Soon.

Hurry, Jen. Before Bart gets here. The roofer was scheduled to meet Andi at seven-fifteen to sign the contract for the new roof.

"I thought you'd be pleased to go shopping with Jenny, Ida Jane. Last night you said you couldn't wait to pick out a dress for the wedding."

Ida took a slice of toast from the plate and smeared it with peanut butter. "What wedding?" she asked suspiciously.

The queasy feeling so common in Andi's belly lately returned. *Is this how an ulcer starts?* "Jenny and Sam's wedding," she said slowly and succinctly. She watched her aunt's face to see if they were on the same page.

Ida seemed to think a minute. "Oh, for heaven's sake," she exclaimed, dropping the toast untouched to the table. "Of course. Where is my brain? I think I'm losing my marbles."

The relief that washed over Andi was almost equal to the dismay that hit when she heard a knock on the screen door and spotted Bart McCloskey, clipboard in hand.

"Oh, there's Bart. Auntie, maybe you should go change. Jenny will be—"

Ida Jane let out a delighted squeal. "Bartie."

Andi wasn't the only one who cringed.

Unable to avoid the inevitable, Andi opened the door.

"Hi, Bart. I'll be with you in a minute."

"Bartrum. Look how you've grown," Ida Jane exclaimed, hugging him with relish. "Your mother must be so proud."

Andi put the last of the breakfast dishes in the dishwasher, hen walked to where her aunt had waylaid the contractor. "Ida, Jenny will be here any minute. If you go get ready, you can talk to Bart before you leave. He and I have a few things to discuss."

"Yep, we're finally going to get that roof of yours replaced," Bart said with enthusiasm.

Big mistake. Ida gave Andi a reproving look. "What's wrong with my roof?"

Bart seemed oblivious to the undertones in Ida's voice. "Just about everything," he said, consulting his clipboard. "Those shingles are ready to disintegrate. They won't even make good firewood they're so rotten. You're really lucky you haven't had more water damage, Ida Jane. Of course, the steep pitch helps, but it can only do so much."

"Well, what's this new roof going to cost me?" Ida asked, her eyes narrowing.

Andi had seen this stance before—usually right before Ida Jane creamed whomever Ida suspected of cheating her.

Bart consulted his notes then stated a figure.

"Why, Bart McCloskey!" Ida Jane exclaimed. "You ought to be ashamed of yourself, trying to take advantage of an old lady. I'm going to tell your mother about this."

Bart attempted to defend his bid—which Andi had found quite reasonable—but Ida would have nothing to do with it. "I suppose those big ugly trash bins outside my window belong to you, too, don't they?"

Bart nodded.

"Get rid of them. I want them out of my sight by this afternoon or I'll...sue you." The last came out as an afterthought. As if she'd been groping for the right word.

Andi looked out the window just as a dust-colored minivan pulled into the parking lot. "Jenny's here, Auntie. You're not going to wear your nightgown to go shopping, are you?"

"Oh, dear," Ida Jane said, moving with surprising agility, given her hip problems. "I don't want to miss my hair appointment."

Hair appointment? That does it. I'm calling her doctor.

"Bart…"

"Andi…"

She let him speak first.

"I'm not gouging anybody, Andi," Bart complained with justifiable frustration. "You walked this roof with me. You saw how bad it is. Roofs like this are difficult. I'm not even charging you for any of the underlayment that needs to be replaced."

"I know, Bart. I'm sorry. I'd hoped to have the job done before Ida came home from the ranch, but…she came back sooner than expected. She's a little touchy right now. She flies off the handle at the drop of a hat."

Or any time she talks to me.

"Do the job, Bart. Please. As quickly as possible. I'll make sure everything is squared away with Ida Jane."

Bart nodded but he added, "Okay, but I can't afford to have her spreading the word among the Garden Club ladies that I'm overpriced. Word of mouth is my only advertisement and that would kill me."

Andi doubted that. Bart was the only licensed roofer in Gold Creek. "Jenny will talk to her," Andi assured him. "And one good thing is, Ida probably won't remember any of this."

Again with the flippancy. What is wrong with me?

Bart was obviously wary when he left, but at least he'd promised to start ripping off the old roof in the morning. Andi had no idea how she was going to fix this with Ida Jane, but she'd have to try.

Andi finished straightening up the kitchen then went outside to find her sister…and Harley. Jenny had called last night to tell Andi that she'd offered to give Harley a ride to town when he'd come to the office to ask for the day off.

"I can't believe you coerced him into looking for his motorcycle. Aren't you the sweet-talker," Jenny had said, not giving Andi time to set the record straight. "I have a lullaby to sing. Gotta run. See you in the morning."

Andi had tried calling back later, but the line had been busy. On those rare nights when Sam was out of town, the phone at the O'Neal house was occupied for hours at a stretch.

"Hey," Jenny hollered, waving from the open door of the van. "I found a few more of Ida's things. Come help us."

Andi draped her damp dish towel over the railing and trotted down the steps. She'd dressed for today's reconnaissance mission in broken-in battle dress uniform pants—the standard military wear known by its acronym, BDU—and a bright orange T-shirt. Her black lace-up boots, which reached the bottom of her calves, felt like old friends.

"Well, don't you look…armed and dangerous. You're not armed, are you?"

"Believe it or not, sis, the government wanted their weapons back when I left the service," Andi replied.

Her lighthearted reply sounded inane the minute Harley appeared, two brown paper bags clasped in his arms. "Good morning," he said politely. "Where do you want these, Jenny?"

"Just put them on the porch by the back door. Andi can decide what she wants to do with the stuff."

"What exactly is in the bags?" Andi asked, unable to keep her gaze from following Harley as he walked away. His jeans appeared to be the same pair he had on yesterday, but his shirt was different. A much-washed chambray that clung to his nicely contoured shoulders.

Jenny coughed with exaggerated effort.

Andi gave her a look any sister would understand.

Laughing, Jenny grabbed Andi's arm and led her off in the opposite direction—toward the bordello's front porch.

"Wait. I want—"

"He's not going anywhere. You've got the car, remember?" Jenny said softly. "I just need a minute."

Andi relaxed. Her original timetable was shot to hell anyway, so what would a few minutes more matter? "Okay."

"Ida called me on my cell phone a few minutes ago."

Andi almost tripped over the curb. "You're kidding."

Jenny frowned. "She was upset. She said you were trying to drive her to bankruptcy."

A flutter of panic ruffled through Andi's chest. "She was in the kitchen when Bart stopped to sign the contract to replace the roof. We'd agreed on a price. This was just a formality. But Ida freaked out. She said the roof was fine."

Jenny looked upward. "It looks pretty bad to me."

Andi nodded. "Believe me, I don't want to do it. It's coming out of my—" She stopped. She hadn't been completely honest with her sisters about Ida Jane's financial woes. Partly because by the time Andi arrived home, Josh had been so sick, she hadn't wanted to add to Jenny's burden. And Kristin was seldom around and seemed to have some problems of her own. Plus, their personal history hadn't included sharing each other's troubles for many years.

"I've got it covered," Andi said. "But I don't seem to handle Ida Jane well. At all. In fact, I can't say anything without her acting like I'm trying to undermine everything she's worked so hard to accomplish. Maybe there's a gene missing in my makeup or something."

Jenny, who'd pulled her long hair into a stylish twist, wrapped one arm around Andi's shoulders. They were nearly the same height, but built differently. Jenny was long-bodied, willowy, Andi more compact and solid. "Honey, don't say that. I used to envy your relationship with Ida. You both liked to do the same things. You loved puttering in the workshop and sprucing up the antiques." She made a face. "I hated the dust, and the smell of tung oil made me retch."

Andi relaxed slightly. That was true, but it didn't explain why she and Ida had been at odds almost since the day Andi returned from Virginia.

As if hearing her unasked question, Jenny said, "You're the new regime, Andi. She recognizes that, and it's hard to let go. Give her time to adjust. Whenever Ida and I talk about what's going on at the bordello, she always seems fine with your decisions."

"With you, maybe. Not with me."

"Whoo-hoo," a thin voice called. "Girls, I'm ready."

The sisters looked toward the rear porch. Ida was standing at Harley's side, looking as perky as a young woman on a date. And festive enough for a luau. She'd changed from her robe and slippers into a Hawaiian-print muumuu that probably hadn't been out of the closet in thirty years.

"Oh, my Lord," Jenny murmured.

Andi bit down on a smile. "Suddenly, I don't feel so sorry for myself. I'm going for a stroll in the mountains, and you get to go shopping with Mrs. Don Ho."

She flinched when her sister pinched her on the back of the arm, but even the pain didn't dampen her good mood.

"WE'D BETTER PICK UP the pace," Andi said two hours later. The sun felt hotter than she'd expected—a fact that could be attributed to the elevation and the lack of shade.

Andi knew the dangers of both. She'd helped rescue her share of ill-prepared day hikers who wound up lost, disoriented and suffering from heatstroke.

It irked her that she'd lost some of her edge.

"Do we have to walk the whole road today?" Harley asked from a foot or two behind her.

Andi heard the breathless quality in his voice and mentally reprimanded herself. Even the fittest flatlander needed time to acclimate to the mountains.

"No. Of course not. I'd like to cover as much as possible," she said, scanning the vista that stretched for miles. "But it's your dime."

In the far distance, she saw the white-capped Sierras. She'd spent two incredible summers working in Yosemite's Tuolumne Meadows, but she hadn't found time for so much as a camping trip since her return.

Harley slowly trudged to her side. "Well, if that's all I'm paying you, then let's slow down."

Andi chuckled. For a man who was obviously not used to this kind of hiking, he'd held his own. True, he hadn't shown any real enthusiasm for the task, but he hadn't complained either.

He'd removed his shirt and had stuffed it into the backpack he carried; his white undershirt bore the logo of a beer company and sported a small rip in one sleeve. A thrift-store purchase, she assumed. Unpretentious in both dress and manner, he resembled neither cowboy nor biker. He was an enigma, and Andi had to admit, he fascinated her in a way that didn't seem wise.

"What's poison oak look like?" he asked, absently scratching his forearm.

"'Leaves of three, let them be,'" she quoted a poem she learned as a child. "I read somewhere that it would only take a quarter ounce of the poison-oak toxin to infect everyone on earth.''

Harley scratched more vigorously. ''I had a rash on my neck for a while after Lars picked me up. He thought it might be poison oak. Maybe we should call this search off.''

Andi took a deep breath. ''We can. If that's what you want. But…'' She wished she had more self-control. After all, it wasn't any of her business if he didn't want to find his bike.

He tilted his head, waiting for her to finish her thought. The sun accentuated his golden-tinged waves, and Andi pushed her sunglasses tighter to her nose. It wasn't fair that he was so darned handsome, and she was so attracted to him. The timing couldn't have been worse—even without the matter of his missing past.

''It's not going to get any easier, is it? I know this must be hard for you, but will putting it off help?''

His shoulders stiffened. ''I didn't say I was canceling the search for good. I just don't want to contract another case of poison oak. It itched like hell.''

His peevish tone made her smile. ''Well, it won't kill you. At worst, it goes systemic and you swell up like the Elephant Man, but I've only seen that happen once.''

The look of horror on his face made her regret her teasing. She brushed the backs of her fingers across his arm. ''I'm kidding. You're safe up here on the road. It will only become an issue if we spot something down in one of these ravines. But I don't expect you to do any climbing, and I've developed an immunity.''

Andi had hiked this area many times in high school as a member of the sheriff's volunteer Search and Rescue team. By the look of it, the rugged terrain hadn't improved over the past ten years. Two of her recoveries had included searching for cars that had gone off the road. Cars were difficult enough to spot, given the density of foliage. The chance of seeing a motorcycle—which could be in fragments by the time it hit the bottom of some ravine—wasn't promising.

"What do you say we try for the next ridge?" she asked, nodding toward a plateau about half a mile away.

He looked undecided.

She reached out and took his hand, holding it upright between them. "This area is like a W," she said, forming the letter using his first three fingers.

"We're here," she said, poking the base between his index and middle finger. When had his hands gotten so strong and work-worn? She'd always been attracted to men with powerful-looking hands, but the nicks and scars, blood blisters and calluses on this hand seemed almost a sacrilege. Didn't Sam provide gloves for his crew, she thought, momentarily distracted.

She swallowed loudly. "We'll stop here," she said, drawing her finger up the soft inside flesh to the tip then bending it at the knuckle to make the distance half as long. When she looked into his eyes, the tiny bit of saliva remaining in her throat and mouth disappeared.

"What if this is just a big waste of time?" he asked. His cream-colored hat shaded his face. The front rim was creased in an awkward fold not found in more expensive hats.

Andi found the wrinkle oddly endearing. She'd learned a long time ago that clothes did not make the man. Neither did expensive cars or substantial bank accounts. It was heart and head, grit and soul that determined worth. So far, she liked Harley's heart, grit and soul. It was the missing stuff inside his head that worried her.

"It's my time," she said, letting go of his hand. "And believe it or not, this is like playing hooky for me. In fact, it's exactly what I did when I was a kid and skipped school.''

"You went looking for lost motorcycles?"

She started to lead the way up the hill. Normally, Andi didn't like to talk about herself. There really wasn't much of interest to tell, she figured. But Harley was a good listener.

"Actually, I'd pretend I was an explorer. Like Kit Carson or Jedediah Smith. I'd take off with a topo map—which was cheating, of course—a compass and my lunch.''

"Wouldn't your teachers report you as missing?"

"Jenny's handwriting is *just* like Ida Jane's. You have no idea how handy that was,'' she added with a wink.

Before she could turn back, he reached out and took her arm, making her stop. "Why are you doing this? And don't say for exercise. Your sister told me you jog ten miles a day.''

Andi moved sideways slightly so he was forced to let go. Habit, she figured. She'd never liked men crowding her space. "Run,'' she corrected. "Jogging is for sissies. I'm a marine. I run.''

His grin lit up his face. "Sorry.''

She shrugged. "Easy mistake. But my sister is wrong. I haven't run for days. Partly because I stubbed my toe on the leg of an oak nesting table, and partly because I've been busy meeting with contractors. So this is the first decent exercise I've had in a week.''

He didn't look entirely satisfied with her explanation, but she turned away and resumed walking.

"You still haven't answered my question,'' he said close behind her. "Why are you doing this? There are other forms of exercise that don't waste a whole day. You hardly know me, so it's not like you're helping an old friend or a long-lost relative.''

"We could be related," she said, trying to keep her tone light. "Cousins, maybe. What if your mother was my grand-father, Bill's, sister? Ida said she never knew anything about Bill's family. He came from back East. You might have been sent by the family to find us."

When she looked at him, he shook his head slowly, as if to deny the thought. Before she could say anything else, the sound of a car engine—roaring as it climbed the steep grade—filled the air.

"Traffic," she said, drawing Harley closer to the edge of the road. She braced for a dust cloud but luck—and the breeze—was with them.

A Subaru Outback with a thick layer of grime obscuring its forest-green color pulled alongside them and stopped. The passenger window slid down. "Hey, there, need a ride?" the driver called.

Andi ducked down and looked inside. "Hi, Mr. Camp-bell. Jonas."

Ron Campbell was the high-school music teacher. On Sundays, he acted as music director at the Methodist church. His other children were married and living in the valley. Jonas, who was Andi's age, was mentally disabled and still lived at home.

"Well, Andi Sullivan, bless my soul, we haven't seen you in ages, have we, Jonas? You remember Andi, don't you? She's the girl who rescued Pooh Bear Kitty from the tree after that big windstorm."

Andi glanced at Harley, who gave a questioning look. Dropping her backpack in the dust, she squatted beside the door. "How'ya doin', Jonas? Still making wooden toys? I'd be interested in selling some at the Old Bordello if you ever have any extra."

"Okay," Jonas said with a wide smile. His round face

and slightly slanted eyes were unlined, innocent. "Okay, Dad?"

Ron made a broad gesture. "We've been donating them to Valley Children's Hospital, but it couldn't hurt to sell a few. Maybe we'd make enough money to buy more material." He leaned around his son to get a better look at Harley. "Say, aren't you the fella from the Rocking M? The one Lars Gunderson rescued."

Harley reached inside the car to shake hands with both men. "That's me. Harley Forester," he said, introducing himself.

Andi blushed at her social gaffe.

"What kind of wood do you use, Jonas?" Harley asked. "We have a bunch of leftover pieces at the ranch. Mostly cedar, but there's some pretty redwood and a little bit of hickory, too."

Andi felt an odd flutter in her chest. *Kind and generous. Two primary requirements on my Daddy List.* The thought distracted her until she heard the roar of male laughter. "What'd I miss?" she asked.

Harley accidentally brushed against her shoulder when he lowered himself to one knee beside her. "Mr. Campbell said you and your sisters used to play in the band. Somehow I can't picture you with a tuba."

The merriment in his tone made her skin tingle. *A sense of humor had been on the list, too.* "We drew straws. I lost."

"She was a valiant tuba player, I'll give her that," Ron said. "Never missed a practice unless she was out helping with Search and Rescue. When Andi Sullivan says she's going to do something, she does it," he stated emphatically.

Andi felt herself blush again. She stood up and dusted off her knees. "Well, nice talkin' to you, Mr. C. Tell Mrs. C. I said hello."

After a little more chitchat, the station wagon pulled away. Andi and Harley huddled, backs to the dust until it was safe to turn around.

"Mrs. Campbell had a stroke a couple of years ago. She doesn't go out a lot anymore," Andi said, suddenly feeling an odd tug on her heartstrings. "She used to make the most heavenly fudge. Whenever the band traveled, she'd send each band member little individual packages."

He studied her as if trying to read her mind. "It's hard watching someone you care about suffer," he said.

Andi pushed away the image of Ida Jane looking confused and fretful this morning over whether today was Monday.

"Hank told me his mother suffered a severe stroke when she was fifty-five and needed full care for nearly eighteen years," Harley said. "He and his brother ended up having to sell the family farm to pay the bills." He frowned. "You're worried about Ida Jane, aren't you?"

Andi didn't try to deny it. "She was the best mother any kid could have hoped for. People thought she was crazy taking on three tiny babies at her age, but Ida told me she never thought twice about it. Our mother was like a daughter to her. Our grandparents were dead. There was no one else."

"What about your father's family?"

"He emigrated from Ireland as a teenager. His parents are gone now, but he has four brothers and two sisters still living there. We met them—and a swarm of Irish cousins—when we were fifteen. Ida Jane took us to visit. Jenny and I had fun but couldn't wait to get home. Kristin begged Ida to let her stay."

"Really? How come?"

"I don't know. Kris is different. She moved there right out of high school. Worked as a caregiver for a year or so then returned to the United States to share a place with two of our cousins.

"But I know why Jenny and I were so anxious to get home."

"Why?"

Andi hesitated. It was one thing to admit this to yourself, quite another to share it out loud. "In Gold Creek, we were the Sullivan *triplets*," she stressed the word. "In Ireland, we were just three more Sullivan kids. Believe me, it was a rude awakening to find out you're not as special as you thought you were."

He closed the gap between them, automatically taking the outside position like a gentleman of old. His bare arm brushed against hers. The innocent contact produced a not-so-innocent response in her body. "You *are* special, Andi," he said with a rueful smile. "I knew that the first time I met you. Even without a wide frame of reference."

Andi was very tempted to test the boundaries of this attraction, but a relationship wasn't part of her plan. "Thanks. I'll remember that." She hadn't meant to sound so snide, but she could tell by the way he dropped back, she'd cut him down.

Amazingly he caught up with her a few steps later and asked, "Is Ida's memory getting worse?"

"We're not sure what the problem is," Andi admitted. "A few years ago she was diagnosed with high blood pressure. We thought she was managing it with medication, but when she fell and broke her hip, the doctors discovered an imbalance in her electrolytes. They blamed the diuretic she was taking.

"Now she's on some other medications, but Ida got it into her head that the pills were to blame for her problems, so sometimes she simply doesn't take them."

"That can't be good."

"Even worse, she'll feel guilty later then take a double dose. One doctor said this could cause a stroke." Andi couldn't stand the thought. "That's one of the reasons she's been staying at the ranch. So Jenny could dispense her meds.

"We also need to keep an eye on her *toddy* consumption. Ida's always been fond of a mixed drink or two in the late afternoon. But the doctor has limited her to one glass of wine a day."

"What does she think of that?"

Andi made a face. "She's not happy about it, but at least with Jenny she's cooperative. I don't know what will happen now that she's back at the bordello. Ida gets very defensive when I try to help her. We used to be close, but now she treats me like Nurse Ratched in *One Flew Over the Cuckoo's Nest.*"

She remembered too late that he probably wouldn't know what she was talking about. But he ignored the movie reference, saying instead, "You really have your hands full, don't you?"

The sympathy in his tone left her slightly undone. Picking up the pace, she marched toward a turnout where a fallen bull pine rested at a sixty-degree angle.

"That looks like a good place to stop."

She needed water, a snack, something to shake her out of this funk. A ten-mile run was a piece of cake compared to this slow-paced soul-searching that seemed guaranteed to stir up memories. And since he didn't have any, she thought grimly, the entire exercise was one-sided.

THIS TIME when she took off, Harley made up his mind to keep up—even if it killed him. He didn't think of himself as particularly macho, but Andi was definitely in better shape than he was, and it irked him.

When they reached the fallen tree—carved with layers of initials and funny-shaped hearts, he could barely breathe. Tiny silver dots zipped across his vision. He groped for a worn limb to keep his balance.

"Dang," he wheezed. "Tell me it's the altitude. Even if you have to lie."

Andi dropped her backpack on to the flattened weeds at the base of the pine then hunched over, hands on her knees. Harley was gratified to see her shoulders heave. Sweat had darkened a spot on her T-shirt between her shoulder blades. After a minute, she dropped to a squat and opened the bag to retrieve a water bottle. "It is."

She offered it to him first.

"Not yet."

Her nod seemed to hold respect, as well as understanding. Harley's chest would have swelled with pride if he could have managed a deep breath.

As the sound of their gulping air lessened, Andi rose and hopped to a seat on the log. She juggled the half-empty plastic bottle between her hands as if looking for a message in the water. An odd image struck. Harley pictured himself holding a black ball in his hands. A much younger voice called out an ambiguous, but mysterious-sounding message.

Rolling his head to ease the tension in his neck, he pushed the image away. If it was a memory, it might bring on a headache—which was the last thing he needed here. "You didn't want Ida Jane to move back to the bordello, did you?"

She offered him half of her granola bar, which he declined. "The timing sucks. The roofer starts tomorrow. I have an electrician coming in next week. Ida's not too steady on her feet, you know. She could trip again. Get hurt."

He sensed this was the truth, but not the whole truth. "How does she feel about all this work?"

The look she gave him said *Bingo*.

"You haven't told her?"

"She met Bart, the roofing contractor, this morning." Her expression told him the meeting wasn't satisfying. "Jenny and I have both tried to keep her up to speed, but it's difficult. Some things we tell her don't stick. Other times she goes ballistic for no reason. When I mentioned replacing some windows with dual-pane glass, she came unglued." She frowned. "Wanna guess what my December utility bill was?"

When she mentioned the dollar figure, Harley gave a low whistle. "Even if Ida doesn't understand the rationale behind your improvements, it sounds like you have a handle on what needs to be done. For everyone's benefit."

The look she gave him was filled with doubt, and for the first time since he'd met her, Andi Sullivan appeared vulnerable. In need of a friend. The thought seemed diametrically opposed to what he knew of her. But what *did* he know?

He still didn't know why she was helping him. Just to avoid a confrontation with her aunt? He didn't think so.

She re-capped her bottle, stuffed the granola bar wrapper into her pack, then hopped to her feet. "Shall we press on?"

Harley stopped her with a hand to her bare forearm. The contact made her freeze. Harley felt a current pass through him. Her skin was slick from exertion, which he found incredibly sexy. He could picture the two of them naked and sweat-drenched after making love.

"Maybe we should turn around," he suggested, struggling to keep his voice level. The farther they climbed up this hill, the less he wanted to be there. Instinct told him to top, but he couldn't very well admit that to Andi—who was eyeing him as though he'd just suggested they elope.

"It's your call," she told him, "but I guarantee this will be my last window of opportunity for a long time." She made a negating gesture. "Of course, you can always hire somebody else."

Harley reviewed his options—as he had much of the night while tossing and turning. He reminded himself that finding his bike—if there was a bike—might lead to him recovering his memory. Which was a good thing, right?

A sudden surge of red colored her cheeks. She looked down and kicked a stone with the toe of her hiking boot. "I'm sorry, Harley," she said softly. "This is your life, not mine, and I don't have any business pushing you to do something you don't want to do."

She looked flustered. He liked her flustered. It made him feel as if he had a chance to get under her armor.

"Maybe I'm just as much of a busybody as Gloria Hughes—you know, the lady who writes the gossip column. I mean, it's not like this is *my* problem—I have enough of those waiting for me at the bordello."

She sighed. "Do you want to know the *real* reason I volunteered to do this?"

No. "Tell me."

"Because I've seen your eyes glaze over when the other cowboys start talking about their rodeo exploits and bar fights. Maybe working at the Rocking M is enough for you at the moment, but you don't belong there."

Harley's male response to her sex appeal warred with his intellectual response to her challenge. He knew at a gut level he wasn't living the life he'd lived before, but something kept him from venturing beyond the safe little world he'd created for himself at the Rocking M. *Fear?*

"It's good enough for your brother-in-law," he argued.

"Soon-to-be brother-in-law," she corrected. "But Sam's a rancher, and he knows you're not. He told me he thinks you're using the Rocking M for therapy—to heal and get your bearings."

It annoyed him to think that people were speculating about his state of mind behind his back, but Andi put her hand on his arm and said, "Small towns are like families, Harley. We talk about each other because we care. It's only natural to worry about the people in your life. And however you arrived—crashed motorcycle or alien invasion—" her grin made her look about ten "—you're a part of our lives."

Her fingers were callused. He wanted to turn her hand up to investigate, but she stepped away, burying both hands in the pockets of her fatigues. "Sorry. That was me on my high horse again."

"If you were suffering from amnesia, you'd have been searching for your past from day one, wouldn't you?" he asked.

Her shoulders rose and fell. "Hard to say. I'm an action kind of girl. Downtime is pure hell for me."

"So I've noticed."

Her smile was as feminine and enticing as he'd ever seen, but the look in her eyes was serious. "This is your business, Harley. Not mine. It's your call whether we go on or not."

Go on. To where? The future or the past?

"What did you want to be when you grew up?" he asked, stalling while he tried to calm the trepidation building in his belly.

She blinked once then said, "A veterinarian. A smoke jumper. A pilot. An FBI agent. Not necessarily in that order."

Her smile looked curious, but she didn't return the question. What good would it do? he thought bitterly.

"Lately," he told her, "I've been wondering if, as a

child, I might have dreamed of being a cowboy and this is my way of fulfilling that fantasy." He took a deep breath of clean, pine-scented air. "I mean, think about it. If you woke up tomorrow with no memory or obligations—virtually a clean slate, you could pretty much pick your life, couldn't you?"

Her eyes opened wide, as if the thought had never crossed her mind. "We all have obligations, Harley. That comes with being born."

He liked the way she argued with him. "But mine belong to my old life. To the person I was. Since I can't remember that person, he doesn't exist, right?"

She frowned in thought. "But you do exist." She punched him lightly. "In body."

"But this isn't the same body that woke up at Lars's cabin with the mother of all headaches. And while I might not be much of a cowboy, thanks to my job, my body is a heck of a lot more fit than it was when I first got here."

Her eyes did a quick toe-to-head scan, and she nodded. "That's true. You've toned up a lot. But we're more than just muscle and bone. What happened to the old you? Where'd he go?"

A pulse point of light flickered behind his eyes. A warning. "I don't know. I admit there's a whole side of me that doesn't fit this life. Little pieces that don't belong to this puzzle. Not memories exactly, but impressions."

She stepped closer. Her scent—something fresh and natural—reached him. "Like what?"

The sharp sensation in his brain oscillated. He moved backward until his hip brushed against the log. Finding a flattened-out spot that had obviously served as a resting spot for other butts, he sat down, letting his legs dangle. His feet felt hot inside his secondhand black Ropers, now tan with dust.

As tempting as it might have been to reel Andi into the space between his knees, the suggestion of a headache made him rest his elbows on his thighs.

"Let's see," he said, trying to think of how to answer her question. "The other night at the Slowpoke. After you and your friends left. I got into an argument with the bartender."

Harley's memory of the incident was vague. Not because he'd had too many beers, but because he'd blacked out after he'd snapped. According to the story circulating in the bunkhouse the next morning, the mouthy bartender had made a comment about Andi "screwing Ida Jane out of the antique business," and Harley had reacted by trying to shove the guy's tonsils down his throat.

"Oh, yeah, I heard about that," she said.

"You did?"

She chuckled. "Probably ten minutes after it happened. Donnie stopped by for a cup of coffee and told me." She shrugged. "Like I said, this is a small town. People talk."

Harley sighed. "The image I have of myself—as Harley—doesn't include public brawls. I mean, in order to be consumed by rage, don't you need a background, history, passion?" He couldn't bring himself to say what he was thinking. *I don't have any of those things in my life.*

Andi lightly cuffed his shoulder. "Don't sweat it. Rollo's a self-medicated, undereducated idiot. Whatever he said to provoke you was undoubtedly stupid. I threw a beer in his face last fall, myself."

"Really?" Harley wondered if she knew what some people were saying about her motives for making the changes at the bordello.

"Right after we started the 'Haunted Bordello' advertising campaign, Rollo said something like, 'Who cares if some slut was murdered? She probably deserved it.'"

"You tossed a beer in his face?"

"A Guinness, no less. Broke my heart to waste good beer on a jackass."

He chuckled. "Remind me not to piss you off."

As if embarrassed, Andi suddenly dropped to one knee and dug in her bag until she produced a pair of binoculars. "Maybe I'll just take a peek around. Since we're here."

When Harley failed to acknowledge the suggestion, she paused in the process of removing the protective lens caps and looked at him. "Unless you really want to call the whole thing off."

He looked at the ground. "I like it here in Gold Creek. I like you. I don't want to screw that up."

She went very still. "I like you, too, Harley. The past-few-months you. But I know I've barely scratched the surface of who you really are."

Something about her tone made him ask, "Are you saying you won't get involved with me unless I find out the truth about my past?"

She brushed a lock of hair off her forehead. Her shoulders lifted and fell with casual grace, but Harley sensed her answer was filled with import. "I don't know. But whatever comes from finding your bike—*if* I can find it—is for your benefit, not mine. I have no idea how it will change things."

He crossed his arms. "But things *will* change."

"I agree, but..." She drew out the word. "Isn't it better to find out *now* instead of a year from now?"

CHAPTER FIVE

WHILE ANDI WAITED for Harley to make up his mind, she stepped closer to the edge of the precipice and moved the powerful binoculars in an arcing motion just below treetop level. An errant hint of color caught her eye, and she paused.

Just as she brought the image into focus, a woodpecker peeled away from the tree he'd been about to plunder. She lowered the glasses and was startled to find Harley standing just a few inches away.

"Did you see something?"

His proximity sent a weird flutter through her chest. Her instinct was to shove him away—a defensive move perfected when she'd been the only woman in an office filled with horny marines, but she stifled the impulse.

"A peckerhead," she said, trying not to breathe in his scent. If his cologne was a popular brand, it wasn't one she recognized. More woodsy and fresh, like soap and the great outdoors with just a teasing hint of patchouli.

He turned his chin, a question in his eyes.

Andi had to swallow to work up enough moisture in her mouth to speak. "A woodpecker," she clarified. *Have his eyes always been this blue or is it just because the sky is so clear at this altitude?*

"Ah," he said, smiling.

Oh, God, no. Don't let him smile.

Andi stepped back, almost tripping over the soles of her

heavy hiking boots. Her clumsiness stirred up a cloud of grayish-brown dust.

"They're destructive birds," she said, focusing on anything but what she was feeling. The intensity of her reaction unnerved her. She was not a *chemical reaction* kind of girl. She chose a man by his qualities, not by the way he made her head spin.

And what do I have to show for that?

"They peck holes, fill them up with acorns, then fly off and forget about them, so they have to peck more holes. Stupid birds," she said with more passion than the subject called for.

"Not fond of woodpeckers, I take it?" His teasing tone made her blush.

"According to Bart, it's going to take an extra day to repair the woodpecker damage at the bordello. Extra day means extra bucks."

He nodded more soberly. "I understand. It's personal."

"Pretty much."

She put her hands on her hips and faced him. "So? Are we doing this or not?"

He looked around, his gaze sweeping across the panoramic vista. A vast patchwork of greens and grays stretched westward with occasional scarlike lines, indicating a power line or fire trail.

"Let's give it another hour. I'm afraid that's all my legs can take."

His honesty—and his willingness to take risks—were aspects of his personality that she found extremely appealing. Which, she reminded herself, was not a good thing.

She turned back toward the road and set off, motioning for him to follow. She'd intended to put some space between them, but Harley dogged her heels.

"I may have mentioned this before," he said, "but I admire what you're doing to help your aunt. You and your sisters are part of the Sandwich generation—young adults who are faced with raising children and caring for aging relatives at the same time."

Sandwich generation? Once again, Andi was struck by his intelligence. Sure, he could have heard this theory stated somewhere on the news, but it stayed with him, and he applied it to his observations.

"What choice do we have? We're talkin' family."

He was silent a moment. "That's one of the subjects I try to keep out of mind. If I think about people…connected to me…worrying about me…"

Andi heard the distress in his tone. His amnesia fascinated her, but it frustrated her, too. There were so many avenues of normal conversation that were closed to them. "Where'd you grow up?" "What did you want to be when you were a kid?" "What are your parents like?"

"I've noticed that you tend to think the worst about your past, Harley, but what if…you're a scholar or a surgeon or someone vital to national security?"

His laugh reminded her of her first crush—Bob Sanders, her junior-high-school math teacher. He'd made Andi's secret list—Potential Husbands. Until he married Miss Jerrond, the French teacher.

Breathing hard again, Harley pointed to a plateau a quarter of a mile ahead. "Water break. Up there."

They squeezed under the minuscule area of shade afforded by a scrawny oak. A lone granite boulder—probably left behind when the road went in—offered a fairly level bench for their rest stop. After graciously helping her get settled, Harley hopped up beside her.

He slouched forward slightly, his back an attractive curve. He took a drink from the water bottle he'd pulled from the backpack, then held it out to her. Andi shook her head. She wasn't ready for that kind of intimacy.

"For a while when I looked in the mirror, I'd see a stranger. Now, I've slowly gotten to the point where my face is starting to look familiar. I work with people I've come to know. People in town wave at me. It's the level of recognition a person wants in his life. The thing that worries me about digging up my past is that I won't fit anymore. I'll have to deal with a whole slew of strangers who know me and expect certain things of me. But I won't know them. What if the new me doesn't meet their expectations?"

Andi made a fist to keep from reaching out and touching his face. Dang, he had great skin. Hardly a beard to speak of. Sandy-colored eyebrows and lashes. Even his half-moon scar was attractive.

"Since I can't remember anything about my past, I only know who I am now. And I like myself." He gave her a halfhearted smile that seemed to ask for her approval. "What if I don't like the man I was?"

Andi made herself focus on his plight instead of his body. "I'm trying to understand, Harley. But the idea of starting a second life when the first one is still out there somewhere seems…I don't know. Incomprehensible, I guess."

She put out her hands, frowning at the remnants of cherry-wood stain that hadn't washed off. "It's true you might have been a lobbyist for the tobacco industry in your other life," she said, trying to keep her tone light. "But what if you're a researcher on the verge of finding a cure for cancer?"

A flash of something that looked like pain clouded his eyes. "I was only joking, Harley. I'm sorry."

He nodded. "There's the rub, Andi. I could be a good guy or I could be wanted by the police."

"But your prints would have shown up on the police records," she argued. "And Donnie said they were clean."

When he looked at her with a question in his eyes, she explained, "Donnie told Sam and Sam told Jenny, who told me."

He nodded. "I guess I should find the results of that check reassuring, but we both know the system isn't perfect."

Andi couldn't think of anything supportive to say that wouldn't sound as though she was diminishing his fears. He had every right to feel this way, and she couldn't begin to understand what he was going through. After all, her past was an open book. In fact, thanks to Gloria Hughes, much of Andi's past was documented in the annals of the *Gold Creek Ledger*.

"Don't get me wrong, Harley. I wouldn't trade places with you, but sometimes a little anonymity sounds heavenly."

He smiled again. "Let me guess. You're saying it was hard to be a chameleon in the marines?"

Andi chuckled. "There, too."

"How come you don't talk about your military career?"

Suddenly feeling restless, she sloughed off her backpack and stood up. Keeping her knees flexed, she walked the uneven surface of the boulder until she had a clear view of their surroundings.

The mountain ridges were staggered like knuckles. A gray-blue haze softened the outline of those farthest away. Overhead, the sky was a cerulean blue that reminded her of Harley's eyes.

Since he'd been so frank with her, she decided to talk about her military experience. "I went into the marines for the wrong reasons. Ida and the Garden Club ladies were pestering me to transfer from junior college to the university, but I was tired of school. Burnt out. Bored.

"Then I met a guy at a party who was on leave from the marines. He'd been all over the world. Had a cool car and money in the bank. It sounded like a great opportunity." She looked at him and said, "And, believe me, the corps is perfect for *some* people. I don't regret my experience, I just couldn't make a career out of it."

"Why not?" he asked, his gaze trailing up her legs.

Something in his all-male look made Andi glad she'd shaved her legs, even though she was wearing long pants.

She took a breath. "I missed my old life," she said, knowing how that might be interpreted. "I liked the order and stability of the Marine Corps, and the feeling of being one of an elite few. But in the end, I realized I needed my family.

"At some level, I thought the Corps would take its place, but that never happened. I never had a close woman friend the whole time I was in the service. The women I worked with were extremely competitive."

Out the corner of her eyes, she spotted something that looked out of place. Dropping to her haunches, she put out her hand. "Pass me the glasses."

Harley leaned over to dig in her pack. Andi's hand hovered an inch above the smooth white material stretched taut across his back. He was lean but not skinny. She liked the way his shoulder muscles moved—contoured and sinewy under the soft cotton. Her fingers itched to touch him, but as he straightened, she moved her hand to the right to take the binoculars.

Standing, she lifted the small, powerful glasses to her nose but didn't hold them to her eyes until she'd checked what had attracted her attention in the first place. Moving in minute increments, she slowly scanned between the grayish-green needles of bull pines, around the dense blue-black cluster of live oaks. The purple velvet nubs of the red bush would soon give way to glossy green leaves that would obscure even a very large target.

"I saw something shiny. But I can't—" Another tantalizing glimpse taunted her, but it took three or four seconds for the image to make sense. Because it was upside down. In a tree. Back wheel caught in the Y of a branch like a dead fish suspended twenty or thirty feet above the ground. "I found it."

"It?" Harley barked, jumping to his feet. "My bike?"

Andi swept right and left to get her bearings before lowering the glasses. "A bike, but how many lost motorcycles have you heard of in this area?" She grimaced. "Never mind. Forget I asked. Let's get closer so we can see if it looks new or if it's been there since before either you or I were born."

"Were they making motorcycles back then?" he asked with a grin.

Andi pretended to swing at him with her binoculars. "Watch it, fella. I may be an *ex*-Marine, but I survived MCT—that's Marine Combat Training—at Camp LeJeune, so I'd be a bit more careful with the insults, if I were you."

"Yes, sir, ma'am." He gave a goofy salute and a smile that looked sexy as hell.

She felt a quiver of trepidation. What if that bike did belong to Harley? What if he turned out to be married with six kids? *Then you're doing his family a service. So shut up and get busy.*

She hopped down from the rock, hefted the strap of her backpack over one shoulder and started walking. She needed to put the attraction she felt for Harley out of her head.

Perhaps once his past was settled, and he turned out to be a dot.com millionaire with a glam wife and three adorable kids, or an uptight lawyer with half a dozen ex-wives, she'd be able to get past this attraction. Unfortunately, none of those possibilities made her feel better.

Andi lengthened her strides. If she was going to lose him, she might as well get it over with before she did something stupid like fall in love.

HARLEY LAGGED behind. His brain was having trouble processing the possibilities. This find would change things. For better or worse? That was the question.

As if attuned to his dilemma, the woman ahead of him paused. She'd charged up the steep incline like Teddy Roosevelt at San Juan Hill, and now faced him, chest heaving from the exertion. She had a lovely body—fit and trim with enough curves to make him stare—especially when a gust of wind made her nipples stiffen against the bright-orange fabric of her T-shirt.

Bold, bright, beautiful. He liked her a lot, was drawn to her, but he'd be a complete and utter fool to think it might lead anywhere.

Suddenly, an image made him stagger. A bleak, hostile landscape the color of bleached bones. Pockmarked craters gave it a moon-surface look. Twisted hunks of steel were scattered like children's jacks. And at the rim of one jagged saucer was the broken body of a child. Limbs charred. Unrecognizable beyond its human form.

"Harley?" Andi called.

A river of ice water passed through his veins. The thrumming in his head reverberated like a drum riff run amok. Was it really so important that he find out whether the image was real or imagined? Dr. Franklin had mentioned something about "false memories." *Please, God, let that one not be real.*

"Are you coming?"

Harley still lacked the ability to answer.

Andi apparently put her own spin on his reticence. "When I was in Search and Rescue, my team leader used to say I had the nose of a bloodhound and the same amount of social skills," she said as she walked toward him. "This is a huge deal for you, if this is your bike. Would you like to go first?"

She held out the binoculars as a peace offering.

Damn, he liked her. *If only—*

Harley cut off the useless thought before it could develop. Dr. Franklin had warned him that depression was common amongst amnesiacs. It came from having too many variables outside his control.

"I once heard a quote that might help you," she'd told him. "*The main thing is to keep the main thing the main thing.* It applies to a lot of things in life, but particularly what you're going through."

"Prioritize," she'd advised him. "Let the rest of the world catch up with you, instead of you trying to catch up with it."

A pain radiated under his breastbone, and Harley wondered momentarily if he was having a heart attack. He tried not to breathe too deeply. A memory—if that's what it was—seemed to hammer at the edge of his consciousness, but it brought with it the white, consuming pain that always left him sick and humbled.

He couldn't handle a second headache episode in Andi's presence. "No," he said. "I can't do this."

She stepped toward him, both hands resting on the strap of her backpack, which was slung over one shoulder. The sunlight glinted off her wind-combed bob—the richest mix of reds and gold he'd ever seen. Her sunglasses were pushed back on the crown of her head like a tiara.

"It's up to you," Andi said, lifting her chin to look him

in the eyes. "We can turn around right now, if that's what you want but…"

He was almost afraid to ask. "But what?"

She looked down as if ashamed of her thoughts. "I know the SAR helicopter pilots who scouted the area said their infrared equipment didn't pick up any signs of life, but by the time Lars brought you to town the whole area was under a couple of feet of snow."

Her sympathetic look made him brace for what was coming. "This question sucks, Harley, and I'm sorry. But, what if you weren't alone that night?"

Harley ground the heel of his hand against the tender scar at his temple. Lars had asked him that question the morning after the accident, and Harley had answered honestly, "I don't know."

Andi's hand on his bare arm pulled him back from the brink of darkness. "Harley, forget it. I shouldn't have brought that up. Lars told us he was pretty sure you were alone."

Her touch soothed, but he couldn't allow himself the intended comfort. Although he'd pushed the idea from his mind these past months, the possibility existed that he'd abandoned someone—buddy, wife or girlfriend—that night.

"That's what I want to believe," he said. "I tell myself if there were someone else, I would have remembered, right? What kind of monster—"

She cut him off. "No. Don't do that to yourself. You can't help it that you can't remember."

But what if I can? For the past few nights, he'd had a dream. At first, he thought it was another of the gruesome nightmares that had plagued him. But unlike those, this one felt connected. Real. Maybe because the images were, in fact, memories of his accident.

"Two nights ago I dreamed that I was falling down a

deep fissure. My body bounced off rocks, rolling over and over, out of control. I didn't know where I was or why I was there, but I opened my eyes to total blackness.

"Cold. I was so cold I thought I was dead. But there was a red-hot pain in my head. And I could smell gasoline." He closed his eyes, trying to reel in the memory. The image remained disjointed—mixed with the panic he'd felt upon waking up.

"It felt like days passed. No one came. The only sound was a constant drip. Like a leaky faucet."

Andi's eyes grew big. "You think it's a memory of your accident?"

"Maybe. I don't know. Usually pain and nausea accompany any kind of memory. But this dream was so intense I woke up shivering."

He closed his eyes picturing the moment he'd awakened. Swamped by feelings he couldn't decipher. "One thing that stayed with me was the sense of being all alone, and knowing that if I didn't do something to help myself I was going to die."

Andi squeezed his arm supportively. "So you did it. You saved yourself."

"I guess so, but I can't *remember* the accident, Andi. I can't remember driving a motorcycle or being a passenger on a motorcycle. I don't even have any memory of Lars picking me up or my first night at the cabin. Nothing— except for that dream."

She moved her hand to the middle of his back and rubbed it, much like a mother might do to a child. "I wish I hadn't said anything. Me and my big mouth. I'm sorry."

He straightened. He didn't deserve her sympathy. The fact that he'd blocked the possibility that someone else might have been hurt from his mind didn't say much about his character.

"No. You're right." His words were clipped, his throat tight with emotion. "I told myself that searching for my bike was a hopeless cause. But maybe I was just trying to postpone the inevitable."

"Harley, it can wait. We don't have to..."

"Yes. We do. *I* do. I can't put it off any longer." He gripped her hand—for luck. For strength. For hope. "Let's go get that damn bike."

AFTER PULLING OUT a variety of clamps, fittings, hooks and who knew what from her backpack, Andi stepped back to survey the mess. Her smile held a distinct air of satisfaction. Harley felt as useful as a cowboy at a quilting bee.

He shoved his hands into his pockets and waited for her cue.

She lifted her chin and looked at him. "You know, there's something we neglected to get straight."

"What?"

"My finder's fee." The impish look in her eyes told him she was kidding. "I mean, what if you turn out to be the guy who invented Velcro?"

His bark of laughter echoed in the trees. He would have given anything to kiss her. Right there. Middle of the road. No future, no past involved. But he took control of his emotions. He didn't want to leave Gold Creek with even more regrets. If this turned out to be his motorcycle, he knew it would be only a matter of time before he was yanked back into his old life.

"Somehow I doubt I'm a big money man. I didn't have one thin dime on me when Lars found me."

"Says Lars." Her eyes sparkled sassily. "What if next week he shows up in town claiming to have hit the mother lode? Uh-huh. Sure. We'll know where it really came from, won't we?"

Harley laughed outright. "Like I said, I kinda doubt it."

She put her hands on her hips and faced him. "Okay. Here's the plan."

Harley liked the way she described each step in the process, making certain he understood her. He listened carefully, but nothing she said about the rappelling process rang even the slightest bell in his memory. He knew he had to trust her experience and expertise to accomplish this.

She drew his attention to a break in the mound of gravel at the edge of the road. "That could be where you went off the road." She'd dropped to a squat and appeared to be studying the ground as if it were a book with a story to tell. "I think you must have been going back down the hill. There's no way you could have gone off at that angle if you were climbing. Is any of this coming back to you?"

He tried to picture himself on a motorcycle, but aside from a throbbing sensation just behind his eyes, nothing else appeared. "No."

He followed her to the edge of the road. The hillside at their feet fell away at a sixty-degree incline and disappeared into underbrush so thick it was impossible to follow it more than twenty feet from where they were standing.

"Look at that broken branch," she said, pointing. "And there's another. Deeper in. My gut says this is the place, but I can't see a thing. I'm going down for a closer look."

Harley looked over the ledge and was hit by a sudden wave of panic. Raw, stomach-turning panic. His skin turned clammy, his respiration shallow, his vision blurred.

"No. I can't let you do it. Let's just mark the spot. I'll hire a crew to recover the bike and whatever else is left. Even if—God forbid—there is someone else down there, a few days won't make any difference."

Andi spun around. "Harley, this is *my* find. I don't want to hand it over to somebody else."

"But it's *my* bike," he shouted. He needed to get away from the ledge, and he wasn't going without Andi.

He grabbed her arm.

She yanked back. Harley's grip faltered, and she seemed to lose her balance. Her right foot stepped backward...into space. Her expression went from anger to consternation, as if she didn't have time for a bothersome little tumble down the side of a cliff.

"Andi." Ignoring the rush of fear that deafened him to the sound of his own cry, Harley reached for her. His fingers felt numb but reflex made them clamp on the material bunched at her waist. This kept her upright long enough for his other arm to swoop behind her shoulders and haul her close.

Bodies in motion—they fell backward to what he knew was safe, level ground. They hit hard, his left shoulder taking the brunt of the impact. Small stones pierced his skin, but Harley didn't care. Pain meant they were alive. Andi was safe.

Neither moved as the dust settled. Harley ignored the screaming fury in his shoulder. The weight resting on his chest more than made up for any ache. She was awkwardly clasped against him, but she felt wonderful—and smelled of fresh air and herbal shampoo.

Andi lifted her head then braced one hand on the ground beside his jaw to push up. "What the hell was that?"

Harley opened his mouth, but it took several seconds to produce the necessary mental state to speak. It didn't help that her midsection was resting squarely against his own. "I thought you were going to fall."

"So?" She arched her neck as if working out a kink. Her breasts—just a few inches from his face—rose with her breath. The movement added to Harley's problems.

"You could have been killed," he said, his tone husky.

Her lips flattened then gave way to a grin. "You were trying to save my life?"

Harley didn't like her condescending tone. "I *did* save you. At no small cost to my own body, I might add."

She rolled to her hip and sprang into a squat beside him so fast Harley barely had time to blink. "You're hurt? I'm sorry. I thought you were goofing around because you didn't want me to go after the bike."

It bothered him that she seemed totally unaffected by the sexual overtones of their encounter. He sat up stiffly, trying not to wince. "I'm fine, but I'm not letting you go down into that ravine."

She rocked back. "You're not."

It wasn't a question. "No."

He didn't try getting to his feet. His vision blurred, and he felt a bit queasy. *Not another damn concussion,* he silently muttered. Andi would probably want to carry him to the car—on her back.

"This has nothing to do with finding your past, does it?" she said, her tone frosty. "You're turning all macho because you think this is too dangerous for a girl."

He didn't like her tone—or the direct hit.

"Harley, I'm an experienced climber. I spent two summers working in Tuolumne Meadows, and I did 5.11 face climbs and 5.10 crack climbs. This isn't even a challenge. Trust me."

He didn't understand the jargon, but he believed her.

"I'll just drop into the gully and snap a couple of pictures. It might not even be your bike, and you would have wasted all that time and money on nothing."

"Fearless Andi Sullivan. Tell me, are you afraid of anything?" He moved cautiously so as not to aggravate the pain in his back. Finally he was sitting.

Andi sat, too—after adding a few inches between them.

"Sure. Most social situations make me jittery. Put me in front of a crowd and my brain freezes solid."

He didn't believe her, but before he could say so she went on, "And I'm afraid of losing my aunt's business." Her gaze dropped, and she tucked in the hunk of shirt that he'd pulled loose.

Were Ida's financial woes really that bad?

"Last week I got a letter from a company called Meridian, Incorporated. They want to buy the old bordello."

"Do you want to sell?" The idea made him uneasy, but he couldn't say why. What did the demise of a run-down old building matter to him?

"Of course not. It's our home. But then I realized it's not my call to make. Ida Jane's name is on the deed. Maybe everything I'm doing is for nothing."

"Have you talked to her about it?"

Andi shook her head. "Not yet. I called a local realtor. His wife is a friend of Ida Jane's. He said there's big money moving into the area, but not to do anything until he'd investigated the company."

"Sound advice," Harley said, surprised by the sense of relief he felt.

Andi rose. "Why are we talking about me? This is your show," she said. "Are we doing it or not?"

Harley took a deep breath. He couldn't put it off forever. "Okay," he said, reaching around to massage his aching shoulder. "But nothing fancy. No shinning up the tree to perform some kind of inverted Evil Knievel trick."

Her quick peck on his cheek made it tough to stay focused, but that, he promised himself, would be his goal. Maybe his unconscious mind was afraid of heights. Maybe his past was about to catch up to him. Maybe he was falling for a woman who was twice the man he was, but he refused to think about any of it. Focus on keeping Andi safe, he told himself. That's all.

TWENTY LONG MINUTES LATER, Andi had two half-inch braided ropes secured to the trunk of a pine as thick as a watermelon. "I'd rather use an oak tree—their roots go all the way to China," she explained, hoping to dispel some of Harley's obvious unease, "but this guy will have to do."

Harley didn't say anything, but he gave the tree a stern look.

"I'll be back in a flash," she said, securing a bright purple anodized clip to her guide rope. She used her teeth to pull on a pair of leather gloves then started walking backward toward the ravine. "All you need to do is keep an eye on my line so it doesn't get twisted. I'll holler if I need anything."

Her pulse was charged, nerves primed. She hadn't been climbing in months, and she had to admit it was fun to show off for a nonclimber. With a jaunty wave, she hopped out and back, dropping a quick three feet over the precipice. Her boots landed cleanly, knees bent to absorb the impact. Once she made certain her lines were clear of debris, she slowly eased downward. Her boots sank into layers of decayed leaves, sending up a moldy smell that reminded her of the bordello's basement. A cluster of bristly, grayish-green bushes grabbed at the long-sleeved, heavy canvas shirt she'd pulled on to protect her arms. The bright-orange garment was left over from her Search-and-Rescue days. She'd dug it out of the closet at Ida Jane's.

"What do you see?" Harley called from above.

She knew he was embarrassed about his acrophobia, but it was a common fear. Jenny and Josh had been avid hikers, but Josh had hated heights. When the three of them hiked to the top of Half Dome, Andi had walked right to the edge of Yosemite's famous landmark. The nearly-five-thousand-foot drop to the valley floor was scary but exhilarating, too. Jenny and Josh had snapped pictures from the safety of the football field–size center plateau.

"Lots of broken branches," she called. "Tons of poison oak. Stay put."

Andi heard a noise above her. A river of shale rained downward. "And keep away from the edge."

"Sorry," he called out, his chagrin obvious.

She liked him way more than was smart. Too bad the future looked even less stable than the ground under her feet.

Almost simultaneous with that thought, the earth gave way and she had to hop, skip and jump the remaining thirty feet to avoid twisting an ankle. Breathless, with adrenaline pumping, Andi took a moment to calm her nerves. As she did, she glanced around.

A debris field—twenty feet ahead and about the same distance in diameter—reminded Andi of a hastily abandoned picnic. Scraps of faded and torn cloth adorned bushes. Small piles of paper and personal items created pockets in the bright-green grass. She tilted her chin and looked skyward at the source of the refuse.

The picture seemed even more impossible from this angle. The massive bull pine consisted of two trees that had grown together at the base and parted at a point about twenty-five feet in the air forming a Y. The branches criss-crossed like a net. A net that had snagged the motorcycle.

"The bike looks like a giant Christmas-tree ornament," she called out.

Harley's reply came a moment later. "Is it new?"

Andi moved closer. Dusty, streaked with grime and pine tar, the bike seemed in amazing shape, given its precarious position. "Brand spankin'—give or take a wrecked fender, two flat tires and a nasty dent in the gas tank. Looks like it's deep burgundy, but it's hard to tell with all the shadows. Gonna take a helluva winch to get it out.''

"Can you see the license plate?'' They'd discussed the possibility of tracing the bike, if moving it was problematic.

"Not yet.'' She shook out more line and stepped clear of her ropes. "I need to get right under it.''

"Be careful,'' Harley shouted. "Don't risk it.''

"Don't worry,'' she called out. "This baby isn't coming down without help. Looks like you had a couple of leather saddlebags on the back. There's stuff all over the ground.''

Andi walked with care amongst the remains of Harley's past. She felt like a crime scene investigator—although thankfully, she could report that no body was in view. She looked upward. "A second helmet is still attached to the bike, Harley. You couldn't have had a passenger.''

She didn't hear his response, but she felt his relief. As she moved directly under the bike, she spotted a small brown hunk of leather. *A wallet.*

Kneeling, she picked it up. Stiff and discolored from the weather, it was fairly well preserved. Her hands shook as she flipped it open. The tiny photo on the Missouri driver's license made her breath catch in her throat. She told herself she was being silly. Foolish. Of course this was Harley's bike. Harley's wallet.

She used her thumb to clean off the condensation on the plastic frame that held the license. Same face, different name.

"Find anything?'' Harley called.

Andi heard the edge of worry in his voice. Stifling her inner disquiet, she stuffed the billfold in a pocket in the leg of her pants and buttoned it for safekeeping.

"There's a mangled laptop,'' she said, moving on. Water seeped from its insides. "It's toast.''

Keeping a running commentary, she shouted out her finds. "Clothes are everywhere." She used a stick to poke at a mound of mildew-splotched briefs. "All rags now." She picked up a long-sleeved blue oxford button-down, faded and torn, but serviceable for her purpose. "Pretty ritzy labels. You didn't buy this at a thrift store."

"What?" Harley called. "I can't hear you."

She quickly scanned the area for anything personal. Under a clump of soaproot shoots, she found a leather-bound book. A journal, she thought. Without peeking inside, she tossed it on top of the shirt.

A little more poking turned up a platinum-encased TAG Heuer watch. A ruined cell phone and a couple of electronic gizmos Andi couldn't identify. "He's not as poor as he thinks he is," she mumbled under her breath. "Unless the bike was stolen, of course."

When she kicked over a clump of mushy newsprint, she unearthed what at one time had been an elegant black velvet jeweler's box. Her fingers were trembling—*from the dampness*—as she pried open the rusted hinge. An engagement ring. A big, flashy diamond surrounded by six smaller jewels. While obviously expensive, the rock didn't appeal to Andi's taste, but she knew women who'd swoon at the sight of it.

"Oh, great," she muttered. "He was on his way to propose to some woman."

She made the snarling noise her sisters called the *bad* sound, then tossed the rest of her discoveries onto the blue shirt and tied the arms together to form a knapsack. With a spare clip, she hooked it to her belt.

"Coming up," she said after snapping a few pictures of the bike and the scene below it.

Instead of the thrill of victory she'd been expecting, Andi felt let down. She'd accomplished her mission, but now what? Like so many other times in her life, she'd leaped without looking. Actually, she had looked ahead—just not far enough. She'd done the smart thing, the right thing, but now she was going to lose a man she'd come to care about.

And he *would* go—just as soon as he remembered the beautiful blonde and the two adorable kids in the photo in his wallet.

CHAPTER SIX

SNAPPING BRANCHES and several muttered curses heralded Andi's ascent, but Harley kept his distance. Just peeking over the top of the ridge was enough to make the pressure build behind his eyes. He chose to pretend that sitting beneath the pine tree watching the tension on her rope amounted to helping her.

A minute later she scrambled over the hump of loose gravel at the side of the road, dusting off leaves, bark and dirt from her pants and shirt. "Made it," she said with a grin. "And I've got a present for you."

He barely heard her words because he was trying to talk himself out of kissing her.

She stepped free of the ropes, then peeled off her gloves, dropping them to the pile of gear. "Look at this," she said, handing him an object from the top pocket near her thigh. A wallet.

Harley's stomach turned over. "Mine?" he croaked. The weight of possibilities pressed on his chest, making it hard to draw a breath. That little leather square in his hand might tell him everything. Was he ready?

"It was lying near some clothes and books and a mangled laptop. Most of the stuff was beyond saving, but I brought up what I could carry," she said, unclipping a funny-shaped cloth bag suspended from her belt. "Animals got everything, I suppose. And weather. This whole area probably spent a couple of months under snow."

She shrugged off her heavy shirt, folding it inside out, then used the hem of her T-shirt to wipe the sweat from her face. Harley caught a tantalizing glimpse of her belly.

Even though the timing was undoubtedly terrible—and the action foolish—he reached out and put his free hand on her shoulder.

She didn't resist when he pulled her to him, although her eyes were wide with surprise. But her lips parted before he lowered his head, and she seemed to welcome his kiss. Harley hadn't kissed a woman since his accident. Whom he'd kissed last and when that might have been were pure guesses, but Harley was willing to bet he'd never experienced anything sweeter and more intoxicating than kissing Andi Sullivan.

Her lips were soft—a little salty. Her tongue wasn't the least bit shy, which didn't surprise him. The way she closed her eyes and the small sound she made were so feminine, so irresistible, he felt a surge of desire rock him.

He wrapped his arms around her and tilted his head to taste her more fully. With eyes closed, he entered a world of lush texture, beautiful colors and scintillating music.

She put her arms around his neck; and the stiff leather object fell from his fingers. He was instantly reminded of why they were standing in the hot sun in the middle of nowhere. Even as her body melted against him, and his body responded, Harley felt the cruel slap of reality.

He dropped his arms and stepped back, breaking her hold around her neck. "I'm sorry, Andi. That was out of line."

She blinked twice. "Was that hazard pay?"

A great comeback, but the little tremor in her voice robbed it of any flippancy. "No. That was me being an idiot. I'm a stranger—a nobody—and my past is *this* close to catching up with me," he said, bending to pick up the billfold.

She sighed. Her expression showed a range of emotions, none he could easily interpret.

He blew the dust from it, then studied the weather-damaged exterior, whitened by moisture and brittle around the edges.

"You'd probably like some time alone to look at this stuff," Andi said, shouldering the coil of rope. As she passed by him, she handed him a red cotton bandanna. "Tie this to a limb before you leave. We'll need help to recover the bike."

Too overwhelmed to express what he was feeling, Harley could only nod.

"I'll wait for you at the car." She turned to leave, but paused. "Harley, I did a little reading about amnesia, and it probably doesn't pay to get your hopes up. Maybe this stuff will trigger a whole flood of memories, but it might not. That doesn't mean you'll never remember."

Her concern touched him. And he knew she was right, but he couldn't quell the double-edged thrill of anticipation coursing through him. Harley waited until the sound of her footsteps was nothing more than a soft whisper, then he dropped to his haunches and opened the wallet.

The first thing he spotted was a driver's license protected by opaque plastic. Fingers trembling, he worked the laminated card free. A state emblem he didn't recognize was his first clue this wasn't going to be the miracle cure.

I'm from Missouri? The question produced a humming in his head. A dangerous sound. One he usually shied away from. But he rose, holding the object to the sunlight.

The photograph was definitely the same face he saw in the mirror each morning—a bit younger, perhaps. The statistics fit: blue eyes/brown hair, six-foot, one-hundred-eighty pounds. It took him a few seconds to calculate his age. Thirty-two. He would turn thirty-three in August.

A Leo, he thought, recalling his conversation with Ida Jane.

Dropping to his haunches, he gave a cursory glance at the items Andi had recovered. Intellectually, he knew that each article was a clue—and he should be dancing with joy, but it was difficult to get excited about the possibilities this find offered when his head was pounding.

He massaged his temple. The faces matched, but what did that mean? Was he Harley Forester? Or Jonathan Jackson Newhall?

ANDI WAS TWIDDLING her thumbs to the sound of Huey Lewis and the News when she spotted Harley slowly trudging down the road. She'd become a master at thumb twiddling during her years in the military; she'd also become adept at reading a man's body language. The man approaching her great-aunt's beloved Cadillac was hurting. Big time.

Andi opened the door and got out. "No bells or whistles?" she guessed.

His head swiveled from side to side, but his gaze seemed fixed on the car's grille. Andi's heart went out to him. If Jenny or Kristin were here, they'd know what to do. Andi would probably blow this, but she'd have to try.

She motioned to the passenger side. "Come on. I'll buy you a beer."

He moved like a sleepwalker. She could tell by the squint around his eyes that he was in pain. Once he was seated, she took a plastic bottle of Extra Strength Motrin from the glove compartment and offered him two gel caps. He swallowed them without water, even though Andi had a water bottle handy.

"I'll be fine," he said, his voice strained.

The wallet and the blue-shirt satchel rested on the seat between them.

Andi started the car and carefully backed the beast into a three-point turn. Rosemarie hadn't been new when Ida Jane bought her twelve years earlier, but after her christening, she'd become a member of the family.

"Can you talk about it?" Andi asked once they were headed back toward the main highway. "Even if there was no instant recall, there must be stuff in the wallet that can help you find out about your past. Credit cards, photos."

Andi didn't want to think about the photo she'd spotted during her quick perusal of the wallet. Unfortunately, she'd been able to think of little else. So far, she'd come up with a dozen scenarios to explain both the engagement ring and the beauty with two kids at her side. None made her feel any better.

Harley let out a sigh. "I didn't look beyond the driver's license. What was the point? I didn't recognize the name on it."

"You're sure it's your wallet?"

"Actually, it belongs to a guy named Jonathan Newhall. But he looks a lot like me."

The frustration in his voice was tinged with dismay. She tapped the signal lever and stepped on the gas. A few miles later she pulled onto a gravel road leading up a sharp driveway to a rustic conclave of bungalows scattered on the steep hillside and connected by decks and wooden walkways.

She parked in front of one set of buildings then grabbed her purse. "Come on," she said. "And bring the booty. I'm good at puzzles."

The Yosemite Bug Hostel's Recovery Bistro was housed in what had originally served as a mess hall for young men who'd stepped outside the boundaries of the law. A pair of Bay Area entrepreneurs had converted the forty-year-old dormitories to a youth hostel, and eventually the swell of business had necessitated building new suites to cater to a more moneyed clientele. Weekend barbecues now attracted diners from all over, locals and tourists alike.

Since Harley seemed immersed in an introspective fog, Andi ordered two Bug Brews and carried both to a little table overlooking a wooded gully not unlike the one she'd just scaled. "Sit. Drink," she ordered.

He pitched the wallet on to the table then sat down, placing the blue carryall on the extra chair. He sighed weightily before picking up his glass. "I guess at some level I expected this to open the door to my past. Just like magic."

He took a long gulp then looked at Andi. "Thanks."

Andi sipped her beer. She preferred iced tea, but this beer was a prop. She knew from experience guys opened up when they had a brewsky in hand. "I'd be disappointed, too. That's only human. But it doesn't mean the key isn't here." She tapped the wallet. "It just hasn't made it to the lock in your brain. Mind if I take a look?"

Harley shrugged then polished off the rest of his beer. "I need another. How 'bout you?"

"Not yet." She waited until he left the table before snatching up the billfold. She gave the outside a cursory scan—*not cheap*—then opened it. She removed the driver's license and looked at the signature. She'd read somewhere that even people with the kind of amnesia that wiped out all past memories—retrograde amnesia, she thought it was called—often retained the same handwriting.

Jonathan signed his name with a flourish that rendered it almost illegible.

"Jon," Harley muttered, sitting down a moment later. "Could I possibly have a more ordinary name?"

"It's not J-O-H-N," she said, smiling. "It's Jonathan. That's not so common."

"Hmmph. You have a beautiful name. Andrea."

He said it with a lover's lilt.

She felt herself blush. "Only problem is I've been Andi ever since the fourth grade when I told the school secretary I wouldn't come back if anyone called me that sissy name again."

"I like that sissy name."

"You would...Jonny." Her teasing earned her a smile, but it disappeared when she turned the wallet sideways to open an accordion file of photos. These hadn't fared as well as the laminated driver's license and half-dozen credit cards. Most of them had gotten wet and were a smeary mess sticking to the plastic. A couple in the center had fared better. She looked for the one she'd seen earlier.

"This could be your family," she said in a small voice. She ran her finger over the plastic rectangle. The image of a woman with long blond hair flanked by two towheaded little girls was clearly visible. Andi guessed the children to be about six and four.

Harley anchored his elbows on the table and sat forward. She spun the wallet around to give him a clearer view. "You're right," he said dispassionately. "Those could be my kids. Which would mean that for some reason I abandoned them in Missouri—if the address on the driver's license is legit—and they don't know if I'm living or dead."

Andi's heart ached for him. He was a good man, despite how damaging the scenario he'd just described might sound. "Let's call information in Bainbridge, Missouri, and find out," she said, leaning down to dig the cellular phone out of her purse.

She thought Harley was going to stop her, but he sank back in the chair and took a big gulp of beer. Andi gave the operator the name and address on the license. "Nothing?" she exclaimed at the news. "Okay. Thank you."

"Maybe she gave up and moved away," he suggested.

Andi rolled her neck. "Oh, pul...lease," she said, taking

a drink of beer. "If this woman loved you enough to give you two adorable children, she sure as heck wouldn't just take off. Not if there was any hope at all that you might show up. I know I wouldn't," she added without meaning to.

Her words made him smile, and some of the anxiety left his eyes. "There could be another explanation," he said. "She might be my sister. Or a friend."

Andi thought about that diamond ring she'd found. "Have you looked at the other stuff yet?"

"Nope." He eyed the bag as though it held snakes and scorpions. After a full minute, he picked up the knapsack and dropped it on the table. "What's inside it?"

"Guy stuff. Rusted electric shaver. A book of some sort. An expensive-looking watch."

That made his eyebrow shoot up. "Really?"

He took another drink of beer before drawing the bag closer to his side of the table. Andi held her breath as he opened it. The damaged material made a ripping sound as his masculine fingers manipulated the knotted sleeves. "This shirt has seen better days," he said.

"It was handy."

The first thing to fall out of the bag was the jeweler's case. Harley blinked in surprise. "What's this?" He popped it open. "Wow. That's a nice ring, isn't it?"

Andi tried to ignore the weird emotions racing through her. "I'd say most women would swoon if somebody gave it to them."

He plucked the small sparkling symbol of love out of its protective bed and held it between his fingers. He lifted it to the light as if looking for engravings.

White gold or platinum—she couldn't tell which. A full carat at least. It sparkled like fire. "It's...pretty."

He returned it to the box, snapped the lid closed and

tossed it aside. "I wonder what I'm doing with it. I suppose it could be stolen."

Andi stifled her reprimand. "I sincerely doubt that."

He didn't appear to hear her. He'd opened the leather-bound volume next. "Look at this," he said, turning the open leaf so she could read an inscription. Although the ink had been muddied by moisture, the text was still legible. *From Dad, with love. Christmas 1998.*

"You have family."

"Or had in 1998," he corrected.

Only a few of the elegant ivory pages had been written on—as if the journal writer had just begun to log his thoughts before being interrupted. By a motorcycle accident, perhaps. On the inscribed pages, the ink had bled into blue rivers running parallel across each page. Some pages were stuck together like wet money.

Andi reached out and turned the book over. In the bottom corner of the cover were gold-leaf initials: JJN. "This is a very classy gift. Inscribed, no less."

Harley didn't offer an opinion.

"How's the headache?"

"Still there, but, at least, I don't feel sick to my stomach."

Andi sympathized with him. She couldn't begin to understand what he was going through and she felt powerless to help. Because she had to do *something,* she reached out and brushed her fingers along his jaw. The gesture wasn't meant to be anything but supportive. Unfortunately, a spark of current seemed to spring to life from the contact. The memory of their scintillating kiss made her sit back in her chair. She wasn't good at flirting, and this wasn't the time or place, anyway.

"Maybe Sam could help, if you take this stuff to the ranch. He's smart, worldly. You could try Donnie Grimaldo again, but working with the sheriff's office is like opening a can of worms.''

He cocked his head. "Why do you say that? When Sam took me in to run my prints, Donnie seemed quite personable.''

Andi nodded. ''Donnie's a genuinely nice guy, but he and Kristin had a thing in high school and it ended badly. We sort of do our best to avoid him.''

Harley's sandy-colored eyebrow shot up. ''How do you manage that in a town this size?''

Andi shook her head. ''It isn't easy. Last year at Josh's funeral, Donnie handled the traffic for us. But I figured that was because Josh and Donnie were friends. Everybody loved Josh.''

"So I've heard. Did you love him?''

Something about the way he said the words made her answer bluntly. ''Of course. He was the brother I never had. But from the minute he spotted Jenny, there was never another girl for him.'' Andi stifled a sigh. She'd always hoped for that same kind of love-at-first-sight romance in her life, but so far it hadn't worked out. The closest she'd ever come was the crazy sense of rebellion she'd felt when she'd dated Tyler Harrison during her senior year of high school. Until Kristin had batted her big blues at him.

"Donnie's a good man and a decent cop, but I wouldn't blame him if he still held a grudge. Kristin really set this town on its ear when she backed Ty's version of their altercation over Donnie's.'' She shook her head. "It's old news—except when Gloria Hughes rehashes it in her gossip column.

"I swear that woman is part elephant. She never forgets. Of course, it doesn't help that she's Ty Harrison's mom.'' She made a negating motion. ''Never mind. It's a long story. We should probably hit the road. I'd like to be home when

Ida and Jenny get back from shopping. Maybe if Jenny's there, the two of us can help Ida understand that the new roof is absolutely necessary.''

''Okay,'' he said. ''But maybe we should talk about that kiss—''

She knew what he was going to say. ''Don't,'' she interrupted. ''That was more about triumph than boy-girl stuff. The timing isn't right for either of us. But I consider myself your friend, Harley, and I want to help.''

He sat back and took a drink before speaking. ''Actually, you're wrong. That kiss was *all* boy-girl stuff—for me anyway. But you're right about the timing. And I need all the friends I can get.''

His smile did things to her she wanted to ignore and his voice had an unprecedented effect on her libido. True she'd been celibate for over a year, but now wasn't the time or place to get carried away.

''Unless, of course, we discover something sordid in my past. If it turns out I'm an ax murderer or something odious, you're under no obligation to be my friend.''

Suddenly furious, she reached across the table and grabbed a fistful of T-shirt. ''Just stop it, Harley. As your friend, I won't sit back and let you think the worst about yourself. Your past may be unknown. But the man I know is a great guy—the kind of man who chauffeurs old ladies and stops to fix a flat tire for tourists. So, quit running yourself down, okay?''

She released her hold and sat back, temper spent.

Harley looked down at his shirt, then without lifting his chin looked at her and smiled. Something raw and hungry surged through her body. Damn. She wanted this man—even if he was married to the beautiful blonde in the picture or about to be engaged to some other lucky woman.

"Andi-amie," a cheerful voice boomed. "Whatcha doing in this neck of the woods, *ma petite?*"

Andi looked over her shoulder. A Goliath of a man—well over six foot with snowy hair and a rotund belly framed by bright red suspenders—clomped into the room. He had to duck to clear the threshold. At his heels trailed a golden retriever with white whiskers and a jaunty red, white and blue bandanna around her neck.

"Pascal," Andi exclaimed, jumping to her feet. She hugged the older man with joy then dropped to her knees to embrace the dog. "Belle. Hello, girl. I've missed you.

"Harley, this is Pascal Fournier, my old—excuse me—*former* English teacher. Pascal, my friend Harley Forester." She sort of stumbled over his name because it suddenly occurred to her that he wasn't Harley anymore. "Can you join us?"

"Oh, no, *chérie*. Wish I could, but I'm picking up take-out dinner for Waldo and Frenchy and myself. They're my brothers," he added for Harley's benefit. His craggy eyebrows wiggled in self-deprecating humor. "Somehow—in the cruelest of ironies—we've ended up together in our old age. Three Frenchmen who never learned to cook because we smugly told ourselves we'd have women falling over themselves to take care of us in our twilight years."

Andi hugged him again. "You know you were at the top of my list for years."

"Ah, missy, if you only knew how often I've regretted turning down your offer. Perhaps if it had come from Ida Jane instead of her niece we might have worked something out," he said with a wink.

Pascal looked at Harley, and in true teacher form, proceeded to explain in great detail about Andi's mission to find a man for her great-aunt to marry. "Nowadays, if a student walked around with a list of teachers' names in their notebook, someone would probably call the police,'' he said sadly. ''How is Ida, by the way? I heard she'd moved home from the ranch.''

Andi gave him a quick briefing then added, ''You're coming to the wedding, aren't you?''

He made a face. ''Alas, the Fournier brothers will be in Chicago. A family reunion.''

A young server from the kitchen signaled Pascal that his order was ready, and the man said his goodbyes. Andi gave the big, friendly dog another hug then returned to her chair.

Harley was eyeing her with a serious look on his face.

Andi felt herself blush. ''What? Ida Jane told you about my Daddy List.''

''I know, but I just realized what a determined person you are. You see a goal and map a course to take you there.''

Andi detected an undertone she didn't recognize. Trying for a lighter take on the subject, she said, ''Setting a goal is one thing; achieving it is another. In case you hadn't noticed, I never succeeded in finding a husband for Ida Jane. I'm not an officer in the marines, and, even though I found your bike, I didn't help you get your memory back.''

He reached out and took her hand. His calluses were somehow reassuring—they made him more Harley than an unknown entity called Jonathan.

''Aren't you the person who gave me a hard time for bad-mouthing myself?'' he asked. ''Number one, you can't make a person fall in love—no matter how perfect the potential candidate. Two, you chose family over career—not an easy choice, but an admirable one in my book. And three, there are no miracles where amnesia is concerned. My doctor says the mind heals at its own rate. This—'' he tapped his temple ''—is out of your control, sweetheart.''

Harley squeezed her fingers then let go. She felt oddly

unsettled and a little sad. If she were looking for candidates for a husband list of her own, she knew who'd shoot right to the top.

HARLEY PAUSED at the door of the old bordello. Jenny's minivan was in the parking lot, so he had no choice but to go inside if he wanted a ride to the Rocking M. But at the same time he was hesitant to share the news of Andi's find.

"Cold feet?" Andi asked, just inches behind him.

Her soft snicker made him want to grab her and run in the other direction. Ever since she'd handed him the make-shift knapsack filled with someone's personal belongings, Harley had felt as though he were slogging through quicksand. He now possessed a name, several credit cards and photos of people he didn't recognize. He could walk into a video store and rent the latest flicks—if he owned a TV and VCR. He could pay for gas with plastic. He even had an ATM card. If only he could recall the code, he'd have access to funds.

But none of those things brought him any closer to understanding who he was. He might not be Harley Forester, but he sure as hell wasn't Jonathan Newhall.

"Come on," she cajoled, lightly touching his shoulder. "It's not going to get any easier."

Harley bit down on a grin. One thing he'd learned about Andi Sullivan—she met life head-on, and she took anyone loitering in her path with her.

Harley followed her to the parlor he'd been in earlier. An assortment of lamps—including a 1920s molded-brass figure of a naked woman holding aloft a fringed lampshade—cast the room into warm shades of gold. Jenny and Ida Jane were sitting on the velvet settee, their booty at their feet.

"You're back," Jenny exclaimed. "How'd it go? Did

you have as much luck as we did?'' she asked, motioning toward the boxes of shoes and garment bags.

Andi dropped her gear just inside the door. She motioned him forward. ''I'll let Harley—or should I say, Jonathan?— tell you about it.''

Her bombshell had the desired effect. Jenny leaped to her feet and flew across the room. ''You found your bike?'' she exclaimed, hugging him enthusiastically. ''Congratulations. That's fantastic. Did seeing it trigger your memory?''

Ida Jane rapped a shoe box against the spindly-looking end table. ''Give the man a moment to catch his breath before you bombard him with questions. Goodness me.''

Jenny stepped back. ''Sorry. I just didn't expect—''

''You didn't think I could do it, did you?'' Andi challenged, her hands on her hips.

''It's not that. I just thought it would take longer. That area is practically all wilderness.''

''Sit down,'' Ida ordered. ''I want the whole story.''

Harley took a chair near Ida Jane. The armchair was upholstered in animal hide of some kind; its springs were so weak his bottom sunk to within an inch of the floor. His elbows on the armrests were higher than his shoulders.

''Uh-oh. The bad chair,'' Jenny said. ''Auntie, I thought you sold that chair to Pete Petersen.''

''I did,'' Ida Jane replied. ''How'd it get back?''

''Maybe it's a homing chair,'' Harley quipped.

The trio was laughing, when a knock sounded at the door. Harley saw the sisters exchange a look. Apparently, they weren't expecting visitors. Before either could respond, a voice called out, ''Anybody home?''

Jenny's face lit with joy. ''Sam,'' she cried, disappearing in a flash.

Andi looked confused. ''I thought he wasn't due back until tomorrow?''

"Hank told me Sam was shooting for today," Harley told her. "If his meeting ended early enough."

Harley knew his employer was a family man—and something of a recluse—who hated to be away from Jenny and the twins. He'd undertaken a campaign to alert the public to the dangers of grassland wildfires and had been asked to speak on behalf of legislation introduced by his local congressman.

A few moments later, Sam and Jenny entered the room. Jenny's cheeks were a pretty pink, her lips showed telltale signs of kissing. Sam looked as happy as Harley had ever seen him. "Hello, Andi. Miss Ida." He crossed the room to give the older woman a kiss on the cheek, then turned to shake Harley's hand. "Don't get up—even if you can. I've gotten stuck in that chair once or twice myself."

Sam and Jenny squeezed together on the sofa, then Sam looked at Harley and said, "Jen tells me you've found your bike."

"Andi found it."

Andi made a preening motion, then winked. "Piece of cake. There's only one road."

Sam chuckled. "That twists and turns for ten miles. No small feat. Congratulations."

Harley smiled at her blush. He wished he didn't like her so much.

Knowing there probably would never be a better time to discuss their discovery, he dug in his hip pocket for the wallet. "The good news is I've got a driver's license. The bad news is I've probably got a couple of hundred overdue parking tickets somewhere."

Andi gave him a stern look.

"Turns out my name is Jonathan Jackson Newhall."

"That sounds vaguely familiar," Jenny said.

"Wasn't there a Newhall family that lived on the old

Ragsdale place when you girls were in school?'' Ida Jane asked.

Andi shook her head. ''Newhouse. Charity and Carla. Char was a junior cheerleader.''

Ida looked ready to argue the point, but Sam spoke first. ''What about the bike? Is it salvageable?''

Andi rose from where she was sitting to hand Sam the wallet, then perched on the arm of Harley's chair.

Harley smiled at her back and said, ''Ask the daring young woman who dangled from a rope on my behalf. One thing I learned today is I'm not partial to heights.''

Jenny laughed. ''Me neither. Josh and I were both cowards when it came to high places. Sam wants us to get married on the summit overlooking the ranch, and I get a little queasy just thinking about it.''

''My brother may have hated heights, but he loved a great view. He wanted me to build the ranch house on the summit, but it wasn't practical. I think he'd be pleased to see us exchange our vows up there.''

Harley spotted the tender, loving look Jenny gave her intended. Although he didn't know the whole story behind their relationship, he sensed it was founded on true respect and love. He wondered if he'd ever known that in his life. Somehow he doubted it.

''Before we get sidetracked into wedding talk,'' Andi said, ''Harley will need a little help retrieving the bike. It'll take a crane to haul it out. Right now, the bike doesn't look bad—it's thirty feet up in a tree, but if it falls…splat.'' Her graphic hand slapping made everyone jump.

Sam's mouth dropped open. ''A tree?''

''Hanging nose down. Harley's lucky to be alive given where the bike landed up.''

Sam gave a low whistle. ''Downright miraculous. Why don't I give Ron Jensen a call in the morning?''

"Beulah's grandson?" Ida Jane asked.

"His salvage company is the best in the area."

While Jenny, Ida Jane and Sam discussed the Jensen family's trials and tribulations, Harley focused on blocking the noise in his head. His ears felt hot and his scalp itched—even though he'd left his hat by the door. Watching Sam's casual examination of the wallet was triggering some kind of emotional response.

"I take it this didn't produce any miracle memories," Sam said.

Harley stretched against the tension in his neck. "Nope. Not even a glimmer."

Jenny took the wallet next. She quickly flipped through the pictures, studied the driver's license briefly then checked the money compartment. "Hmm. Not bad. Three big dogs and six Andrew Jacksons."

Andi passed it back to Harley. "I think he should go on the Internet and see if his name is on any list of missing persons. Maybe his family has a Web site set up," she said.

Jenny nodded. "Good idea. And I bet Donnie could help you—now that you have a name to run through the data banks."

Harley and Andi exchanged a look.

"Maybe actually touching the bike will trigger something," Sam said. "When do you want to go after it? Tomorrow?"

Harley was overwhelmed by the generous offer. "What about your wedding plans?"

Jenny answered. "The wedding is under control. We're keeping it simple—for obvious reasons. The ceremony will be small—family only. We've combined the reception with the annual St. Patrick's Day bash, and the Garden Club is handling that. So we can certainly make time to help a friend."

Harley looked down. He wanted to ask how any of them knew he was worthy of their friendship, but the words wouldn't come.

As if reading his mind, Sam said, "Harley, I learned a long time ago not to judge a man by his car, his house or his bank account. His wife, his horse and his dog are a lot safer bets, but even those can be misleading. Since you started out with none of those things, I had to go with my gut. And my gut tells me you're a good man. Reliable and smart. And I consider you a friend."

Harley was moved. "Thanks, Sam. I don't know how I got so lucky. No memory. Not much more than the clothes you see and a few bucks in a tin can, but I'm not complaining. Today I feel rich."

Sam held out his hand. "Hell, buddy, you could be rich. I don't know too many paupers who drive a Hog."

Harley looked at Andi. "It might be stolen."

She slugged his arm. Hard. "Or you mighta paid cash for it. I guess we won't know till we get it out of that tree and run the serial number on it, will we?" Her tone dared him to contradict her.

"Let's drive to the site tomorrow and take a look," Sam said. "I need to stop by the Blue Lupine, anyway, and make sure Lars knows he's expected at the reception."

"Good," Harley said. He'd swung past the mine last Thursday after delivering some hay, and Lars hadn't been around. Only Sarge, Lars's hound dog had been there, baying as if Harley were a robber out to sack the place. Dogs made him nervous, so Harley had headed on without even getting out of the truck.

Suddenly, Harley's headache returned. Anxious for a little privacy, he tried to get out of the chair. Andi came to his rescue—again. She braced her feet a shoulder width apart then held out her hand.

He had no choice but to accept. "Sam, do you want Harley to take your truck so you can ride home with Jenny?" Andi asked. Harley had had the same thought, but wouldn't have dreamed of suggesting it.

"Good idea," Sam said. "The keys are in it."

Harley tipped an imaginary hat to Ida Jane. "Miss Ida, take care."

She smiled and nodded, but Harley thought she had a preoccupied look about her. As if she might be trying to place him. His heart ached for Ida Jane and her family.

"I'll walk you out," Andi said. "Your other stuff is still in the car."

She wasn't about to let Harley slink off without a pep talk. She'd seen how powerfully he'd reacted to Sam's suggestion that they proceed with the recovery operation. Things were moving fast, and he needed to know that everyone was in his corner.

She slipped her arm through his and escorted him back the way they'd come. The hallway was narrow and they had to squeeze together to walk abreast. "Are you okay?" she asked softly.

He sighed. "I feel like I've got one hand on the lip of Pandora's box and the other on an unbroken stallion trying to pull me in the opposite direction."

"Spoken like a true cowboy."

His wry chuckle was pure Harley. Andi guessed that in the weeks to come this new identity would slowly become more real to him. What that meant was anybody's guess, but there was no turning back now.

"Do you believe in destiny, Harley? I thought I could change mine by leaving Gold Creek, but it didn't work. I'm back where I started, running my great-aunt's antique shop."

They stopped—as if by mutual consent—in the shadow

of an artificial palm. "You might not know this, but Ida went to college somewhere back East. She had a good job in Oakland, but when her parents needed her, she came back to Gold Creek. She opened the store and years later made a home for my mother after my grandmother became ill. Then we came along. That's why I'm here. It's my turn, and I'll stay as long as she needs me."

He was close enough that she could smell the beer on his breath. "And when Ida's gone?" he asked.

"Haven't a clue." Which, at the moment, was true. She'd had a plan once, but that was when she'd been young and cocky. Now she understood that even the best-laid plans were subject to change.

When he pulled her to him, Andi didn't hesitate. Yes, it was a dumb idea, but it felt right. Her arms went around his neck; her body leaned into his. His kiss was tender and inquisitive. She might have been tempted to ask him upstairs if a sudden knock on the door hadn't interrupted them.

Andi jerked back. Harley dropped his arms to his sides. She looked into his eyes. Instead of chagrin or embarrassment, she saw desire.

The knock came again. Louder. A man's voice called, "Andi, open up. It's me. Donnie."

Through the etched glass oval in the door, she could see the fuzzy silhouette of a man in a tan-and-black uniform. She recognized the voice. "Hi, Donnie," Andi said, throwing open the door. "What's going on?"

Donnie had retained his quarterback physique. His broad shoulders and powerful build combined in a handsome, very masculine way that had driven the girls in Gold Creek High—including Kristin—crazy. When he removed his hat, Andi spotted a few silver threads in his closely cropped hair. For some reason a snippet of Gloria's most recent column came back to her—something about Donnie's ex-wife's

European sojourn and Donnie's struggles with being a single parent.

"I was on my way out to the Rocking M when I spotted Sam's truck."

Donnie had a deep, resonant voice. Not as sexy as Harley's but pleasant nonetheless. He'd served as Andi's Search-and-Rescue unit commander until he graduated—a year ahead of her and her sisters. They'd been good friends—until that disastrous party they all wanted to forget.

"Is something wrong? Sam and Jen are in the parlor."

He stepped inside but went no farther. "Actually, I haven't come to see Sam." Suddenly all business, Donnie stated in a very cop-like voice, "Harley Forester, I have a warrant for your arrest for the murder of Lars Gunderson."

CHAPTER SEVEN

HARLEY STARED at the painted block wall across from him. The pockmarked texture reminded him of a moonscape, except for the color—a cross between beige and institutional green. It might have been the color of the moon if it were really made of cheese, he thought.

The view hadn't changed in the fourteen hours since his arrest. He'd been apprised of his rights and had met with a court-appointed attorney who'd advised him to plead not guilty.

Not guilty of what? Harley had longed to yell. He only knew the basics. Lars was dead. A witness had placed Harley at the scene at the time of death.

Dead. While he understood the concept, Harley couldn't name a single person of his acquaintance who was dead. He didn't doubt for a minute that his alter ego, Jonathan, could name a few, but *Harley* hadn't even handled a dead animal in his tenure on the ranch.

How did Lars die? He'd wanted to ask, but his attorney—a man of twenty-six with a blond goatee and thick glasses—had only a smeared copy of the arrest warrant to go by.

"Death from trauma," he said after reading for a few minutes.

"Could you be more specific?" Harley had asked sarcastically. "All deaths are traumatic."

His comment had earned him a lecture. "Homicide is

serious business. We don't get many in this county and everyone is playing it close to the vest and by the book.''

Harley would have commented on the mixed metaphors but he had a feeling it would have gone over the young man's head. "Is this your first murder?" he'd asked.

"Alleged murder," the man corrected.

"No," Harley had returned. "I may be the *alleged* murderer, but the murder happened. Period. A man is dead. A good man. A friend of mine. And someone else killed him.''

A noise at the door of his cell drew his gaze from the acne-scarred wall. Donnie Grimaldo, the man who'd arrested him last night, opened the door and stepped in. "'Morning. How'ya holding up?''

Harley sensed a basic goodness in the man, who had treated him kindly and with solemn respect the night before. While the booking process had been long, detailed and demeaning, Donnie had gone out of his way to facilitate the procedure. Harley had been too numb, too sad to question the special treatment.

But it was at the top of his list of questions this morning. "Can I ask you something? Why are you being so nice? You barely know me.''

Donnie chuckled and looked around. "This is a cell not a hotel room, in case you didn't notice. Those black smudges on your fingers are from ink. I wouldn't call this a deluxe booking.

"I just wanted to lay things out for you. Sam woke me up at five this morning to say he was replacing your public defender with a top-notch criminal attorney. He'll get you out on bail. Sam's prepared to personally guarantee you're not a flight risk," Donnie said. Harley could smell his aftershave and suddenly craved a shower and clean clothes.

"I have to say, though, your amnesia could work against you with the judge. You have no real roots in Gold Creek.

He's a decent man, but he crucifies anyone who goes fugitive on him.''

"Where would I go? It's not like I have a lot of resources," Harley said. "I don't even have a car, and my bike is up a tree.''

"That's true. On the positive side, though, I talked to Andi, and she's agreed to take me to your motorcycle.''

Harley's eyebrow shot up. For some reason that sounded slightly treasonous.

As if reading his mind, Donnie said, "That Andi is one sharp cookie. She was a member of the Sheriff's Search and Rescue team for years, so she knows the system. She figured if we regarded the bike as a potential source of clues to you and your past, we'd undertake the recovery operation at our cost. Probably save you a bundle.''

A grin formed on Harley's lips. "She *told* you that?''

"No. I just know how her mind works. I used to date Kristin. Those Sullivan girls are something else.''

Harley would have asked for more details, but a voice in the corridor interrupted. Donnie turned to leave. "I've got a mountain of forms to fill out before we can go after the bike. Your arraignment is this afternoon. Andi said to tell you she'd be by this morning with clean clothes. Orange jumpsuits aren't terribly convincing when you're trying to look innocent.''

"Do you think I'm guilty?'' Harley asked.

Donnie looked at him for a full minute. "Andi insists you couldn't have done it. Guess we'll find out soon enough.''

Soon enough. What did that mean? A month? Six months? A year from now? Yesterday he'd found the first tangible link with his past, but what good would it do if he was going to be spending his future in jail.

ANDI'S MORNING had started with a predawn chat with Ida Jane. Luckily, Ida seemed more like her old self. She listened to Andi's explanation about the roof, especially the part about preventing future damage to the ceilings. With a resigned sigh, she'd agreed to let Bart begin the work.

While brewing the coffee for the customers who would be knocking on her door as soon as the rolls and biscotti were delivered, she made phone calls, including one to Donnie Grimaldo.

Now she had ten minutes to organize her thoughts. Jenny had agreed to open the store. Then Linda McCloskey—Bart's mother and Ida's friend from Garden Club—would take over. Jenny couldn't stay all day because she had the twins and a lot of wedding details to take care of. Linda, who'd recently retired, enjoyed a little part-time work. And as a former nurse, she was especially attuned to Ida Jane's problems.

Andi's main goal this morning was to see Harley. Donnie had said Harley was handling the arrest well but seemed a little depressed. Big surprise there, she muttered as she prepared to unlock the door.

Just as she reached for the knob, a figure appeared on the landing. A shadow from the overhang combined with the frosted design in the oval glass kept her from identifying the person, but she figured it was Jenny. "You're early," she said, yanking open the door.

"Not too early for coffee I hope," a deep voice said.

Andi stared. A stranger stood before her. In his sixties, his clothing—shirt and slacks, no tie—told her he wasn't a tourist. "May I help you?"

"James Rohr. Attorney. Sam O'Neal asked me to meet him here." He held out his hand. "May I come in?"

Andi kept the handshake quick. "Certainly. I'm expecting Sam any minute. Is this about Harley's case?"

"Yes."

She ushered him inside, but before she could ask a single question, Sam's truck pulled into the parking lot. Both Sam and Jenny got out. They hurried up the steps of the bordello. "Jim. Good to see you," Sam said, addressing the attorney. "Thanks for getting here so fast."

He made short order of the introductions, then hustled them to the corner table of the empty coffee parlor. "I really hated to pull you out of retirement, Jim. But this case called for big guns."

The man looked genuinely pleased to see Sam. "Trust me, Sam, retirement is not all it's cracked up to be. I'm glad to help."

Jenny delivered three coffees to the table, freshened Andi's cup then took the chair beside her husband-to-be. "Did you call Kristin?" she asked Andi.

Andi, who'd been eavesdropping on Sam and the attorney's small talk, answered without really thinking. "Yes. She was sorry to hear about Lars, and she suggested taking Ida Jane back to Oregon with her after the wedding."

Jenny looked surprised. "Really? That's a first."

Kristin had never invited anyone to visit her. Ida Jane believed that Kris was embarrassed about her standard of living. Andi figured it had more to with her lifestyle— maybe a live-in boyfriend she wanted to keep secret. Regardless of the reason, Kristin's decision to renew her familial ties couldn't have come at a better time in Andi's opinion.

"Does Ida want to go?" Jenny asked.

"Yes. She wanted to start packing, but I told her to wait until you got here."

"Gee, thanks."

Andi spotted the serious look on Sam's face and turned her attention to the two men. "Sam, when you mentioned calling a lawyer last night, I thought you meant Dave Dunningham.''

Sam shook his head. ''Dave doesn't do criminal law. Jim is an old friend from way back, and I knew he'd come if he wasn't out on his yacht.''

The attorney made a negating wave. ''That sounds so pretentious. It's a glorified fishing boat. Now, tell me about Harley Forester.''

Sam started with the facts, which included a copy of the arrest sheet, although he declined to share how it came to be in his possession.

''Lars found Harley walking down the road in the middle of a storm. Lars said he was too drunk to risk another D.U.I. so he took Harley home with him.''

''So Lars was a drinker,'' the lawyer observed.

Sam looked uncomfortable. ''From the little he told me about his past, I'd say he was a Vietnam veteran with some long-term problems, both physical and psychological. He was stoned most of the time and he got drunk whenever he came to town.''

Jenny added, ''Ida Jane dog-sat for Lars the winter before last when he was in the VA hospital up near Yountsville. I don't know what the trouble was, but he was gone three weeks.''

The lawyer scribbled notes on a yellow legal pad. ''Andi, tell me everything you know about Harley.''

He's serious, funny, gentle and a great kisser. ''Aside from the logistical facts that Sam has given you, there's not much I can add. But I can show you what we recovered from the accident site yesterday.''

She looked at Sam and added, ''I did what you suggested and called Donnie. They're going after the bike as evidence.''

Sam and the lawyer exchanged a satisfied look.

While the others talked, Andi dashed upstairs to her room to retrieve the bag of Harley's possessions. Before dropping into bed last night, she'd reexamined every item, hoping something meaningful would pop out at her.

Against her better judgment, she'd tried on the ring. A perfect fit. She hated it. Or loved it, she wasn't sure which.

Forty-five minutes later—as the morning rush hit, Sam and the attorney left. Andi helped get Jenny organized then she drove to Beatty's Menswear to look for a suit for Harley.

Her task became more difficult the moment Gloria Hughes walked into the store.

"Andrea Sullivan," the sixty-something woman exclaimed. She rushed across the small, cluttered shop like a starving dog in a meat market. "I just heard the most distressing news. That amnesia man was arrested last night."

Gloria Harrison Hughes had a way of asking questions without making them sound like questions. Andi knew there was no escaping the columnist's tractor beam once she had you in range. She made an impulsive decision. Setting aside the suit she was examining, she bravely faced the queen of local gossip.

"Good morning, Mrs. Hughes," she said, feeling twelve again. "Isn't it something? That poor man just can't catch a break, but the good news is we found his bike and his name isn't Harley Forester."

The woman's eyes rounded behind her small, stylish glasses. Her blushing-pink lips—a color of lipstick Andi had tried and shunned when she was a teen—formed an O. "Really? How do you know?"

Andi ignored the question. She didn't want her role in this operation discussed. "His real name is Jonathan Jackson Newhall." She spelled it to make sure the columnist got it right.

"Oh, my word," the excited woman muttered. "I wonder why he did it."

A powerful urge to grab the old shrew by her scrawny neck and shake some sense into her left as quickly as it arrived. Instead, Andi faked a *Jenny* smile and said, "I don't believe Jonathan—" she emphasized the name "—is capable of such a malicious act. He's such a sweet man. Ida just adores him."

Gloria's eyes narrowed like a cat ready to pounce on an unsuspecting rodent. "Why, Andi, I do believe you're smitten."

Smitten. A derivative of smite? I wonder.

There'd been numerous times lately that Andi had felt as though someone or something had whacked her upside the head.

Andi knew from experience that the best lie was one close to the truth. "I have to admit I like him. As a friend. That's why I'm shopping for a suit for him to wear to court." No doubt Gloria would have surmised this on her own and attached her own interpretation. "A person needs all the friends he can get at a stressful time like this. Sam and Jenny are standing by Jonathan, too. And Sam was Lars's closest friend."

That seemed to give the woman pause. Andi returned to her shopping. She found several nice suits, but the price tags were out of her range. On the sales rack she finally located one that might fit. Five minutes later she had a shirt, underwear, socks, belt and shoes to complete the outfit. She put the belt back— it probably wouldn't be allowed in jail— then paid for the whole ensemble with her credit card.

As she was leaving, she looked around for Gloria, but apparently, the columnist had accomplished *her* shopping; she was nowhere in sight.

Andi hoped the lawyer's strategy was right.

"The first thing we need to do is create a different image for Jonathan," he'd told them. "Instead of drifter on a motorcycle, we must portray him as a professional on vacation who'd suffered an accident. Wrong place, wrong time. A very unfair coincidence."

Before leaving the old bordello, James Rohr had contacted a private detective to begin tracking down leads pertaining to Jonathan Newhall. From the little Andi had gleaned last night on the Internet, Jonathan was an investigative reporter who wrote under the name of JJ Newhall. He didn't have a personal Web page, but she'd managed to find three of his articles—bitingly cynical pieces published in major newspapers. How that image jibed with the gentle, back-to-nature kind of guy she knew—and possibly loved—was still to be determined.

But Andi hadn't given up hope.

"BAIL DENIED."

The words seemed to echo in the cavernous chamber of the second-floor courtroom. Harley had passed by the turn-of-the-century—the *previous* century—building many times, but he'd never pictured himself on trial there.

His lawyer—a terse, intense man with all the bells and whistles of a modern, *wired* professional—closed his slim electronic notebook computer with a firm click. "Don't worry. I'll have that changed before the week is out."

Harley wanted to believe him, but in all honesty, he could understand the judge's reluctance to grant bail. Who could trust a guy with two names, a minimum-wage job, no phone, no car and no family? The judge's lone moment of hesitation came when he'd looked at Andi and said, "As much as I'd like to rule strictly from the recommendation of my children's former baby-sitter and captain of the girls' volleyball team, I'm afraid I need facts. Line up some ducks, Mr. Rohr, then we'll talk.''

Harley looked over his shoulder. Andi was deep in conversion with Sam. Jenny was nowhere in sight—most probably handling the store in Andi's absence.

At a faint beeping sound, his attorney removed a tiny cellular phone from an outer compartment of his briefcase and hunched over to talk privately. The bailiff, an older man with a shuffling gait, was conferring with the judge at the raised oak dais. Harley felt invisible, but he doubted that would last long enough for him to slip through the rear doors and make a run for it. Besides, where would he go?

"How are you holding up?" a voice said from behind him.

Harley turned in the old-fashioned wooden chair. It made a creaking sound. "Okay. A bit of a headache." Andi's eyes widened. "Not that kind of headache."

"The suit looks good." She started to reach out but curled her fingers in a ball and lowered her arm. Maybe she'd been told not to touch the prisoner.

"Thanks for buying it. Great tie." He fingered the sober red and navy silk. There was so much to say, but his tongue was no longer attached to his brain. "I wish…"

She nodded. Her hair looked freshly washed. He wanted to run his fingers through it; he knew it would smell like green apples. "I printed some stuff off the Internet last night. About your past. Who you were—*are*—damn, this is confusing," she said. "I gave copies to Mr. Rohr."

Harley knew that. He'd glanced through them while waiting for the charges against him to be read.

Sam joined them, and the lawyer, who slid the phone back into its compartment, turned to face the huddle. "That was my investigator. He's faxing his preliminary reports to your shop, Andi. I should have enough to turn this around before the judge leaves for the day. At the very latest, to-morrow.''

Andi made a small sound of frustration.

''Don't worry, kiddo,'' Sam said, touching her shoulder supportively. ''We'll get him out in time for my wedding.''

Harley wished he was the one touching her. But he wasn't in a position to make his feelings known. ''I appreciate everything you're all doing for me. Is there anything I can do?''

''Read,'' his attorney said. ''You've got Andi's stuff from the Internet, and my investigator is putting together a file on your life—your old life. Maybe something will ring a bell.''

Jim Rohr then looked at Sam. ''I need the name of the doctor who saw Harley—forgive me, Jonathan, after his accident.''

Jonathan. The name landed in a pool of acid in his stomach. Who was he really? From the pitch his lawyer had made in his defense a few minutes earlier, Harley would have thought he was as trustworthy as Jimmy Stewart, as misunderstood as James Dean. But after glancing over the articles with Jonathan Newhall's byline, Harley found the guy opinionated, self-absorbed and not particularly likable.

''It's gonna be okay, Harley,'' Andi said softly. ''We'll get through this.''

He wanted to believe her, but the steady throbbing in his head—a pain no amount of aspirin seemed to help—made him question that assumption. Although he hadn't mentioned it to Rohr for fear of making a fool of himself, Harley was convinced that Andi's discovery yesterday had opened the door to his memory. His dreams last night had been filled with images that seemed significant, although he couldn't completely identify them.

An older man sitting behind a wide desk. His look of

disappointment had made Harley cry out a name—*Andrew*. But he hadn't realized its significance until he spotted it in the article Andi had printed. Harley's father was Andrew James Newhall, a retired newspaper publisher. A widower, now remarried and living in Florida.

"Sam, are you handling Lars's funeral?"

"They won't release the body until the coroner is done with the autopsy. Then it will be cremated. Lars told me years ago that he wanted his ashes sprinkled around the mine. No service."

His expression said he was recalling another not-so-distant funeral—his brother's. "Jenny and I thought we'd include a small eulogy after the wedding. Just the good memories. He wouldn't have wanted anything weepy."

Before anyone could say more, the bailiff interrupted. Harley rose without being asked. He nodded goodbye and walked away. His new suit helped him maintain his pride— just knowing Andi cared enough to buy it for him strengthened his resolve. He'd get through this.

He glanced over his shoulder. Sam and the lawyer had disappeared, but Andi still sat there, her gaze on him. At the last minute, she gave him a small *Andi* smile, and his heart took flight. With her behind him, anything was possible.

AFTER WHAT had possibly been the longest day of her life, Andi crawled into bed ready to sleep for a week. But before she could turn off the light, she needed to sort through the faxes that had arrived while she was helping Donnie scope out the recovery site.

Settling against her puffy feather pillows, she picked up the top sheet. A copy of a newspaper clipping.

Does progress grind to a dead standstill because a small group of motivationally challenged citizens are about to face changes to their comfortable status quo? "Stop!" they cry with fake concerns for the environment. I'll buy that argument when I see the last of their aerosol cans hit the garbage in paper—not plastic— bags.

The terse opinion piece dealt with some regional, inter-state commerce issue in the Midwest. She couldn't have chosen a side based on the column. While the arguments made sense and were well-written, the writer's antipathy seemed directed at both sides.

She selected another. As she read, Andi's distress grew. After a long, emotionally draining day, the last thing she needed was confirmation that the person she was working so hard to save was someone she'd never in a million years have been attracted to if they'd met under normal circumstances.

Jonathan Jackson Newhall was an educated man of means. A respected investigative journalist with ties to some of the largest newspapers in the country. According to Mr. Rohr's investigator, Jonathan had taken a leave of absence for personal reasons last November and hadn't been heard from since. Apparently no one found this alarming, given the man's lone-wolf attitude.

"We just assumed he'd rented a cabin in the mountains to hunker down and write his great American novel," an editor at one paper was quoted as saying.

Andi glanced at her bedside clock. Ten-thirty. Ida Jane was sleeping peacefully. According to both Jenny and Linda, Ida had had a good day. No flights of fancy, no temper tantrums. At dinner—a delivered pizza—Ida had expressed her pleasure about being invited to visit Kristin in Michigan. Andi didn't bother correcting her. Kristin had moved so many times, who could keep track?

As she reached for the lamp, the phone rang. It was Kristin.

"How's Ida Jane?"

"Fine. She had a good day. Even with all that's happening around here."

"Maybe she just needed to be home."

Both Jenny and Kris handled Ida's aging problems better than Andi did. Andi wanted to be understanding like Jenny or kindhearted like Kristin, but instead she argued with her aunt. She wanted to turn back the hands of time and she wasn't very good at it. She needed help even if it meant swallowing her pride and reaching out to her sister.

"Listen, Kris, you don't want to hear this, but I think you should move back to Gold Creek."

Andi heard her sharp intake of breath. "I have a life here, Andi. In Oregon."

"I know. But you have family here. In California."

She pictured all the empty rooms in the bordello. Any one of them would make a perfect massage studio. "You could set up shop here. Free rent. Or maybe the basement. When I was down there the other day I thought it would make a cozy office space for someone."

Kristin didn't speak for a moment. "Aren't you forgetting something? Gloria Hughes."

Andi reached for the copy of the *Gold Creek Ledger* that had been in her mailbox when she returned home from the courthouse. She scanned the half-page column until she spotted her name.

"I don't know what you're worried about. The old crone has it in for me, not you. Listen to this. 'Glory has learned that an extensive modernization of one of Gold Creek's most disreputable, but well-loved buildings, is under way. Let us hope Andi's coffee sales justify such a massive undertaking.'"

"She called the bordello *disreputable?*" Kristin exclaimed. "Them are fightin' words."

Andi chuckled. It suddenly struck her that she'd missed this easy-going repartee. She and Kris hadn't talked like this in years. "Maybe the *well-loved* part was supposed to ease the blow. I only hope the old bat goes easy on Harley. I mean, Jonathan."

Kristin asked for an update, then commented. "Well, I wouldn't worry about Harley getting any bad press unless Gloria finds out you're in love with him."

Andi choked on the sip of water she'd been about to take. The glass wobbled in her fingers and spilled a big puddle in the middle of her down comforter. "Who said anything about love, for heaven's sake?" she cried. "He's a friend. I'm just trying to help."

She slapped the water off her lap.

"Andi," her sister said with a sigh, "aren't we too old to play games? You care about the man. Admit it."

If I do, will you make a play for him? Immediately ashamed of her thoughts, Andi pretended to make light of her sister's suggestion. "Who is this again? What if you're not really Kristin? You could be spying for Gloria."

Kristin laughed. "I could prove it's me but that would mean telling truths both of us would prefer to forget. Like the time you put a box of ants in Jane Fenway's pantry because you thought she was too mean to her dog, Fred."

"Ferd," Andi corrected. "The dog's name was Ferd. And Jane wasn't nice to anybody. And you helped collect the ants."

"He was a good dog."

Andi felt a weight lift from her shoulders. Suddenly it was possible to say, "You may be right about my feelings, Kris, but I've got to tell you I'm really confused, too. For one thing, I'm not sure who he is. You wouldn't believe all the stuff the lawyer dug up and it's only been one day.''

''Bad stuff?''

''Not exactly. He's smart and successful, but the things he writes are kind of cold. In a way, he reminds me of Gloria Hughes,'' she said, trying for a lighthearted tone.

''Really?''

''No. I was kidding. Sorta.''

Kristin made a sighing sound. ''Well, I wouldn't worry about it too much. You only have to deal with that person if he gets his memory back, right? Until then, he's just Harley with a different name.''

Andi sat up. ''Wow, Kris, that's pretty smart.''

Kristin's chuckle held a wry note. ''I do my best. Listen, I've got to go. I'll see you Friday. And I'll think about what you said, but there are certain…complications.''

Andi sighed. ''Life is complicated. But Ida Jane isn't getting any younger, and, frankly, I'm out of my league.''

After she hung up the phone, Andi got out of bed and walked into the bathroom across the hall for a towel. The planking beneath her feet creaked in a comforting way. She loved this rickety old house of ill repute. She loved her sisters, too. Maybe if Kris were closer, she and Andi might finally talk about the stupid fiasco that had shattered their relationship in the first place. Two sisters, one guy.

The irony of her present situation wasn't lost on her. This time there were two men—in the same body.

CHAPTER EIGHT

JAIL, HARLEY THOUGHT, is a great place to think. In the three days since his arrest, he'd used the time to "find himself." The New Age phrase took on a different meaning when applied to his situation, he decided.

Harley now had a report that chronicled his life—all the highs and lows. His mother's death in a car accident. His scholastic achievements and occasional brush with the law. "A rebellious youngster acting out," his lawyer had termed it. His father's second marriage. The sale of the family business—a newspaper that Jonathan's great-grandfather had started.

Like acid eating its way through steel, the past crept into his awareness. It started in his dreams, then exploded in fragmented bursts accompanied by blinding headaches into his consciousness.

Dr. Franklin, who'd visited him at his lawyer's behest, had given him new insight on his form of amnesia. She told him that she'd done a little research on frontal lobe amnesia. She believed he might never completely recover the "factual" memory of his life prior to the accident.

"The brain operates in two hemispheres, Harley. The left and the right. To put it simply, the left side deals with facts, the right is more creative. Since your injury took place on the right side—which controls the left hemisphere—your mind is going to rely on the right half to fill in the details that it finds hazy," she'd told him.

The explanation made perfect sense to him. Since the crash, he'd slowed down, found joy in nature and the world around him, instead of rushing through life at a breakneck pace to get the jump on the next story as JJ Newhall apparently had. Her theory explained why headaches hit when he tried to push for left-brain "perfect" recall.

"Your mind is integrating what was lost with the new way you've learned to look at life, Harley," the doctor had said.

She'd also suggested he try meditation to mitigate the pain of the old memories coming to the surface. "Relax. Breathe slowly and deeply. Concentrate on the images and block out the pain. Given time, your brain will come to grips with the pictures these memories produce, and will find a way to make sense of them. They'll no longer feel foreign and obtrusive."

He'd taken her suggestion, and quickly discovered he could bring to mind a collage of images from the past—like stills, as they said in the newspaper trade. Gradually, he could integrate them into a chronological picture that made sense.

He recalled experiences from his career. He figured out what it meant when someone called him an investigative reporter. For the past few years, he'd worked as a freelance journalist, traveling around the world, sometimes with Oshi Kienda, a photographer he liked and trusted.

One vivid image that came into his head was of an argument he'd had with his father. It had taken place in an office—his father's presumably, but Harley didn't know where that was. Or when the shouting match had happened. But, the subsequent image showed him buying a motorcycle.

If he closed his eyes, Harley could almost smell the new leather. And he *remembered* the feel of the wind on his face as he drove, but he had no idea why he'd chosen California as a destination or why he'd turned on the long, winding road that would take him to Lars Gunderson's Blue Lupine mine.

At times Harley felt as though he'd stumbled into a theater and was watching a movie without any idea of the plot or who the characters were. He was slowly regaining Jonathan's memories but couldn't honestly remember living them. He was healed, but he wasn't whole.

Nor was he alone. As he'd predicted that day with Andi, this new identity brought people eager to reconnect with him. So far, he'd had phone calls from his father, his father's second wife and their two young daughters—the trio in the photo in his wallet, and a former colleague and friend, Oshi Kienda, whom Andrew had contacted on Jonathan's behalf.

"There's the rub," he said under his breath. To the friends he'd made in Gold Creek—the caring souls working diligently to secure his release from jail, he was Harley Forester. To the people on the other end of the phone, he was *Jonathan*. Son. Brother. Friend.

"But who am I really?"

"You're a free man," a voice said. "Or you will be after this one last detail."

Jim Rohr and Sam O'Neal walked up to the painted bars. Sam carried his spotless Resistol. The other man, his ubiquitous briefcase.

"This is it," Sam said, shaking Harley's hand through the bar. "We're springing your ass today."

"Is Andi outside with a couple of horses and dynamite?" Harley joked.

"My way's less messy," the lawyer said. "My cleaner hates it when I get dust on this suit."

The joking ended when Donnie arrived to open the cell door. Ten minutes later, they were seated at a table in the law library, two doors down from where Harley's arraignment had taken place. The judge in his black robes strode in, a file in his hand. All three men rose without being told.

He glanced their way and nodded for them to sit down. "So, Mr. Forester-slash-Newhall, it turns out Lars Gunderson was your uncle."

Harley would have missed the chair and wound up sitting on the floor if Sam hadn't been there to catch him. The upsurge of noise in his head felt as if it might spill out through his eyes. "I...I beg your pardon?"

The judge stared at him as if trying to divine whether or not he was acting. Harley didn't care about that; he wanted to know if what the man said was the truth. He turned to his lawyer. "What's he mean? Lars was my uncle? How can that be? I read the report. My last name is Newhall, not Gunderson."

Jim Rohr said calmly, "Your mother had an older brother. The two siblings didn't have the same surname because your grandmother was widowed shortly after your mother was born, and when she remarried, her new husband adopted your mother. Lars, however, refused to give up his father's name. Apparently, he never got along with his stepfather. He joined the army at seventeen."

Harley's mind barely had digested that news when the attorney said to the judge, "After speaking with Mr. Newhall's father, we've determined that Mr. Newhall's journey to California was prompted by his father's suggestion that he go in search of his uncle. The sad irony is that while Mr. Gunderson was acting as a Good Samaritan, he didn't know the young man he was helping was really his nephew. A fact made even more bittersweet when you take into account his will."

"What will?" Harley croaked. He pressed his knuckle

into the furrow between his eyebrows. The pain hammered at his consciousness like a five-year-old with a snare drum.

The judge cleared his throat. "Mr. Gunderson left behind a hand-written will naming you his beneficiary."

Despite the pain, Harley shook his head. "Why would he do that?"

"Maybe he guessed you were related," his lawyer said.

"I know he liked you," Sam said. "He called you a straight shooter. That was high praise in Lars's book. He said you reminded him of himself."

"A line in the document notes that you—like Mr. Gunderson—were all alone in the world," the judge added.

A surfeit of emotions added to the chaos in Harley's head. He wondered if this headache would include nausea—bolting for the door was probably not an option.

He looked at the judge. "Do you think I killed him to inherit a worthless old mine?"

The man's eyes narrowed at the volume that echoed in the room. "People have been killed for less, but no, Mr. Newhall, I don't believe that is the reason Lars Gunderson is dead." He picked up the file. "Bail is set at five thousand dollars." He made eye contact with the clerk, whom Harley hadn't even noticed sitting in the corner of the room, then nodded at the three men at the table.

Harley couldn't decide whether to laugh or cry. He cussed instead. It felt good for some reason, which surprised him mightily, because as far as he could remember, he never swore.

"YOU KNOW they're meeting with Judge Haskell this morning, right?" Donnie asked. "I thought you'd want to be there, instead of on the mountain eating dust and wind."

"I'm here to make sure you guys don't screw up," she said, only partly in jest. Donnie gave her a knowing look.

Andi glanced at her watch. "The meeting was ten minutes ago. Think he'll get bail?"

Her nose curled at the whiff of diesel exhaust that came her way courtesy of a stiff breeze. Rain was predicted and Donnie's crew was working as quickly as they could.

"Yes, I do, as a matter of fact," Donnie said. He was dressed in civvies instead of his uniform.

"Is this your day off?"

He nodded. "I switch to nights starting Sunday."

A thought crossed her mind. "Didn't I read in Gloria's column that your ex and her hubby are out of the country?"

His rugged features changed to stone. "So what?"

"So who watches Lucas when you're at work?"

"Mom. Why'd you ask?"

"Just curious. Kris asked the other day. I guess it stuck in my head."

Andi was certain she saw a momentary spark of interest at the mention of Kris's name, but he turned away to squint at the sky before she could be sure. Wouldn't it be wild if all these years later Donnie was still holding a flame for her sister?

"Is she coming for the wedding?" Donnie asked softly.

Andi nodded. She didn't envy either of them, if that was the case. Unrequited love didn't have the same romantic appeal she'd once thought. For the past three days she'd felt a rift developing between her and Harley, shutting her out.

Jenny suggested his problem might be depression. And she could be right, but Andi feared it was something else. Or rather, someone else.

That diamond ring in his pack was a sure sign that there was another woman in Harley's life.

Jonathan, she corrected. *Keep it straight.*

The sound of a revving motor drew them closer to the edge of the ravine. Work crews had cleared a path through the bushes. A team of dogs and handlers had scouted the area for other clues, and every speck of Jonathan's possessions had been safely bagged.

Andi's stomach had almost emptied itself of half-digested pancakes when she first spotted the fractured helmet that must have been on Jonathan's head the night of the crash. It seemed miraculous that he'd survived with merely a concussion.

"The bike's in amazing shape," Donnie said.

She nodded, her breath trapped in her throat as the motorcycle swung free of the branches. The crane, with its anchors firmly gripping the uneven terrain, groaned under the load, but the cables held.

The huge metal arm swung toward them; Donnie pulled her out of the way. "That bike's done enough damage without nailing you, too, kiddo."

Andi chuckled softly. Donnie was a terrific guy. Too bad his history with Kris precluded any chance that he might become Andi's brother-in-law. "When will you release the bike?"

Donnie shrugged. "Haven't a clue. But I'm willing to bet things start popping once Har…Jonathan's father arrives."

"His father is coming?"

"Yes. We had a little trouble tracking him down since he was on a fishing boat somewhere off the Florida Keys. Mrs. Newhall was a bit reluctant to contact her husband. Apparently Jonathan and his father had words before Jonathan left. They had no idea he was missing."

Andi felt saddened to hear that.

"Once Mr. Newhall got back to shore and contacted me, he made plans to get here immediately. Sam invited him to bring the family and stay at the Rocking M, but he said his daughters couldn't come because of school. And when he heard about the wedding, he opted to get a motel room."

Andi followed Donnie to the orange-and-white SAR van across the road. "I read about the family online," she said. "Third-generation newspaper publishers. Jonathan's dad sold the family paper last summer and moved to Florida. He and his wife have two young daughters. Jonathan's mother died in a car accident when he was ten." Although there weren't photos to support the article, Andi had allowed herself to hope that the gorgeous blonde with the kids in Harley's wallet was his stepmother and much, much junior siblings.

"That's what my sources said, too."

"What else did your *sources* say?"

He reached into the driver's-side area and pulled out a black, brick-shaped walkie-talkie. "Nothing I'd care to share with you. What are you doing here, anyway?"

"It was *my* find."

"Well, now it's mine. Get lost." His big-brother tone was starting to wear on her nerves.

Andi gave him a serious look. "Someday you're going to run for sheriff and you're going to need my vote, mister. And I'm going to remember this moment."

Donnie threw back his head and laughed. "Is that a threat?"

A sudden crackle on the radio made her jump. She'd never been good at interpreting static-charged radio communications, so she had no time to prepare for Donnie's next comment. "Harley's bail came through. He and Sam are on their way here."

Andi gulped. Soon, she'd have a chance to throw her arms around the man who slept with her—in her dreams—every night. Unfortunately, her momentary burst of joy was accompanied by an impulse to run. Their stilted conversations of late told her Harley wasn't Harley anymore.

WHILE SAM CALLED Jenny to give her the good news about the judge's decision, Harley used the chance to talk to his lawyer alone.

"I appreciate all that you've done, James. I didn't kill Lars and I hope like hell you can prove my innocence, but—"

Rohr interrupted him. "Actually, the prosecution has to prove you committed the crime, not the other way around. Fortunately for us, the D.A.'s case is built on supposition and greed. I have absolutely no doubt we'll be able to prove that you had neither the motive nor the inclination to commit murder."

Harley swallowed sharply. "I wish I could be sure of either of those points, but I can't. All I know is I didn't kill Lars."

The man's crow's-feet became more pronounced when he squinted. "What are you trying to say?"

"Ever since the crash, I've had nightmares. Violent. Ugly images. Gutted buildings. Slain bodies," he added harshly.

His lawyer didn't bat an eyelash. "Perfectly understandable given your career. You were in Bosnia, the Middle East and Central America. One of your last pieces was on serial killers. I'm no shrink, but I'd say that kind of stuff gets repressed then jumps out when you least expect it."

Harley shook his head. "Although I've read those articles, I don't remember writing them. A part of me—I guess that part that's Harley—can't conceive of *wanting* to write those kinds of stories. I turn off the news whenever I get the chance. I hate fighting. I can't wait to get back to the ranch. It's peaceful there. Why would anybody live anywhere else?"

His lawyer smiled slightly. "I guess it's all in your perspective." He glanced at his Rolex. "Your father will be here later this afternoon, maybe he can help fill in some of the gaps.''

Sam joined them. ''Jenny needs Andi back at the bordello right away—something to do with the wedding.''

''Did you try her cell phone?'' Harley asked.

''Can't reach her. Maybe she rappelled down into the ravine again,'' he suggested with a casual shrug.

Harley's stomach flip-flopped. ''If you're headed that way, Sam, I'd like to ride along.'' He looked at his attorney. ''Are we through here?''

They made an appointment to meet on Monday or Tuesday of the following week to discuss strategy. After shaking hands with Sam, Rohr headed to his Lexus. ''Nice car,'' Harley said idly, to fill the silence. He and his boss hadn't been alone since this started. He didn't know where to begin.

''You have a Mercedes in storage in Missouri,'' Sam said matter-of-factly.

''I beg your pardon?''

''Jim showed me a list of inventory from a climate-controlled storage unit you rented before heading west.'' He gave Harley an odd look that ended with a smile. ''You've got money. Property. A farm that belonged to your grandparents.''

''A farm?''

''It's rented out. My point is, you're not my employee anymore, Harley.''

''I'm fired?''

Sam chuckled softly. ''You're a man of means. You don't need to work at the Rocking M.'' He gripped Harley's shoulder and squeezed. ''But it's your home for as long as you want.''

Harley was too choked up to speak.

"Should we go?" Sam asked then turned away without waiting for a reply. Harley followed.

The trip to the accident site was much quicker in Sam's four-wheel drive truck than in Rosemarie. Neither man spoke much. Harley appreciated his boss's restraint. But one question needed an answer, "Who do you think killed Lars?"

Sam shook his head. "Donnie hasn't given up looking. Our esteemed D.A. was hoping for a quick conviction to help with his reelection bid, but Donnie's one smart cookie. He doesn't take the easy way out or succumb to political pressure."

"That's comforting."

"It should be. I trust him and so can you."

As he turned on the gravel road that led to the recovery site, Sam cleared his throat in an ominous manner. "There is one thing I need from you, Harley."

"Anything."

Sam looked at him. "Without sounding too melodramatic, Jenny and I'd like some assurance that Andi doesn't come out the loser in this…situation."

A sunburst of pain exploded behind Harley's eyes. He grimaced, rubbing the heel of his hand against his forehead. "What do you mean?"

"Bluntly? Andi cares about you, Harley. You'd have to be blind not to see it. But the moment you get your memory back, you'll be Jonathan. A stranger. And Jenny's worried what that will do to her sister."

Me, too. None of what he'd read about his former life suggested that he was the kind of man who would be good for Andi.

Harley didn't know much about love—either the concept or the feeling—but he could tell by the cynical tone of JJ Newhall's articles that Jonathan was no fan of the emotion.

Any way you looked at it, the decent thing would be to nip this *relationship* in the bud. For Andi's sake. But could he? His memories of being with her were the only ones that held any true significance.

Maybe he could go back to his old life, but did he want to?

ANDI SPOTTED the extended cab pickup the minute it pulled up to the barricade, but neither Harley nor Sam made any effort to get out. Even from a distance, they looked grim. Andi's stomach tightened as she headed that way.

Sam apparently saw her and said something to Harley. Her future brother-in-law opened the door and hopped to the ground. As he walked toward her, he said, "Hey, beautiful, you're needed at the bordello." He held out the keys. "Your cell isn't working, so I told Jen I'd track you down."

Something about his demeanor put her on edge, more than she already was. "They're just about done here. Shouldn't I drive Rosemarie?"

He kept walking. "I want to talk to Donnie a minute. Are the keys in it? I'll take the old girl."

"The big pink keybob is on the seat." She looked toward the pickup. Harley was watching her. Her heartbeat sped up. For some reason, she felt nervous.

She took two steps then paused. "Sam, is there anything I should know?"

His sympathetic smile made her knees buckle, but he shook his head. "Go home, Andi. Tell Harley I'll pick him up there on my way to the ranch."

Andi wiped her damp palms on her jeans. She fluffed out her hair, loosening the moist curls at the nape of her neck and her forehead. Although the sun had felt blistering for a few minutes, she actually hadn't started to sweat until now.

What am I supposed to say? She went for casual. "Hi.

How's it going? Sam said to tell you he'd pick you up at the bordello," she said, hopping into the driver's seat.

She started the engine, and easily backed up the truck.

"I asked him to give us a few minutes alone," Harley said.

Even though she knew it was her imagination, Andi's first thought was he's changed. *His voice is different.* She tightened her grip on the steering wheel. "I heard the judge set bail."

Out of the corner of her eye, she saw him nod. Dang, he looked good in a suit. The charcoal-blue made his eyes even more intense—or maybe that was the emotion behind them. She swallowed loudly.

"My lawyer thinks the charges will be dropped. Lack of evidence. Especially if we get a change of venue."

"Good," Andi said, the word getting strangled by the tension in her throat. "That's great."

For a man who'd just been given a get-out-of-jail-free card, he didn't look terribly happy. "Is something else wrong?" she asked. "As if an impending murder trial wasn't bad enough?"

"Can we stop someplace and talk?"

She didn't like the sound of that. "Sam said Jenny needs me at home. It might be something to do with Ida Jane or the twins."

"Wedding issues. Not life-threatening."

Why did she get the impression what he wanted to say was going to hurt? "Okay. There's a fire station right up the road."

Neither spoke until she pulled to a stop beneath a sprawling buckeye tree. She turned off the engine. "What's up?"

He didn't answer right away. The sun made the air inside the cab warm and intoxicating—filled with Harley's scent. She knew it wasn't cologne, and she doubted that the Gold

Creek county jail provided exotic soap or shaving lotion, so it had to be him.

"Harley, cut to the chase."

"I'm not Harley."

She nodded impatiently. "Okay. Jonathan."

"No," he said, his tone bleak. "It's not okay."

Andi sat back. "I don't understand."

He made a gesture she'd never seen him use before—he scratched the nail of his index finger under his jaw. His forehead was creased. "I appreciate everything you've done to help me, but—"

Pain of unbelievable magnitude pressed down on her chest. *This is the brush-off.* She wouldn't have believed it possible to feel this empty. She couldn't even cry. Besides, she was a marine. Marines didn't cry.

"So, that's it? We're history. Short but sweet?"

His erect posture gave way, and he slumped, his chin facing the window. "I don't know. Sam said it wouldn't be fair to you if I couldn't declare my intentions. But, how can I do that when I don't know what they are? All I know for certain is I don't want to hurt you."

By his rough intake of breath, she knew he wasn't happy, either. "My father is arriving today."

The words seemed ominous. "Donnie told me. What then?"

"I don't know. On the phone, he suggested I needed to see the best psychiatrist in the country." He laughed ruefully. "I don't think he meant that to sound like a slam, but it's hard to know, because I can't remember our relationship. I can't remember how I feel about him. You provided the facts, but I'm still missing the emotional connection."

Andi heard the aching loneliness in his voice. It wasn't difficult for her to imagine what she'd feel like if she became estranged from her family. *Like Kristin.*

He went on. "Logic seems to dictate that—at some point—I'll leave. We both know—hell, you knew before I did—that I'm not a cowboy. I've been told I have commitments. An agent."

He made it sound like a disease.

This was the downside she and Jenny had discussed that morning. "You knew he wasn't a simple cowboy, Andi. You ran the risk of losing him the minute you set out to find his bike, but you had no choice. It was the right thing to do."

Somewhere in her head, she heard a voice say, "And the truth will set you free." She didn't believe it for a minute.

I wish... But Ida Jane always said wishes were for the weak. The strong went out and made things happen.

"This isn't about how I feel, Andi. It's what I *need* to do. For your sake."

She started to turn the key, but Harley stopped her. His hand covered hers. His touch made her toes curl inside her hiking boots. She tried to jerk back, but he closed his fingers, trapping her in a shell of warmth.

"*My* sake? This is some kind of charity breakup?" She yanked harder. "Hey, don't do me any favors, all right?"

He released her hand, but instead of backing away, he leaned across the console between the seats, crowding her. "This isn't easy for me, Andi. I like you. A lot. I like my life here, and I thought I had a chance..." His voice faded.

"A chance to start over? What's stopping you, Harley?"

His handsome face contorted in pain and frustration. "Didn't you read those articles you gave me? Couldn't you sense the kind of person I was—*am.*" He swore. "I don't even know which it is anymore. But that person sounds like a cold, arrogant ass. You wouldn't like him."

Andi started the engine. "If he's anything like you're

being right now, then, guess what? You're right. I don't
like him.''

Once they were on the road and she had her breathing
back under control, she said, "I'm not some loopy romantic,
Harley. I know from experience that the primrose path is
mined, but I was willing to risk it because I like you.''

"You don't know me.''

"You're right. I don't. So we'll just leave it at that.''

"Okay.''

Not another word was spoken until the car pulled into the
parking lot at the bordello. Andi quickly scanned the area.
Two obvious rental cars, possible shoppers, but the bulk of
the vehicles belonged to the construction workers who were
very nearly done with her new roof. And it looked great.
Thank goodness one thing in her life was going right.

She turned off the engine and pocketed the key. As she
started to open the door, her passenger suddenly sat up
straight. She braced herself for more bad news. "What?''

Harley pointed to the two figures standing on the porch.
One was her sister, the other a stranger. "Who is it?''

He looked at her, his blue eyes glittering with unfamiliar
sharpness. "I'm not sure, but I have a feeling that's my
father.''

CHAPTER NINE

"THEY CALL THIS a newspaper?" Andrew Newhall barked. A rude snort and a rustling sound of paper being scrunched in a ball followed his rhetorical question.

In the six hours that Harley had spent in his father's company, bits and pieces of memory had begun to filter through the screen of his amnesia. He'd caught a glimpse of an iron-willed workaholic who'd never seemed to have time for his son, but there was also an image of the same man—an older version this time—playing hide-and-seek with his young daughters.

"The *Ledger's* the only game in town," Harley said. Newspapers seemed like a neutral topic. Safer than any other subject.

"The editor is an opinionated ass," his father complained. "Who the hell is this Glory woman and why does anyone care what she thinks?"

Harley turned from his sentry position at the window. His father had insisted on getting a room at the motel after they'd driven to the Rocking M to pick up Harley's things. It hadn't seemed to matter what Harley's wishes were. Andrew Newhall reminded him of Andi in some ways. He moved forward with purpose, come hell or high water.

"Jonathan, listen to this crap," Andrew demanded. His voice took on a girlish tone that didn't jibe with his dignified persona. At sixty-one, with a full head of silver hair and tanned from the Florida sun, Andrew Newhall still emanated power. "'Murder and mayhem has come to our dear town in the shape of a drifter named Harley Forester, or rather, that's the alias he's been using while worming his way into our good graces. And, Glory, for one, is worried about his relationship with Gold Creek's native daughter, Andi Sullivan, who went so far as to buy him a suit to wear to his murder trial.'"

Harley winced.

"The damn-fool woman doesn't know the difference between an arraignment and a trial? What kind of crock is this? I'm calling the editor and getting *Glory* fired."

"I think she's his wife. Or sister," Harley warned.

"Then I'll buy the damn rag and fire them both."

Harley almost smiled. That sounded like the kind of imperial temper Andrew's son—Harley's alter ego—was renowned for. On the drive to and from the ranch, Andrew had expounded on Jonathan's exploits and accomplishments—his brash temper, his dogged focus when following a story and the awards he'd received for investigative journalism.

When asked about Jonathan's—*his*—social life, Andrew had been less effusive. "You'd just broken off an engagement, which I never saw the point of to begin with. It seemed a cold, bloodless relationship. I spotted more sparks between you and that Sullivan woman than I ever saw between you and…Miranda. I almost forgot her name."

Because Harley didn't want to discuss Andi with his father, he returned to the topic of the *Ledger*. "Gloria's a combination town crier, father confessor and Dear Abby in twenty column inches. You gotta give her credit for trying."

Andrew made a scoffing sound. "She's a small-town gossip on an ego trip. I've seen plenty like her, and so have you—even if you can't remember them."

Curious about the chasm he sensed between himself and

Andrew, Harley turned his back to the window and rested his bottom on the sill. He crossed his ankles and took a deep breath. The room smelled of coffee and newsprint, which brought back a memory from his childhood.

He pictured himself sitting in the knee well of his father's desk at the Bainbridge, Missouri, *Herald-Times*—his childhood playground. He was waiting for his father to return so he could jump out, crying, ''Surprise.'' Sometimes his father wouldn't come back for hours, so Jonathan would take paper from the desk and write stories. Tales of magical places and wonderful heroes who always saved the day.

''If this Glory person was a responsible journalist, she'd alert readers to what's really going on in this town. Let me show you what I mean.'' His father chucked the offending newspaper atop the pile then marched into the adjoining bedroom.

While waiting, Harley glanced around the parlor of the honeymoon suite of the Mountain Comfort Inn. The blue and gray plaid sofa contained a Hide-A-Bed. He doubted it would be a vast improvement over his jail bunk.

He didn't really care. His main concern at the moment was Andi. They'd parted abruptly—his father pulling him in one direction, Jenny's problem—something to do with the florist—pulling Andi in the other. Why had she looked at him as if he'd broken her heart? They barely knew each other.

But he knew that was a lame argument. Time was irrelevant where love was concerned. Andi's bright smile and frank attitude were imprinted on his soul. Correction. Harley's soul. At the moment, he wasn't sure how much of Harley would be left after Jonathan's memories took over.

''Look at this,'' Andrew said, breaking into Harley's reverie. He handed his son a single sheet of typewritten copy.

"I have an old friend who works for the *Sacramento Bee.*
He stumbled across this a few weeks ago.

"Somebody's on the move. Someone big. And they've
got their sights set on Gold Creek. They just haven't bothered to inform the locals. And the *Ledger* is too busy with
local gossip to investigate the *real* story."

As Harley scanned the page—a list of recent property
sales—another memory surfaced. Nothing as clear as his
olfactory regression to the *Herald-Times,* but something that
made his senses tingle. He pictured another time when
someone handed him information, and he'd grabbed his
jacket yelling, "Look out, Mr. Pulitzer, I've got a hot one."

Harley shook his head, not particularly charmed by the
arrogance he heard in that voice. *Jonathan's* voice.

"Sure, these look harmless enough—a ten-acre parcel
here, a convenience store there," his father was saying, "but
a little digging revealed all the purchases were linked to one
holding company—Meridian, Inc."

"Who owns Meridian?"

"No idea."

"Maybe it's the newspaper publisher. He's been pushing
development hot and heavy the past month or so."

His father snorted skeptically. "Anyone who prints that
kind of drivel doesn't have the brains or balls for a move
of this scope. He's probably on Meridian's payroll,
though."

Harley's head started to throb with the worst headache
he'd had in days. He tried to focus on meditating through
the pain, but a rush of images and sensations swirled and
coalesced in his mind. Names, contacts, possible sources
who could help him root out the mystery behind this puzzle.

He rushed to the bathroom and closed the door. In the
grocery sack that held his clothes was a new bottle of as-

pirin. He pried off the lid and shook four into his hand. He washed them down with water scooped from the faucet.

Resting his forehead against the cool mirror, he analyzed the attack. He knew what had provoked it. Jonathan's memories. A response to the kind of stimuli Jonathan welcomed. The kind of game playing Harley wanted nothing to do with. He was out of that rat race for good. He wasn't the same man he'd been before the accident. He might not be a cowboy, but he wasn't an investigative journalist, either. He no longer had the stomach—or head—for it.

When he returned to the sitting area of the suite, his father was hunched forward, a concerned look on his face. "Are you okay?"

Harley nodded as slowly as possible. "Headaches."

Andrew webbed his fingers together. "Perhaps this isn't the right time, son, but I wanted to talk to you about that last meeting we had."

Harley shook his head. "I don't remember it."

His father frowned. "You don't recall tossing a check for a quarter of a million dollars in my face?"

Harley sat in the recliner across from his father. That memory had surfaced once, but it had seemed too staged to be real. Harley couldn't empathize with the fury he'd seen on *Jonathan's* face because he'd had no clue to the motivation behind the argument. "Why was I so angry?"

"I'd just explained about the sale. Instead of giving you the family business, I'd sold it. For a pretty fine profit, if you ask me. The check was your share, but you didn't want it."

Harley closed his eyes, resting his head against the cushion. He could hear raised voices. "As my daughter would say, 'Puh-leeze.' You never wanted the business, Jon. You left town the day after—no, the night you graduated from high school and never looked back."

Then Jonathan's voice. "It was my right—my *obligation*—to carry on the family tradition. I'm the last Newhall male. And I'm a journalist."

"You're my son and you're an excellent reporter, but you've never been a Newhall."

"What the hell does that mean?"

Harley's gut twisted. Now he understood what he'd been feeling that day. Anger, yes. But more than that. Betrayal. Frustration. Hurt. His father had sold his heritage—the Newhall family's string of small but prestigious papers. Andrew planned to retire in Florida with his wife of seven years and their two daughters. Jonathan received a check.

"Jonathan," his father said, his voice low and serious, "You left Newhall Enterprises years ago. You've traveled around the world, interviewed kings, survived mortar fire. Does that sound like the kind of person who could sit at a desk for ten hours a day and not succumb to boredom?"

Harley answered without thinking. "I would have brought a different vision to the company. New energy."

"But why would you want to? Listen to me, Jon. I was trying to save you from a life you would have hated. *My* life."

Harley opened his eyes. He saw something Jonathan Newhall had probably never taken the time to see. A man who'd made mistakes and didn't want to repeat them.

"We fought a lot, didn't we?"

Andrew shook his head. "Disagreements."

"Something about Harvard?"

Andrew looked sheepish. "How come you can remember that but not your little sisters' names?"

Harley almost smiled. "Have I met them?"

"Of course. They adore you. They think you're famous."

Neither said anything for a minute then Andrew spoke. "Jon, I regret a lot things. You should have gone to Harvard. Lord knows you had the grades for it. I just didn't want to see you move so far from home." He laughed ruefully. "I tried to keep you close and only drove you farther away."

Andrew shook his head and continued. "Do you know the true irony of this? As Gwen told me before I got on the plane, for a publisher and writer of some repute, I've never been able to communicate with the one person in my life who mattered the most—my son."

Harley felt sorry for him. But he didn't know what to say. "Gwen is your new wife, right? My stepmother."

Andrew's face lit up, but he said with mock seriousness, "Don't call her that. She hates the word. She's only seven years older than you. But she's wise beyond her years. She's been so good for me."

Harley could tell that just from the look of serenity on his father's face when he spoke of his wife. He asked Andrew how they'd met, and soon heard the whole story. Oddly, his name—Jonathan's name—didn't come up much in his father's narrative.

Maybe I was a lone wolf, off on my travels with no time for family. After watching Andi's connection and commitment to her family, the idea seemed distasteful.

"I guess I'll take a shower," he said, starting toward the bathroom.

A soft knock on the door made him change course.

"Hi," Andi said, pushing her wind-tousled hair out of her eyes.

Her denim jacket covered a plain white T-shirt. Instead of jeans, she had on a denim skirt that stopped several inches above her knees. Her bare feet were clad in Birkenstock sandals.

"Hi," he said, unable to keep from smiling. A mere six

hours had passed, but he'd missed her. Not a very promising start to keeping his distance. "What's going on?"

"I need your help. Will you come with me? I'm prepared to use force if necessary."

Although her tone was light, the look in her eyes was serious. "I don't see a gun," he said.

"I'm an ex-marine. I don't need a gun."

Harley laughed. When was the last time he'd laughed? Pivoting, he reached for the closest jacket—his father's umber-brown golf jacket. "Dad, I'm going out with Andi. I'll see you later, okay?"

He caught his father's look of surprise, which for some reason segued into a broad smile. "I'll be here."

He nodded and closed the door. "Where are we going?"

"A mission of mercy."

As he followed her to the Cadillac, Harley felt an odd sense of lightness. He wondered if it might be joy. Or lust. *Have I seen her bare legs before? Those are great gams. And very nice ankles.*

He got in the car and closed the door. They didn't speak until the outskirts of town gave way to mountainous terrain, then Harley asked, "Can you tell me where we're going yet? I promise not to jump out."

"The Blue Lupine."

"Lars's cabin?" He almost changed his mind about jumping. "But it's a crime scene, and I'm the main suspect."

She made a face. "We have Donnie's permission to be there. Sam got a call from Lars's neighbor lady."

"The one who told the cops she'd seen me on the premises?"

Andi nodded. "Margaret Graham. She's a nice lady. I think she and Lars had a little romance going."

"Maybe she killed him."

Andi's dry chuckle made him frown. "And dragged his body to the mine shaft? I don't think so. She's in her sixties and weighs about ninety pounds soaking wet."

Harley made a dry sound. "I see your point."

"Donnie said not to touch anything. We're just there to pick up Sarge."

"The dog?" Harley's right eyelid quivered. He pictured the large slobbery animal quite clearly, and the image intensified the sudden pain in his head. "Why me?"

"He knows you. You lived with Lars after your accident. Sam figured he'd come to you. Margaret tried to coax him off the porch, but he wouldn't have anything to do with her."

The theory had merit—except for one thing: Harley was feeling a reaction very similar to the acrophobia he'd felt when Andi had been dangling on a rope over the edge of the cliff. He couldn't explain it. He remembered Sarge as a friendly hound completely devoted to Lars. Not the least bit threatening, but now the idea of handling the dog was making him ill.

Andi, who was busy negotiating the turn that put them on the road to the mine, didn't seem to notice his distress. She said, "Sarge is a great dog. He's been living up there alone all this time. Mrs. Graham has been checking on him, supplementing his food, but she's going away for the weekend and she's afraid something will happen to him. She told Sam she heard a mountain lion the other night."

Harley took a deep breath and let it go. *Focus.*

"Is something wrong?" she asked.

Harley rolled his head to loosen the muscles in his neck. "I don't know."

He thought back to his weeks of recuperation at Lars's cabin. The huge, floppy-eared mutt—part hound dog, part coyote, Lars used to say—had slept at Harley's side on a braided rug on the plank floor beside the couch. Once Harley could handle the climb to the loft bedroom, Sarge had positioned himself at the foot of the ladder, as if guarding him. *Or making sure I didn't escape.*

"Are you certain I'm allowed near the property?"

"I told you, Donnie gave me the go-ahead. But he did say to be careful. He said, 'If Harley didn't kill Lars, then somebody else did. I don't want you up there alone.' That's another reason Mrs. Graham is leaving."

"Couldn't *she* drop the dog off in town?"

"Not if Sarge won't go with her." Andi's grin lit up her face. "Besides that, wait till you see Margaret's car. She never goes anywhere without her menagerie. Two birds—cockatiels, I think. Three or four cats, a snake and a standard poodle. Old Sarge would never fit."

"She sounds like quite a character."

Andi nodded. "She is. Just like Lars was."

Harley closed his eyes. Lars was a recent memory. A good one, and returning to the small, rustic miner's cabin was going to hurt. Even if he did have Andi at his side.

ANDI HADN'T VISITED Lars's place in years. Not that it had changed one whit, she decided as Rosemarie approached the clearing. The tiny cabin sat at the edge of a meadow just as she remembered it—a lush green carpet dotted with blue lupines.

A recent rain gave everything a clean look, but there was a sad, abandoned feeling to the house, too.

As Andi had noted, the cabin looked unchanged—except for an obscene yellow necklace of crime scene tape around its middle. It flapped in the breeze with a ghostly crackling sound.

Harley had gone quiet the past few miles. He hadn't seemed as enthusiastic about their mission as she'd thought he would be. She was trying to make herself think of him as Jonathan Newhall, not Harley Forester. But it wasn't easy.

Jenny—once the flower crisis had been solved—had taken a few minutes to give her sister some advice. "In a way, you've lost a friend. Even if he looks the same, his mind is changing. And, trust me, change, even good change, is almost always accompanied by a sense of grief."

Andi believed her sister. She didn't know anyone better qualified to talk about loss and change than Jenny. "But maybe you're giving up too soon," Jenny had said as she'd left for the ranch. "If you get to know him better, you might like this new incarnation as much as you liked the old one."

Andi glanced at her passenger. She'd felt something in their few stolen kisses that she'd never experienced before. Was it love? She couldn't say for certain, but Jenny was right. Andi owed herself a chance to find out.

"Mrs. Graham's place is right around the corner," she said, slowing for the railroad crossing. The traditional white X with the words *Southern Pacific* always made her smile since the narrow-gauge track only connected the mine to the stamp mill where the ore was crushed. "Her house sits up on the knoll, giving her a bird's-eye view of Lars's place— which is how she happened to see the Rocking M truck that fateful day."

As they drove past Lars's driveway, she frowned at the mournful baying coming from the front porch. A few seconds later, she cranked the steering wheel to the left and turned into a steeply banked driveway. The car rocked to a stop at a forty-five-degree incline. She put the gear into park, letting the car idle. "Before we go in, though, I'd like to ask you something."

He sat up a little straighter. Wary.

"Are you planning to leave once the trial—if it comes to that—is over?"

"My father wants me to return to Florida with him. He thinks that by looking at family photo albums and spending time with his wife and daughters, I'll feel more...like my old self."

The wry tone was pure Harley, and Andi could have kissed him. Would have, if he'd made any kind of signal that he'd welcome her kiss.

She gambled. "Do you have to go? I was thinking you might stay and take over the mine. It's yours."

He looked doubtful.

"I don't mean actually mine it. I doubt if Lars made any money at that, but with a satellite dish, you could telecommute."

He shook his head. "I'm out of the newspaper business."

"Then write the great American novel."

His snort was filled with skepticism.

Andi hadn't thought her suggestion would work, but she cared too much to just let him walk out of her life. She took a deep breath, then asked, "What about us?"

He kept his gaze on the view out his side window. "We already talked about this. I don't want you to get hurt. You've grown to care for a man who doesn't exist. Maybe he did for a while, but now I'm part Jonathan, part Harley." He gave a small laugh. "I'm pretty sure I'll be in therapy for years."

Andi scooted across the wide seat and draped one arm across his shoulders. "That's just it. You still *look* like Harley. And I can't shake the feeling that deep down you care for me too. Can we check my theory?"

He shrank back against the door. "I don't think that's such a hot idea."

"Humor me." She knew the risk. If the feelings that had

drawn the two of them together were still there, their relationship held potential. If not...

Just as she lowered her head, a horn sounded.

Harley moved across her protectively. "What is it?"

A gray Subaru Brat with an oversize wooden camper shell drew to a stop a bumper's width away from the nose of the Cadillac. Andi sighed in frustration. "It's Mrs. Graham's car—the Holyroller." She slid back behind the wheel. "You'd think she could wait a minute."

Andi tried to put the car in reverse, but the shifter on the column refused to budge. She put her shoulder into it, but to no avail. She'd forgotten that Rosemarie hated hills.

"Hello," a voice hailed. A scrawny arm in red, white and blue waved from the window like a flag on the Fourth of July.

"Is that her?" Jonathan asked.

Andi returned the wave then sank her teeth into her bottom lip as she tried to coax Rosemarie into gear. Harley scooted over to add his help. When his fingers closed over hers on the shift knob, Andi's heart jumped in her chest. His hand was a little sweaty. *From the idea of kissing me?*

At last, the lever gave. Andi shifted sideways and prepared to back up. His gaze, she noticed, was stuck on her bare legs.

He seemed to collect his thoughts and bulleted to his side of the seat. "What's this woman going to say when she sees me?"

"Who knows? She's a little weird. But in a good way."

Andi backed up until she had a clear view of the road for a hundred feet in each direction. Mrs. Graham barreled down the driveway and pulled to a dusty stop just across from her. "You're late," she complained. "But no matter. Katty-kit had anxiety diarrhea, so that slowed us down." She used her index finger and thumb to mimic a clothespin and squeezed her nose.

Andi glanced at her passenger. He startled when a large apricot-colored poodle with a pompadour haircut suddenly poked its head out the vehicle's back window and started barking.

"Sorry for holding you up," Andi shouted above the ruckus. "This old car isn't fond of mountain roads."

"No bother. I'd have given Sarge a lift into town, but as you can see there's just not enough room. Even had to leave Joe Bob home so we could all fit."

"Who's Joe Bob?" Harley asked, leaning closer to Andi so he could look out her window. His hand was almost touching her bare thigh. The skirt—Jenny's idea—had been a smart move after all.

"My boa," Mrs. Graham answered. She didn't appear to recognize Harley as an alleged murderer. "I left him out of his cage so he could do a little mouse eradication. Gotta go."

"Hmm," Harley said, leaning forward to watch the odd car disappear. "Definitely unique."

Andi knew at that moment the feelings she'd felt for Harley could easily pass over to this new man. With a vocabulary as extensive as his—she'd read a few of his editorials—he could have chosen any one of a hundred adjectives ranging from bizarre to deranged to describe the old lady. *Unique—a Harley way of putting it.*

Instead of trying to back all the way to Lars's cabin, Andi pulled ahead as she had the first time so she could maneuver the car into a downhill position. The Caddie lunged forward, then rocked back and forth while Andi tried pushing the lever upward. "Come on, Rosemarie, you can do this."

"Maybe it needs transmission fluid."

"Well, unless that's an item you carry with you in your pocket, I think we're screwed."

He looked askance at her snide tone. "Lars had cases of the stuff around."

Before she could comment on his resourcefulness, he got out of the car and set off down the road. Andi could have taken the shortcut between the two homes, but she followed him instead. Not such a chore considering how sharp he looked in his new clothes. Navy Dockers with an off-white cotton shirt with rolled-up sleeves that revealed his muscular arms. He'd left the brown windbreaker in the car.

He walked fast. Seemingly unconcerned that a misstep in one of the muddy puddles might ruin his leather topsiders. His legs looked long and powerful. She had to hustle to keep up with him.

"I've got the cell phone in case Donnie gets a break and catches the killer," she said, patting her pocket.

"Won't happen."

"Today, you mean?"

"Here. Lars told me his place was impervious to cellular reception. Sam said he tried to outfit Lars with some kind of two-way radio system years ago and nothing ever worked. Which suited Lars fine. He didn't like people and he didn't trust anybody. Except Sam."

"And you."

He missed a step. "He took pity on me."

"Maybe, at first, but then he got to know you. And like you. Lars was good at reading people."

His shoulders stiffened. "He didn't know me from Adam."

"Then why'd he leave you the mine?"

He stopped so abruptly she almost plowed into him. *Accidentally on purpose,* as Kristin used to say. Just so she could feel his body against hers. "I don't know what he was thinking. I wish to hell I did."

Andi sobered. She'd been so wrapped up in the murder and the bike and her own feelings, she hadn't given much thought to Harley's sense of loss. He'd cared for the old man who'd rescued him, and now Lars was dead.

"Sorry," she said. "That was insensitive."

He started to say something but the woeful baying began again, making the hair on her arms stand up. Sarge might not have been a purebred, but his vocal genes belonged to the Baskervilles.

"If I check the machine shed for the transmission fluid," Harley said, his tone strained, "could you deal with the dog?"

The dog? Andi didn't understand this sudden tension in his voice. She remembered seeing Harley interact with Sarge the day Lars dropped off Harley at the Rocking M. Perhaps not as enthusiastically as a dog-lover might, but certainly there'd been no antipathy between him and Sarge.

Puzzled, she walked to the house. With its aged timbers and thick, uneven mortar, the cabin oozed charm—and neglect. As she neared the building, Sarge's long, sorry howl turned to frantic barking. The dog put his forepaws on the railing and watched her approach. Andi could tell by his nervous posturing, he was hoping someone—probably Lars—would come to relieve him of duty.

"Hey, there, Sarge. Good boy. It's me, Andi. Remember? You're my pal, aren't you, Sarge?" She said his name over and over and approached cautiously until she saw his skinny tail start to swish back and forth. "Come here, sweetheart. Let me give you a hug."

Starved for attention, Sarge's hug became a body slam that knocked her on her butt. His sloppy kisses covered her face, then her hands, which she used as a shield. She was laughing too hard to scold him.

"Sarge," a stern voice barked. "Sit."

Immediately, the dog backed away and dropped his rear end to the ground. Andi sat up, too, brushing her hair out of her eyes. She'd lost her keys in the tall grass and had to stretch to reach for them. Harley made a funny sound, and when she glanced at him and saw his gaze on her bare legs—and no doubt immodest pose—she hastily drew her knees under her. The dampness sent a chill through her.

"Did he hurt you?"

"Of course not. I was just giggling too hard to escape. He's lonely."

The dog stared at Harley with such obvious yearning it almost broke her heart. He was a man's dog; his man was gone. This man gave commands but not the one he was waiting for.

She started to reach out to the animal when Harley said, "Come."

Sarge surged forward but didn't jump up. He seemed to know instinctively that this man wouldn't like it. "Good dog," Harley said, petting the dog.

Andi turned away to keep from letting Harley see her tears. She wasn't a soft touch, but she loved animals. And Harley, without knowing it, had just done something guaranteed to make her fall in love.

"I'll see if Lars has a leash around here," she said.

"There's some rope in the shed. I should have picked it up, but when I heard the commotion, I thought he was going to eat you alive." Harley hadn't dropped to one knee, as Andi would have done. He didn't have his arm looped around the dog's neck. But he did scratch Sarge's ear. Twice. Both times, Sarge sighed as if in heaven.

For the first time, she noticed a small plastic container in his left hand. "You found some transmission stuff?"

"Yes," he said, helping her to her feet.

"Great. Let's get going."

The corner of his mouth crinkled in a typical Harley smile. Although she'd caught a glimpse or two of his alter ego—Jonathan—Andi chose not to think about the two personalities occupying the same body. It was a little creepy.

She shuddered.

"Are you cold?" he asked.

Harley and Sarge followed a few steps behind her. It was obvious no leash was necessary. Sarge would have followed Harley to the moon and back.

"No. Just thinking."

"It's this place," he said, looking around. "It seems so empty without Lars."

"What are you going to do with it?" she asked.

He shook his head. The wan sunlight filtering through the pines made his hair tone darker than normal. He'd combed it differently—too neat for her taste. She longed to run her fingers through it and mess it up.

"That depends on the verdict," he said. "If I'm found guilty, the state will probably take it. Legally, you can't profit from someone's death if you're deemed instrumental in causing it."

Their conversation died as they reached the car. Harley poured in the transmission fluid, then checked the miniature dipstick. After testing it twice, he opened the rear door and pointed to the back seat, which Andi had covered with an old beach towel. Sarge leaped into the space.

Harley closed the door soundly and walked to her. He stood close enough for her to smell a mixture of dog, motor oil and man. Somewhere in that combination was Harley. She felt a prickly sensation in her sinuses.

"We started something we didn't finish," he said.

His tone wasn't the least bit romantic, but Andi didn't find that too surprising. Despite that one sweet *"Good dog,"* Andi wasn't fooled. She knew this wasn't the same man she'd begun to have feelings for. But she owed it to herself to put an end to her X-rated dreams. She would kiss him and put the past away. "Let's do it."

HARLEY TOOK A STEP CLOSER. He knew this wasn't a good idea, but that damn skirt enticed him. And the misty look in her eyes when he'd petted Sarge hadn't helped. You'd have thought he was a saint or something. What man could resist that kind of combination?

He braced one hand on the roof of the old car behind her. The paint felt gritty—and he had a sudden image of a sleek shiny Mercedes. Black with tinted windows. Like some kind of gangster car, he thought, frowning.

"We don't *have* to do this," Andi said peevishly, apparently misinterpreting his scowl.

The sun chose that moment to peek out from behind the thick low clouds that seemed to brush the tops of the trees. The breeze made her curls dance. His hand itched to touch that inviting silkiness, but he crammed his fist into the pocket of the trousers his father had suggested he buy.

"Yes, we do."

"Then don't scowl. I won't bite. I promise."

Her tone was irreverent, spunky, but beneath the chutzpah Harley sensed a hint of trepidation. She had something invested in this outcome. Hope, maybe? That sounded risky.

She lifted her chin in challenge. "So are we going to do this or—"

He lowered his head and pressed his lips to hers while they were still moving. He hadn't taken into account that her mouth would be open. That made it not only easy but also natural to slip his tongue into her mouth and explore the moist warm recess.

And he might not have bothered trying to engage her tongue if she hadn't made such an effort to avoid contact. He closed his eyes to concentrate on the target.

He had no recollection of his hand escaping from his pocket and burying itself in her hair, but he knew the exact moment it did because she gave a small sigh and ambushed his tongue with hers. He acknowledged his victory with a grunt of his own. One that seemed to echo in his head. So loudly, he opened his eyes.

And looked into Andi's assessing green eyes. He knew instantly that the attraction between them hadn't lessened. If anything, the intensity of emotion was stronger. Hotter. He stepped back.

Andi didn't say anything. Maybe she was hurt because he stood there mute instead of making polite romantic chit-chat. No doubt Jonathan would have engaged in some pleasantries, but Harley couldn't think of anything appropriate to say. He moved out of the way so she could close the door, then he walked to the opposite side and got in.

Sarge lumbered to his feet and swung his large slobbery head in Harley's direction. His smell—woolly canine and stringy drool—made Harley's stomach heave. A pulse in his temple throbbed.

"You look sick. If it was from kissing me—"

Harley groaned and rolled down the window. "Headache. They still hit now and then. Not your fault."

He wasn't sure she believed him. She started the car.

Thankfully, it went into gear without his assistance. Moments later they started the downhill journey. Before they reached the cabin the sun disappeared, and huge, fat raindrops began to pummel the windshield.

Harley hastily rolled up the window, taking a last gulp of

wet, clean air. Andi drove slowly to adjust to the pouring rain and bathtub-size potholes. While keeping her eyes on the road, she fiddled with a couple of knobs on the dashboard. "What are you looking for?" he asked, sensing her tension.

"Defog. It isn't Rosemarie's forte," she said with a gulp.

She cracked the window and a wet gust sliced through the opening. Shivering, she hastily cranked it back up then swiped at the condensation on the windshield with her palm. Moisture beaded up, leaving a blurry streak.

"We'll be fine once we get past Snot Corner," she said. "Do you know how it got its name?"

Harley pictured Lars expounding on the navigational pitfalls of this road. "Lars told me there's a strata of clay that runs through this part of the mountain. It crosses the road right at the S-curve. When it gets wet, it turns to slime."

"Bingo," she said. "That's the reason he couldn't take you to a doctor right away. Even though he knew you had a concussion."

Less than a minute later, she said, "And here we are." As she eased the car around the first part of the curve, the back end broke loose. She took her foot off the gas. "I heard Lars tell Sam that The Corner ate a VW bug once. Snapped its drive train or something," she said.

"Should we turn around?"

"How? If we get off the road, we'll get stuck for sure."

She had a point. The hills on either side of the road had turned into grayish-brown waterfalls.

"Maybe you should slow down," he advised.

"I'm going five miles an hour," she growled. "Can you wipe the window? I can't see a thing."

He grabbed his father's jacket and rubbed. All it did was smear the moisture into a streaky mess that forced Andi to duck back and forth in rhythm to the windshield wipers. The motion reminded him of a person dodging bullets.

He scooted closer and tried again. He made one clear path, just in time to see that they'd arrived at the hairpin corner with the disgusting name. ''Tighten your seat belt.''

He glanced down and saw her foot press the brake pedal flat to the floor. Her toes showed the strain of her effort, but the big car was still moving forward—like a skier atop an avalanche.

Harley scrambled back to his side of the seat and snapped his shoulder harness into place, then reached out to tug on Andi's. She spared him a bemused glance then turned all business. He braced his feet on the floor, his hands on the cracked padding of the dashboard. No such thing as an air-bag in this year's model, he thought.

''Hold on, Sarge,'' Andi said. ''This might get funky.''

Harley watched her face. Fear? Yes, but something else, too. Excitement. For some strange, totally ridiculous reason, the only thought that came to his mind was *I think I love her.*

A second later, the car picked up speed and shot into the grade like a marble in a maze. Andi did an admirable job of keeping it from flipping when the back end slid out from under them again, but in correcting the spin, she missed her chance to make the turn. It wasn't her fault. They simply ran out of road. And like a topsy-turvy pinball the car rolled.

CHAPTER TEN

ROSEMARIE WAS BEYOND help. Andi took one last look as they trudged on foot up the muddy incline. The crumpled pink automobile resembled a squashed toy, but, at least, it had landed far enough off the road that it wasn't a hazard to other drivers. And, thankfully, neither she nor Harley had been hurt. But Sarge…

She hurried to catch up with Harley who was carrying Sarge. Although alert, the dog had yelped when they'd freed him from the wreckage. And seemed unable to stand, let alone walk.

"How far?" Harley asked, his breath a harsh hiss through clenched teeth.

The combination of rain and wind put the risk of hypothermia at the top of her list of concerns. "Half a mile? I'm not sure. After we dry off, I'll run up to Margaret's cabin and phone for help."

Hunching her shoulders, she clasped the neckline of her jacket tight to her throat to keep a funnel of icy rain from coursing down her back. The denim provided neither warmth nor protection from the elements. Mud sucked at her sandals, making each step an effort, but she couldn't complain. At least, *she* wasn't carrying a very large dog.

"D-do you want me to take him?" she asked, praying he'd turn her down.

"Yes," Harley said, but he kept walking, shoulder into

the wind. His father's jacket stuck to him like a wet grocery bag.

"Okay," she said, reaching deep for the strength she'd need to carry the dog's weight. The clearing where the cabin sat was barely visible through the steady downpour, which felt as if it might turn to sleet or snow any second.

He gently nudged her with Sarge's paw. "I was kidding. I couldn't let go even if I wanted to. My arms are frozen in place."

He took a step then waited. He wasn't going without her.

Sarge gave a low moan. Andi leaned close and pressed her nose to the dog's ear. "Hang in there, buddy. Harley and I are going to take care of you. We're almost home." She tucked the soggy towel that she'd retrieved from the back seat under Harley's trembling biceps.

Taking a deep breath, Andi mustered the energy she needed. "Let's go. I sure hope the electricity is still working."

It wasn't.

When they finally arrived at the cabin, Andi savagely ripped off the yellow caution tape. She located the hidden key where Harley said it would be then unlocked the rear door. Teeth chattering in harmony, they found the place almost as chilly as outside and a lot darker.

Andi knew from experience that in cases of hypothermia, time was critical. "I'll find some towels. Put Sarge on the rug and cover him with that couch throw for now. You and I need to dry off. Right away."

Shivering nonstop now, she stripped off her jacket and peeled away her stiff, soaking-wet skirt. Her white T-shirt stuck like plastic wrap and announced the fact she wasn't wearing a bra, but modesty was the least of her problems.

Groping in the darkness, she stumbled through the tiny house to where she thought the bathroom might be.

The house smelled of pot, indoor animals and an un-washed miner. She found a stack of scratchy, sun-dried tow-els folded on a shelf in the bathroom. The abrasive texture chafed her skin, but she dried her arms and legs then stripped off her shirt and wrapped one towel above her breasts. She used another, turbanlike, for her hair.

"Dammit, Lars, did you have to buy the smallest, cheap-est towels you could find?" she muttered as she grabbed the rest of the stack and backtracked into the living area.

To her surprise, Harley had started a fire in the potbelly stove that sat atop a semicircle of flagstone in the corner of the room. "Wow! You must have been a Boy Scout."

He shook his head. His teeth were chattering badly. But instead of looking her way, he patiently fed another few pieces of kindling into the cast-iron mouth.

Andi dropped a couple of towels beside him then moved to the big braided oval rug to check on Sarge. She removed the knitted throw Harley had covered him with and carefully dried the dog's legs and body. While whispering encour-agement and praise, she squinted in the half light to see if she caused him any pain.

"Is it his leg or hip?" Harley asked from a spot beside her elbow.

Andi had been so intent on Sarge she hadn't heard him move. She glanced to her left. He wore two towels—one at his waist, one draped over his broad shoulders like a child pretending to be a superhero. His hair stood up in several spots, adding to his boyish look.

"He whimpered when I touched his back leg," she told him. "It could be a dislocated hip. Hopefully, it's just bruised, but, in all honesty, I'm more worried about internal injuries. Those might not show up right away."

Harley made a harsh sound. "Let's pull the rug closer to

the fire, then I'll find us some clothes. Lars kept everything in a trunk by his bed.''

Dragging the heavy rug with the dead weight of the dog on it would have been easier if her towel stayed in place, but every time she tugged, the two halves would pop apart, flashing Harley. His frustration must have matched hers, because he let out a groan not unlike Sarge's low moans.

''I'm sorry,'' she said, retucking the material.

He didn't respond but disappeared the second after they got Sarge situated in front of the now-crackling fire. Andi knelt near the open grate and added two small hunks of wood. A splash of sparks gave a burst of light to the room and she looked around.

She barely remembered the interior of the cabin from her first visit years earlier, but, like the exterior, it seemed unchanged. A small room crowded with a man's life and playthings. Fishing gear and two rifles stood clustered in one corner. Mining magazines, newspapers and a dog-eared copy of *Playboy* lay scattered on the floor near a well-used, brown tweed recliner. The kitchen looked surprisingly neat. Canned goods of every size and shape were visible on several shelves of a pantry. At least they wouldn't starve until help arrived.

A flickering light to the left caught her eye. Harley stepped through the doorway of the adjoining bedroom holding a candle. He'd donned baggy gray sweatpants and a bulky, red thermal pullover. He walked in a shuffling manner due to oversize moccasins that made a scratchy sound against the plank flooring.

''Lars was a big guy,'' he said. ''Size sixteen shoes.''

Andi anchored her towel to her sternum and rose. The warmth at her front versus the chill at her back made her shiver. Harley noticed. He carried his candle to a small cabinet on the opposite side of the room, then hurried toward her. In his left hand rested a stack of blankets with some articles of clothing balanced on top. The *shish-shish* of his slippers made her smile.

He looked at her quizzically. Except for the murmur of rain and the crackle of the fire, the cottage was too quiet. She needed a distraction to keep from thinking about the wreck. How scared she'd been to lose control.

She helped herself to a massive flannel shirt and a pair of thick socks, ignoring the sweatpants. "I don't think Lars's pants will fit. He was a couple of inches taller than you and weighed more than Sam."

She turned her back, dropped her towel and shrugged on the shirt. She might have been more modest if she hadn't lived, slept and dressed in the company of GIs for six years. A bare behind was the least of her problems.

The mammoth shirt hung to her knees and the socks came almost to her kneecaps. "There," she said, spinning on one heel to face him. "Much better."

The look in Harley's eyes said he agreed, but there was something else in his look. Something she wasn't ready to acknowledge. "Cocoa?" she asked, heading for the stove with an ancient teakettle resting on the back burner.

"Whiskey."

"Alcohol isn't as warming as people think," she said, recalling a lecture she'd heard years before in search and rescue training.

"That's not why I want it," he said softly. He walked back to the small cabinet. "There are more candles on the shelf above the sink. Matches, too. Lars said he was always the first to lose power in a storm. The stove is propane."

Andi stepped carefully to avoid the hunks of rock littering the floor in small piles. She guessed these were assays going to or coming back from the geologist in town. Sam once told her Lars made just enough money from his gold to pay his property taxes and buy food. Since he never bothered with income tax, licenses or insurance, he didn't have much overhead.

She found the matches and lit one of the burners on the stove. Instead of cocoa—the only milk she could find was canned—Andi decided to have tea. She lit two more candles, anchoring them in chipped saucers. The soft yellow light gave the place a cozy feeling. The thick log walls made her feel safe and snug. Only the ping and plop of the rain on the tin roof reminded her that she'd just had an accident.

"I wrecked Rosemarie," she said to herself. A ripple of sadness passed through her. Ida Jane loved that car.

"Here," Harley said, holding a small stinky glass under her nose. "You need this more than tea."

She hated whiskey. The taste, the smell. "No thanks."

"Trust me. In a few minutes, you're going to feel the aftermath of the accident. Your muscles will start to shake and your head will feel like it's going to explode and your stomach will heave."

Something about his tone told her he spoke from experience. She took the glass. "How will this help?"

"I don't know. But it does."

She pinched her nostrils closed—which caused Harley to chuckle—then took a mouthful. It scalded the inside of her mouth and she swallowed fast. The burn raced down her throat and blossomed in her upper chest like a volcano. *"Eouw,"* she said, taking a breath. Residual fumes seemed to singe her nose hairs. "I'll throw up for sure now."

"Not if I keep you preoccupied." His tone was soft and deceivingly benign—until she looked into his eyes and saw a fire beneath the blue. She saw a determination there that had nothing to do with crisis management.

He took the glass from her numb fingers and set it to one

side then opened his stance so his legs straddled her. Andi's lower back pressed against the counter.

"This isn't a good time to make out, Harley," she said. "We need to call for help."

"Why? No one can get here. It's probably snowing on the upper pass. And no one is going to make it past Snot Corner."

The mention of the accident site made her stomach turn over. "But we at least need to let people know we're okay. Jenny's probably too busy with wedding plans to be worried, but Kristin is arriving this evening, and she'll worry."

"We'll walk to the animal lady's house as soon as we're warmed up," he said, raising his eyebrows at the double entendre. "In the morning, we'll use Lars's truck. The snow won't last long and the truck has four-wheel drive."

"What about Rosemarie?"

His lips flattened. "Do you have to call her—it—that?"

"It's her name. She's practically a member of the family. Why does it bother you?"

He moved back. "It seems profane."

Suddenly she remembered something she'd read in his bio, and she understood. "Jonathan Newhall's mother—your mother—was killed in a car accident."

His gaze didn't veer, but a muscle above his right eye twitched. She gave a small, spontaneous peep. "You were in the car with her, weren't you?"

He started to shake his head then stopped. "Was I?"

The look of confusion on his face reminded her of Ida Jane at those times when her memory failed her. He closed his eyes and rocked back on his heels, as if dizzy.

Andi took his hand. "I'm sorry. That was me being my usual insensitive self."

He inhaled slowly. "I can almost remember. But I can't quite bring it back...." He paused, his eyes still closed. "I picture a woman. Driving the car. Laughing. The music was playing. She's my mother. She was singing along with a song—the Beach Boys, I think. She liked to change the lyrics to make me laugh. She was quick, and very clever with words.''

He wasn't looking at her. His gaze seemed focused on the candle she'd set on the table.

"She lost control for a second and the tire hit something—a curb, I think—and the car flipped. It landed upright just like the Caddie. Only, we weren't wearing seat belts." He shook his head sadly. "Nobody did in those days."

Andi closed her eyes and groaned. "Oh, Harley, I'm so sorry. This wreck must have felt like déjà hell for you."

Impulsively, she threw her arms around him and kissed the side of his face. He didn't return the embrace. His arms hung limp at his sides. "She put her arm out to protect me— like mothers do when their kid is in the front seat—and her head hit the steering wheel. They said she died instantly."

"And today *I* walked away without a scratch," Andi said to herself.

He looked at her. "Thank God," he said, pulling her to him. "I don't think I could have lived with myself if history had repeated itself. Talk about cursed—"

She didn't let him finish. She pressed her mouth to his, just as he'd done earlier to her. She knew all about survivor's guilt. Even though Andi and her sisters had had no control over the events surrounding their birth, Andi knew the circumstances of their loss had always been a factor in their lives.

She'd read somewhere that the surest way to block hurtful memories was to create pleasant new ones. This wreck was one memory that wouldn't hurt this man ever again—not if she had any say in the matter.

HARLEY WASN'T PREPARED for the onslaught of emotions that hit him. First, the memory of his mother's death. Then the life-affirming joy of Andi's kiss. A powerful need made him jump at the escape Andi offered. "Are we going to make love?" he asked, closing his eyes as she trailed kisses from his lips to the scar on his temple.

"You have anything better to do on a rainy evening?" she quipped.

Her playful tone was too enticing to resist. "At the moment, I can't think of anything I'd rather do, provided we can find...um, what we need."

She gave him an impish look. "A raincoat of another kind, you mean?"

He nodded. "Lars kept a stash in the loft."

"Lucky us. As long as they're still in working order."

Harley laughed and kissed her again. Andi wiggled free. She looked at him and smiled, then took his hand and tugged him toward a large lumpy couch. "The bedroom's right over there," he said softly, nodding toward the doorway a few feet away.

She shook her head. "I don't think so."

Harley understood. "I know what you mean, but I think Lars would be cheering us on. He wasn't one to pass up a sweet deal." He lifted her hand and dropped a kiss on the inside of her wrist. Her skin smelled liked rain. "In fact, Lars once told me, 'Harley, if you're open and receptive, the good stuff will drop right in your lap.' At the time, I thought he was talking about dope."

She laughed. "Well, if you're implying that fate set this up, then it would be a tragedy not to take advantage of the opportunity, right?"

"Sweet logic," he said with a grin. "I love a convoluted mind."

She pressed herself to him and dropped her hands to his

butt. "I've been lusting after your body for weeks. Maybe from the first day I met you."

He'd longed for her, too. But, there were valid reasons why he shouldn't become involved with her. How did a car crash change that?

He stepped back. She had a surprised look on her face, but before she could respond, a shrill siren pierced the air. The teapot sent a plume of steam into the air, along with its whistle.

Andi snatched the vessel off the burner. "Whether we make love or not is up to you, Harley. There's something between us, and I'm tired of pretending it doesn't exist."

She poured the hot water into a cup then set it aside. Before turning around, she lifted the faded gingham curtain. "The rain doesn't look like it will let up any time soon. We may be here overnight." She glanced over her shoulder. "Are we going to settle this or not?"

A part of him—probably the Harley part—wanted to do the honorable thing, but his mind and body were weary. He felt as though he'd been running a marathon—and Andi was the finish line.

He nodded. "Why don't you pour me a cup of that? First, we need to talk."

ANDI TOOK a deep breath. A funny shiver passed through her. She knew the sensation. She'd felt the same thing when she signed her name on her enlistment papers. She closed the distance between them and placed her hand flat against his breastbone. Below the layer of sweatshirt and muscle beat a steady thump.

"I'd rather kiss you," she said.

Harley covered her hand with his own. "This probably sounds like I'm stalling, but shouldn't you call home first?"

"I know this doesn't make any sense. And it's probably

not something you want to hear. But, Harley, when I'm with you, I feel like I *am* home."

He looked into her eyes with a vulnerability she'd never seen before. "I have so little to give you, Andi. I barely feel any connection to my life back in Missouri. And I'm slowly getting more and more cut off from this life. I'm in limbo," he added grimly.

Feeling more confident than she had any right to feel, she kissed the side of his mouth. "That's not true. You're *here*. With me. In the cabin your mother's brother left you in his will. It doesn't matter if your name is Harley or Jonathan. I want to be with you."

"I want you, too," he said, returning her kiss with the same fire she'd felt in their earlier kisses.

Maybe a wise person would have waited until there was an understanding—a commitment—between them. Promise of a future. But at the moment, she wasn't feeling wise. "Is there a bed in the loft?"

He nodded. "It's where I slept once my shoulder and ribs had healed and I could climb the ladder."

"Then that's where I want to go. To make love."

There was a moment, right before she placed her foot on the bottom rung of the ladder that Andi had second thoughts—and third and fourth. A voice in her head argued the merits of waiting until the trial was settled and she knew whether or not Harley planned to stay in Gold Creek, before jumping into bed with him. But Andi wasn't listening to that voice. She needed this man with an urgency she didn't understand and refused to question any further.

"You're grinning." His voice rumbled from below her.

Andi stuck out her butt and sucked in her gut so she could look down. Even though Harley's face was barely visible beyond the hem of Lars's oversize shirt, she guessed he had an unobstructed view of her breasts under the shirt. The knowledge sent a quiver of heat channeling through her limbs. "How could you tell?" she asked. Her voice seemed unnaturally husky.

"Masculine insecurity."

"Never heard of such a thing," she teased, scrambling up the final few rungs. The sleeping platform was nothing more than a landing covered in hideous orange shag carpeting, straight out of the seventies. Dark, hewn rafters provided anchors for spiders to build galaxies of webs. A simple bed—double mattress and box spring—was situated right below a tiny window made opaque by the rain. There was a faded yellow sheet covering the mattress. A stack of neatly folded bedding and pillows sat to the left of the bed; an end table made of two cinder blocks and a piece of plywood was to the right.

Crouching in the dim light, she also spotted an oil lamp, a box of kitchen matches and a Zane Grey novel on the table. She quickly lit the lantern, adjusting the wick to produce a mellow glow. She turned to face him. Her nipples felt chafed by the shirt's soft material and she quickly unbuttoned it all the way. She left it on, but made sure the gap exposed the bare skin between her breasts. It was about as risqué as one could get with flannel.

Her reward came from the heart-stopping smile that lit Harley's face as his head cleared the platform. He hoisted himself into a sitting position with his legs hanging over the edge, his back to her.

"How could a person with a fear of heights stand it up here?" Andi asked. She knew the jittery feeling in her tummy wasn't from acrophobia.

"I never looked down. But maybe we'd better move to the bed—just to be safe."

He wiggled his eyebrows à la Groucho Marx. Andi laughed. First times could be awkward, but she wasn't really nervous. True, he might leave once the trial was over, but she'd deal with that when it happened. Maybe if we're good together, she thought, he'll be tempted to stay.

Harley scooted backward until he was sitting cross-legged on the mattress. Leaning over, he reached for her hand, and with as much grace as a courtier, kissed her knuckles. ''Come,'' he said, giving a light tug. There wasn't room to stand, so Andi moved catlike to join him.

She had to look down to make sure she didn't impede her progress by kneeling on the hem of her shirt. Harley helped by reaching out and pushing the neckline over her shoulders. Then he slipped the right half over her shoulder and tugged the sleeve free. He did the same to the other side. Naked, except for her panties, Andi stayed in her feline position and watched his gaze roam over her body.

For the most part, Andi liked her body. Her hips were a little wide and her legs were layered with the sinewy muscles of a runner, but her breasts didn't sag; her belly was flat.

''I may not be able to remember everything about my past, but I'm certain I've never seen a more beautiful sight,'' Harley said. The look in his eyes started a tremor of desire that turned her knees weak.

It had been a long time since anyone had told her she was beautiful. Desirable. Sexy. She moved closer, straddling him so that her knees framed his hips. She sat—the apex of her legs touching his quite noticeable erection. She moved closer, finding that perfect fit.

Harley made a small sound—air passing through clenched teeth. He jammed two pillows behind his head then reached out with both hands to grasp her waist. When his thumbs stroked her belly, a pool of heat fanned out in every direction, redirecting all thought.

Her nipples puckered, and his hands moved upward in

response. When his thumbs brushed the sensitive tips, Andi couldn't suppress a moan of desire.

"This isn't going to be slow and tender, Andi," Harley warned, his fingers squeezing. "Not this time. I need you too damn much."

She covered his hands with her own and arched her back. "It's the same for me." The movement brought her hips forward. "Why did I put these damn panties back on? And what's with those sweatpants? Why aren't you naked?"

His chuckle preceded a slight bucking sensation that prompted her to move to one side. While she stripped off the scrap of white material, she watched Harley shed the bulky jersey sweats. He untied the drawstring waistband then pulled the elasticized band up and over his erection. His sweatshirt disappeared in one smooth yank.

The warm air rising from the little stove in the living quarters down below had turned the alcove into a cozy nook. Harley got to his knees to meet her face-to-face.

"You are amazing," he said softly. "I've wanted this for so long."

Andi knew she'd never felt this intense a desire. The depth of her need left her a little frightened. But she was no coward. "Me, too," she said, reaching out to brush the back of her hand down his smooth chest.

His nipples puckered. Her hand dipped lower and the muscles of his lean belly tensed.

She closed her eyes as his arms went around her and pulled her close. She caressed his rock-hard buttocks, locking him against her. Naked skin—cool yet steamy—created a language of its own. And Andi's body had no trouble understanding every nuance. She ran her tongue across the hard shelf of his collarbone. He did the same to her.

"Broken," he whispered, his tongue flicking back and forth in the shallow depression. "How?"

"Fell off the neighbor's mule. Kristin dared me. I was eleven. I didn't tell Ida Jane until it was too late for the doctor to do anything. It healed funny."

He kissed the old wound so tenderly her breath caught in her chest. "It's so you," he whispered. "Willful and independent. If we had a child…"

He went no further with the thought.

Andi didn't care. She was engrossed by her exploration. The taste and smell of his skin. His chest was tanned from the warm spell they'd had last month. His belly fascinated her—tight ridges with just the right amount of fat to give it contours.

"You have a beautiful body," she said. As her tongue circled the depression of his belly button, his stomach muscles contracted.

He jerked slightly and her chin brushed against a velvety softness. She could feel the heat radiating from him, the musky scent of desire and male body. She was ready, and he hadn't even touched her.

As if reading her mind, he drew her upright so he could nuzzle her breasts. She gasped with relief when he took her nipple in his mouth and sucked. A sweet pressure built inside her and she threaded her fingers through his hair, pressing him to her. When he switched to the other breast, his fingers toyed with the neglected nipple, pinching softly.

"Harley, please," she whispered. "Touch me. Now."

His gaze locked with hers as his hand found her. His finger entered her and she cried out, melting against him. She'd never felt more consumed with need. "Tell me you found the protection," she growled.

His low chuckle reassured her. He pulled away and reached for the sweatpants. From the pocket he pulled a strip of foil-wrapped condoms. Andi looked toward the ceiling. "Lars, wherever you are, I send my heartfelt thanks," she

said then dropped to a seated position, reclining on her elbows to watch him.

She grinned as Harley impatiently opened the first pack-
age with his teeth then sheathed himself. Next time, she'd
help, but there was something powerfully sexy about the
way he did it.

"I can't promise finesse, Andi," Harley said, his tone
apologetic.

She reached up to wrap her arms around his broad shoulders. "Just make love to me," Andi said, closing her eyes
to better feel every amazing sensation. "I guarantee that will
be enough for me."

"HARLEY," a voice said.

Harley? Who's Harley?

Still half-asleep and drugged from the most incredible
lovemaking of his life, Jonathan had trouble focusing.

Then it hit him. Where he was. Who was running her
fingertips up his spine. Who he was.

He sat up too fast. His breath coming in quick, shallow
gasps made him dizzy. His head filled with a raucous noise
that made him squeeze his eyes shut.

"What's wrong? Headache?"

Her voice was soft, concerned. Harley...Jonathan—whatever his name was—knew something was expected of him.
He'd made love with Andi and now he needed to say something. But his throat was dry and his brain was about to
explode.

"Aspirin?" he croaked.

"Oh, sweetie," she said, massaging his shoulder sympathetically. "Is it a migraine? I'll be right back."

He heard her leave the bed and quickly dress. Her feet
made faint squeaky sounds on the ladder. He sank into the
soft bedding. Once in a prone position, the pain lessened.

From below he could hear her drawing water, speaking to Sarge, adding wood to the fire. A bead of sweat broke out on his forehead. He'd made love with the woman of his dreams. The plain fact was he loved her—or did he? Maybe Harley loved her. Jonathan was incapable of love. Wasn't that what Miranda, his girlfriend of four years, told him when they broke up?

The memory rushed back. Crisp and clear.

He'd been planning to ask her to marry him. But when he arrived at her condo—shortly after his disastrous meeting with his father—she'd made it clear that he wasn't part of her future.

"I used to think we had a chance, Jon," she'd told him, tucking his glittery ring back in his pocket. "But I know now that your father's right. You weren't cut out for small-town life. JJ Newhall doesn't do hearth and home."

The words held a veracity that made him cringe. Yet, a few hours earlier, Andi had suggested he might live here in the cabin that belonged to him and write. But he was a nomad, wasn't he?

"Here's super-duper aspirin. Military issue. Lars had a bottle in his medicine cabinet," she said, materializing at his side. He hadn't even heard her climb the ladder.

He sat up, positioning a pillow against the cabin wall. The blankets pooled at his waist.

She'd mis-buttoned her flannel shirt, making the collar lopsided. Her hair stood up in little tufts. Her skin was cosmetic-free and beautiful. He'd never seen anything more appealing.

She passed him the glass then fished two large white pills from the breast pocket of the shirt. "I'm going to run up to Margaret's and make a few calls while you're recuperating."

Harley swallowed the bitter pills and took a large gulp of

water. "I'll go with you." *Better to move around than lie here and think.*

"No. Rest. I want you in good shape for later."

The humor in her tone could not be missed. Nor the innuendo. Harley took another drink. They'd made love twice. Once with a mindless urgency that made the whole experience end too quickly. The second time had been a languid journey of discovery. But a feeling of remorse had arrived with his headache. Was this fair to Andi?

"What time is it?" Harley asked, reaching for his shirt.

"It's 8:00 p.m. I figure people might be getting a little jittery about our whereabouts. The rain just let up, so I can run to Margaret's and make the call. We aren't getting out of here until morning. The road over the pass is going to be a quagmire—even with four-wheel drive. I don't have to be at the Rocking M till noon for the wedding rehearsal, then Kris and I are throwing a wedding shower for Jenny at the bordello at four. I've closed the shop for the whole weekend."

They'd already discussed using Lars's truck to drive back into town instead of waiting for the tow truck, which would be needed for Rosemarie.

"How's Sarge doing?" Harley asked.

"Not bad. I think he's been bruised. He made it outside with barely any help, but he's still limping. He snarfed down a can of dog food, though. So, that's a good sign."

"Do you still want to drop him at the vet's when we get to town?" Harley had checked on the dog between lovemaking, and Sarge seemed to be resting comfortably. The old dog had lifted his head and licked Harley's hand as if to say thank-you for his concern.

Harley had petted him in return—with mixed emotions. He still felt uncomfortable around Sarge.

"Rich Rumbolt's office is on the way to the ranch," she

said. "I'd feel better if he took an X ray or two. Just to be safe." Andi started to back down the ladder. "Rest. I'll be baaack," she said in a horrible Arnold Swarzeneggar imitation.

For the first time since opening his eyes, Harley felt a glimmer of hope. Maybe, they'd figure this out. Maybe, he could make peace with his past and find a way to integrate his old persona into a new life. But he knew, without a doubt, that Andi was the key to making this happen.

"I'm going with you." Before she could protest, he added, "There's a snake on the loose."

"I'm not afraid of snakes."

He chuckled. "Humor me. I wouldn't feel right hanging out here while you wrestle a boa for the phone. Maybe it's a guy thing."

She smiled. "Oh. Okay, then. The sooner we go, the sooner we can…" The gleam in her eyes was unmistakable.

Harley felt a correlating response. They had the whole night ahead of them. Right or wrong. There was no turning back.

CHAPTER ELEVEN

THE FOLLOWING MORNING there was a chill in the air. "I'm surprised we didn't get snow," Andi said as she led the way to the barn. The crisp fresh breeze made her nostrils crinkle.

Her bare knees tingled, but at least her feet and calves were warm. She'd borrowed Lars's thermal socks. Thick gray tubes with a red band that reached to her knees. Stylish? Not a chance, but that's what happened when you went into the mountains dressed as a girl.

A gust of wind made her wish she'd borrowed one of Lars's stocking caps, too. Without electricity she hadn't been able to dry her hair. Thanks to the resourceful miner who'd built a water tower to provide gravity-fed water to the propane water heater, she and Harley had shared a shower after breakfast—and made use of the last condom in the strip.

Then, without a word of debate, they'd divvied up the chores. Harley had handled the loft, dropping a pillowcase filled with the sheets and the clothes they'd borrowed over the edge. It had landed with a plop that had made Andi jump. Once she'd finished putting away their breakfast dishes, she tamped down the fire and checked all the windows.

As they left the cabin—Harley carrying Sarge—she paused to tack the yellow police tape back in place.

"Are we going to talk about this on the way back?" Harley asked, following a few steps behind her.

She hated mornings after. "We have to hurry. I have a million things to do today. Anyway, what's to talk about? We had great sex. Let's not pretend it was more than it was."

"That's all it was to you?" He had to juggle Sarge to free his hand to grab the hem of her jacket. The dog let out a groan.

Since Harley and Sarge blocked her way to the shed, which was on the far side of the clearing, she couldn't avoid the confrontation.

"Like I said, we had great sex." *Make that an epiphany of love and redemption.* She planned to keep that little truth to herself. *I'm not a complete fool. Say the L-word and he'll run for sure.*

"I don't believe that's all it was to you," he repeated.

His comment irked her. "Okay, then, I'll tell you the truth. The sex was unlike any I'd ever experienced. And I feel an emotional connection to you in a way I've never felt for another man." Andi swallowed. "But I'm trying my hardest to avoid the huge—*humongous*—letdown that is bound to hit when you decide to leave."

He opened his mouth, but she quickly added, "And I don't blame you for not wanting to stay. Small towns aren't always easy to take even if you're born there. They're filled with nosy, well-meaning people who think nothing of giving you advice you don't want. Gossip spreads faster than the flu. And business is so bad...don't get me started. Suffice it to say it sucks."

Since Harley didn't say anything to refute her premise, she stepped off the path—instantly soaking her socks—and stomped toward the shed. "So now you know. Can we please just get going?"

He followed. Once they reached the garage, he carefully

eased Sarge on to a soft bed of packing blankets then faced
her, hands on his hips in a belligerent manner.

"It isn't fair to assume the worst just because you think
you know what I feel."

Andi felt between the grillwork of the truck until she
found the latch then lifted the heavy hood, which was a
patchwork of rust and primer paint. "You told me last night
your father wants you to return home to Florida."

"Florida is not my home. It never has been. He wants
me to go back with him to see an amnesia specialist. I
haven't agreed to go."

She wanted that to mean he was staying here, but that
wasn't what he was saying. "If you stay in Gold Creek
what will you do? Work at the Rocking M?" She answered
her own questions. "Of course not. You're a world-famous
journalist. What could a little town in the Sierras hold for
you?"

He came up behind her and wrapped his arms around her
waist. "You." His breath was warm on her ear and neck.
She wanted to melt against him and never leave their tiny
hunk of paradise.

"Oh, Harley," she said on a sigh.

He stiffened slightly.

She turned to face him, her right hand holding the oil
dipstick, her left a rag. "What's wrong?"

"The name is an issue."

"Do you want to be called Jonathan?"

"Maybe. I'm not sure. At first, it sounded foreign, but
now *Harley* sounds odd to my ear."

"Well, at the risk of sounding flip, let me know when
you've made up your mind. In the meantime, we really need
to hit the road. Jenny sounded pretty calm on the phone last
night, but at the rehearsal she'll have two squirming babies
and a mother-in-law. She'll need my help."

Harley/Jonathan pitched in to help her get the old truck started, then offered to drive. Whether his motive was altruistic or a means to avoid holding Sarge on his lap, she couldn't decide. Being a passenger would give her time to think.

Why is Sarge overjoyed every time Harley gives him any attention, but Harley, no, Jonathan—definitely, Jonathan— looks pained whenever he has to touch the dog?

Andi petted Sarge's big, knobby head as they topped the summit. The snow tires only lost traction once. The sensation made Andi's stomach rise to her throat, but Harley kept the truck under control.

Although the engine noise made it difficult to be heard, Andi was surprised when he chose to put on the radio. "I thought you wanted to talk," she said.

"Um, okay," he said, raising his voice. "Tell me about the wedding plans."

Andi made a face. "Planning large social engagements gives me a headache. That's Jenny's thing. All I do is show up."

"What kind of wedding do you want?"

"Theoretically? The simpler the better. A justice of the peace in Tahoe is more my style. But, at least, Jenny isn't going overboard this time. When she and Josh got married, they invited practically the whole town, plus all their friends from college. It was crazy."

He glanced her way and smiled. "I thought the whole town was invited to this wedding, too."

God, she liked his smile. His Harley smile.

"It's different," she said. "Jenny and Sam are holding a small, private ceremony, first. Then the reception will coincide with the annual St. Patrick's Day barbecue. That's always very well attended because it's so much fun. And the local civic groups—the Garden Club, the Volunteer Fire Department, and the Moose—reap the benefits.''

They traveled a bit farther before Harley spoke. ''So how's business these days? Is the coffee parlor doing as well as you'd hoped?''

Andi sighed. She could lie, but why bother? He knew every other aspect of her life. ''It's holding its own, but my main problem is a glut of slow-moving merchandise. Ida Jane used to be an astute businesswoman, but before I took over she bought a couple of lots of antiques at auction that weren't worth what she paid for them. Now I'm having trouble unloading them.''

''Maybe you need a new approach. I'm no expert, but it seems to me that the Old Bordello Antique Shop is mired in obsolescence.''

''We sell antiques,'' Andi said, aware of the defensive tone in her voice. ''Old is what we do.''

''But obviously you're aware of better marketing strategies. Sam told me about your ghost tours. And the addition of the coffee shop is brilliant.'' He smiled at her and continued, ''I was wondering about the Internet. Maybe you could list certain items on an auction site, like eBay. Do you have a Web site?''

Andi sat up a little straighter. ''I looked into the idea when I first moved home, but Ida Jane flatly refused to discuss it. And when I found out how much it would cost to upgrade our wiring, I sorta put the idea on hold till I'd managed to improve the cash flow.''

She made a derisive sound. ''Like that happened. But the bottom line is the old bordello is Ida's store—not mine, and she wants it kept just the way it is.'' She rubbed her eyebrow with a knuckle. ''Besides, my first priority is a new roof.''

''That's too bad,'' he said. ''If you can't find your footing in the new economy, you'll be vulnerable. Particularly if someone decided to go after the land the old bordello is sitting on.''

Andi would have swung around to face him squarely if not for the dog on her lap. ''What are you talking about?''

His knuckles tightened on the steering wheel. ''Big money is moving into Gold Creek.'' His forehead crinkled; the corner of his lips turned down. ''My father pointed out a story in the *Sacramento Bee* that your local newspaper didn't bother to cover.

''Someone with ties to big business is buying up parcels around town. Didn't you say Ida Jane had been approached about selling the bordello?''

She swallowed. ''A form letter from some company I'd never heard of. I threw it in the trash.''

''Some of your neighbors are taking the offers.''

He rattled off a couple of names. Longtime residents. Friends. A sizzle of fear raced through her. She felt as though she'd been on patrol and just learned that the enemy had struck behind her line. ''Do you know this for sure?''

The dubious tone in her voice must have ticked him off because he answered, ''No, but my dad was a newspaper publisher. I think you can trust his instincts, if you don't trust mine.''

She winced. ''I'm sorry. Maybe I just don't want to believe this stuff. I have heard rumors at the Chamber of Commerce meetings, but small towns are a hotbed of gossip and speculation.''

The hard line of his lips softened. After a minute, he said, ''Andi, about what we were discussing earlier—you were right to assume the worst about me based on what you read in my bio. But something changed last night.''

He took a deep breath. ''I can't make any promises until

we find out who murdered Lars, but once that's settled I plan to stick around. I'm not going to Florida.''

He cares about me.

Suddenly, the future seemed steeped in possibilities. She couldn't wait to get to the ranch to discuss this turn of events with her sisters. They'd tell her if she was crazy to bet her heart in such a risky gamble.

WHEN HE TURNED OFF the muddy access road that linked to the highway, Harley made a decision. He would ask people to call him Jonathan. This interlude in the mountains had shown him one thing—he could run, but he couldn't hide.

He was Jonathan Jackson Newhall. He had a life. And while he didn't remember every aspect of it, he knew the only way to find relief from his recurring headaches was to make peace with his past.

He couldn't simply ignore the real world. His bail bond was real. The murder charges were real. His feelings for Andi were real, too.

He just wasn't sure what to do about them. He'd told her he wasn't leaving. But that had been Harley speaking. A man like JJ Newhall who'd been on the go that much couldn't possibly have felt bound to any one place. The new Jonathan preferred the sense of connection he'd felt as Harley; he wanted to put down roots. But could he make that happen?

When she'd visited him at the jail, Dr. Franklin told him he might never completely recover the ''factual'' memory of his life prior to the accident.

''In my opinion,'' she'd told him, ''you'll never be exactly the same person you used to be.''

She'd offered the assessment apologetically. And for a moment, he'd felt a shaft of fear. But now he was ready to accept the doctor's prognosis. He was a hybrid—Harley and

Jonathan—but since the record of his life on the planet was under the name Jonathan Newhall, that's the name he would use.

"The vet's office is just ahead on the right side of the road," Andi yelled over the engine noise.

He nodded and put on the blinker.

"I wonder how much this is going to cost."

He detected a certain apprehension in her voice. "I'll pay for it. He's my uncle's dog."

It felt odd to say the words, but good.

"Are you sure?"

He recalled an earlier conversation with the man his father had said was Jonathan's accountant. The voice had meant nothing to him, but the cheerful fellow had offered a glowing report about Jonathan's financial situation. "Yes. I'll pay the bill. But what are we going to do with him once he's released? They don't allow pets at the motel. Can he stay with you?"

"I suppose so. But he won't like town life. He's used to chasing his dinner and baying at the moon. My neighbors— and their cats—won't care for that."

Jonathan had to wait for oncoming traffic to pass before he could turn.

"Maybe Sam would keep him," Andi suggested.

Jonathan couldn't picture the hound on the Rocking M. A mob of small, all-business Queensland heelers ruled that roost. Sarge wouldn't fit in there either.

The small, spotlessly clean clinic had a rural-neighborhood look about it. Jonathan carried Sarge to an examination room where a friendly, young assistant took over. While Andi filled out the necessary papers in the ante-room of the clinic, Jonathan thought about the man who was his uncle.

After Jonathan's accident, Lars had nursed him through

blinding headaches and bouts of nausea with amazing patience. In the evenings—after a couple of joints and a few slugs of whiskey—Lars would rant in detail about the government's secret experiments on GIs. But beneath the paranoia and free-floating anxiety was a lonely human being.

Andi took a seat beside him on the vinyl-upholstered bench. There were no other people waiting, and the clerk at the desk was working at her computer.

"Did Lars ever mention his sister?"

Andi's question seemed to come out of the blue, but paralleled his line of thought. "Are you a mind reader?" Jonathan asked. "I was just thinking about him."

"You had a forlorn look on your face—like Sarge."

He gave her the smile she was fishing for. "Lars didn't talk about his past. I got the impression he'd lost touch with his family. When I told him the Internet could help him look for lost loved ones, he clammed up, mumbling something about government spies."

She scooted a little bit closer and said under her voice, "You know, for a hermit, Lars had an awfully big box of condoms."

Jonathan nearly choked on his laugh. Would there ever be a time when he could predict what might come out of her mouth? "Lars told me the veteran's hospital gave him all kinds of freebies. He loved the idea of sticking it to Uncle Sam."

For some reason, the color drained from her face. "When was the last time he visited the hospital? Do condoms have expiration dates? Why wouldn't they? Rubber bands go bad in the drawer. I have things popping loose all the time."

It took him a minute to figure out that she was afraid one of the condoms they'd used might have failed. Which meant this probably wasn't the right time to remind her they' actually forgotten to use protection when they'd made love just before dawn—both of them too into the moment to stop.

"I'm sure everything's fine," he said. "Worst-case scenario we have to get married."

She shot him a look of pure shock. And, he decided, horror.

"That's not the *worst* case these days," she said pointedly. "Do you think we should contact the local health department to get tested?"

His pulse quickened, pain blossomed in his head. *What if I slept around and just haven't found those memories yet? I could have given her something bad. Something deadly.*

"Harley. Breathe. Relax. Let it go. I'm sure the condoms were fine. I'm not terribly experienced in these matters, but we'd have known, right? I overreacted. I'm sorry."

But what if…

Suddenly, the answer came to him. At least he hoped it was a real memory. He'd had a checkup before going to Missouri. He'd wanted a clean bill of health before he settled down to be a publisher and married man.

"I…it's okay…I saw a doctor last September. Right before I…decided to take a cross-country trip on a motorcycle. Honest." He held up his hand. "No diseases of any kind, but you still might be pregnant."

She'd just let go a long sigh then suddenly froze. "What do you mean?"

"Early morning. First light. Not quite awake…"

Her eyes grew large, and her mouth dropped open.

The vet chose that minute to step out of the examination room—without Sarge. He addressed them both. "Sarge is going to be fine, but there's a tender spot in his tummy, and I'd like to make sure his spleen is okay. Can I keep him over the weekend?"

"Sure," Andi answered, scooting past Jonathan without touching him. "Call the bordello when—"

Jonathan interrupted her. "We may have met at the Rocking M, but my memory isn't too good," he said, shaking the man's hand. "I'm Jonathan Newhall. I'm staying at the Mountain Comfort Inn at the moment, but I'll call Monday to see how he's doing."

After they exchanged polite chitchat, Jonathan gave the clerk his credit card and signed on the dotted line. He could sense Andi's impatience, but he wasn't sure if she was in a hurry to get to the ranch or to finish their conversation.

"Thank you," he called as he followed Andi out the door. "Take good care of our boy."

To his surprise, they drove to the Rocking M without speaking. But as soon as he reached the first set of cattle guards, Jonathan made a decision. He pulled off the road and parked.

"Harley, I have to hurry. Jen's expecting me..."

"This will just take a minute. We need to get something settled."

The morning sun made the highlights in her hair sparkle. There was a glow about her that shouted life and vitality. But her green eyes looked wary. "What?"

He took the plunge. "I love you."

She looked speechless. When she tried to talk, words tumbled out. "I...you...probably safe time...never regular like Jenny, but...really?"

He waited to see if any more words were coming, then he answered what appeared to be the only question. "Yes, really."

"You're not just saying that because we slept together and there's a minute chance I might be pregnant?"

He shook his head.

She took a deep breath then let it out. "I don't believe

you. I know you're attracted to me, the feeling is mutual. And you're too good a man not to care for me. And granted, we're amazing together in bed. But love? I don't think so.''

Her logic reminded him of someone from his past, but he couldn't risk a headache by thinking too hard. "I could prove it to you."

"How?"

"I don't know exactly. But I'll do whatever it takes."

She didn't break eye contact with him, so he knew she was both skeptical and intrigued. A heartbeat later, she said, "Well, unless you can accomplish that in five minutes, I'm going to be late for my sister's wedding rehearsal. And she'll kill me, so it'll become a moot point.

"Step on the gas. Now."

"ANDI, thank God," Jenny cried, rushing up to the door of the truck before Andi could get it open. "Kristin and Ida will be here any minute, and I wanted time to prepare you."

Andi lowered her feet to the graveled driveway. Her sister had flown out of the house the instant the truck approached the gated yard, practically stumbling over the newly planted primroses along the walk. "Jen, what's wrong? Are you upset that I didn't come home last night? The roads were—"

Jenny shook her head. "No, It's not that. Or Rosemarie— although the tow-truck driver just talked to Sam and he said she's not worth saving."

"Oh, no," Andi cried. "What will I tell Ida Jane?"

Jenny waved her arm as if the prospect of telling Ida Jane that her beloved car was history was immaterial. "Jenny, what the heck is wrong with you?"

Her sister stomped her foot. She looked at Jonathan, who'd joined them. "I'm trying to *explain*. Kristin came home last night. I'd called her on her cell phone after you phoned, so she'd know that Mrs. McCloskey was staying with Ida until she got there. She said she was bringing along a surprise.

"Then Ida Jane called half an hour later. And, Andi, she wasn't making any sense. I thought she'd had a stroke or was flipping out." She paused dramatically. "She told me that Kristin had brought her little boy to visit."

Andi stopped breathing. An odd pressure built in her sinuses and moisture welled in her eyes. "Her what?"

"Her son. Andi, Kristin has a child. And she never told us."

Jenny looked close to tears, too. Andi inhaled and swallowed the lump in her throat. "For real?"

Jenny nodded, sniffling. Then suddenly they were in each other's arms, weeping. Andi didn't know why she was crying. A child was a good thing. But keeping a baby a secret from your family? How could Kris have done that? Why would she?

When they broke apart a few seconds later, Jonathan was still there, a look of sympathy on his face. Andi took his hand, grateful for his concern. With her free hand, she wiped her eyes and faced her sister. "What did she tell you? When? How old is he? Where's the father?"

Jenny shook her head. "She said she'd explain everything today. That she wanted to introduce him to us in person. And that last night, she wanted him to spend time getting to know Ida Jane."

Andi was overwhelmed. Life seemed totally out of control. One sister was getting married the next day. Her other sister showed up for the wedding with a child in tow. And Andi had a little secret of her own. She was in love.

She decided this wasn't the time to break the news about

Jonathan. There would be time after the wedding—if he was serious. If he stayed in Gold Creek. If he really did love her.

That terrifying, amazing, tantalizing thought was cut short when Kristin's compact station wagon pulled into the yard and parked a few feet away. Andi counted heads. Just two that she could see—Kris and Ida Jane.

Kristin jumped out and hurried around to help their aunt. Neither Andi nor Jenny seemed capable of movement. Andi still hadn't let go of Jonathan's hand.

Ida took a few minutes to collect her purse and cane then she started toward them. Jenny responded by dashing to her side to provide a little extra assistance. Just as they started to walk toward the house, the rear passenger-side door opened and a boy—about 10 years old—unfolded lanky legs clad in sloppy black pants and stood up.

"Holy sh…."

Jonathan pulled her close, whispering something gentle and reassuring in her hair. His support helped her regain her composure. This child was her nephew. Kristin's son.

"This is gonna get messy," she whispered.

Jonathan flicked his finger under her chin and gave her a smile. "Life always is."

"But…" she tried to explain.

He shifted his eyes so she would look to her left. Kristin and the boy were standing a foot away.

Kris's hand rested protectively on her son's narrow shoulder. She said, "Zach, love, this is your Aunt Andrea. Everybody calls her Andi."

The boy kept his gaze on the ground. His white-blond hair was cut razor close around his neck and halfway up his skull, but the long upper locks hung in messy disarray over his high forehead. He was Kristin's clone without any of her bright, soft cuddliness.

"Zach? As in Zachary?"

"Zachariah," Kris answered. "It means the Lord's remembrance."

The boy made a disparaging sound, but no words materialized from his lips.

"It's nice to meet you, Zach," Andi said, mouthing the word *finally* to her sister. "This is Jonathan. Some people call him Harley, but his real name is Jonathan. And that's the name he wants to use." He'd made it clear at the vet's office.

Jenny returned from helping Ida Jane inside, and Andi saw the look of surprise her sisters exchanged at her announcement. Jonathan let go of her hand to put it out in greeting. The boy looked up but didn't shake hands. Although his bangs made it hard to see his face clearly, one thing was evident. Instead of Kris's China blue eyes, her son's were midnight black and filled with silent anger.

"Welcome to Gold Creek," Jonathan said.

"It's a sucky town. I'm not gonna move here. I'm going to stay in Ashland even if I have to live with my friends."

His small, pointed chin lifted defiantly. For the first time, Andi saw the unusual shape of his eyes—almond and slightly tilted at the corners. Ringed with thick dark lashes, they would have been beautiful if not for the angry squint.

A familiar expression. Andi inhaled sharply and stepped back before she could shout out the name that came to mind.

The boy looked her way. His distinctive eyes narrowed. "You don't look like my mom. She's pretty."

He faced his mother. "I thought you were triplets. But that one's tall." He nodded at Jenny, who hadn't even been properly introduced. "And she has red hair." He pointed at Andi. His handsome youthful features—which some day soon would make silly girls do things they'd later regret—contorted in contempt. "So, was that a lie, too?"

SAM MANAGED to diffuse the situation with such aplomb, Andi watched in awe as he escorted Zach toward the barn to view a newborn foal. He'd appeared just moments after Zach dropped the nasty question that had made his mother burst into tears and Jenny wrap her in a protective hug.

At Sam's invitation, Jonathan had joined them, but Andi sensed he was reluctant to leave. She'd encouraged him with a tiny nod that had earned her a smile before he walked away.

When they were out of earshot, Andi closed the distance between her and her sisters and said, "So, let's hear it. He's Tyler's, isn't he?"

"Yes," Kristin admitted tearfully.

Jenny's mouth formed a perfect O. "You got pregnant that night?" she exclaimed. "That one night? No way."

Kristin kept her gaze on her shoes, so Andi couldn't see her expression. Couldn't tell whether there'd been other times. Did it matter? Andi had started dating Tyler after the winter ball in January. She seldom attended formal dances, but going with Ty Harrison—the town's bad boy—had been something of a coup. They'd dated until the triplets' eighteenth birthday in late February—when all hell had broken loose.

"Does he know?" Andi asked.

Kris shook her head miserably. "You always told me the only way to keep a secret in a small town is to tell no one."

Jenny had that hurt look on her face again. "Even your sisters? How could you?" Her eyebrows knitted. "I bet Moira knows about him. All of the Irish cousins know, don't they?"

Andi had never understood her sister's antipathy toward their cousin, Moira, who was their age. Kristin had lived with Moira and her younger sister, Kathleen, in Michigan, after spending a year with the family in Ireland. She'd left home right out of high school—for one very obvious reason.

"They would have been the ones to help her, Jen, since we weren't there for her," she said, putting her arm around Kristin's shoulder supportively.

"We could have helped. She didn't give us a chance."

True, but too late to make a difference. "She's home now. We'll have the rest of her life to bug her about this. Right now, we have to make up for some lost years. Correct me if I'm wrong, but that boy doesn't seem too enthused by the prospect of a ready-made family."

Kristin took a breath and leaned her head on Andi's shoulder. Andi couldn't begin to guess when last that had happened. "I don't know what went wrong. He was such a sweet kid—absolutely perfect, until about a year ago. Then he changed. Hormones, friends, who knows? But it was around the time when I started coming down here to help with Ida Jane."

She sighed. "I suppose I screwed up. Like that's something new, right? I'm Kris—the dumb one."

Andi and Jenny exchanged a look. "The beautiful one," Andi said.

"The sweet one," Jenny added.

Kristin stepped back so she could face them both. She lifted her chin resolutely. "I should have come sooner. When Josh got sick, you needed me and I wasn't as much help as I should have been, Jen. I almost brought Zach home then, but it was such a sad time. It didn't feel right."

They nodded. No one could argue with that.

"Then the twins were born, and Ida fell." She made an encompassing motion with her hands. "I told Zach the truth at that point, and gave him the option of coming with me to meet you, but he didn't want to. I didn't force the issue."

"Isn't that a pretty big life decision for a child to make?" Jenny asked in her "teacher" voice.

"He's a smart kid," Kris answered, her tone defensive. "He even skipped a grade. And he knows what the word *illegitimate* means. Nobody gives him a hard time about it in Oregon, but do you honestly think that would be the same here? In Gold Creek, he'd be talked about, and word would eventually get back to you-know-who."

Jenny glanced at her watch, then started herding them toward the porch. "Doesn't he ask about his father?"

"Not lately. I figure he will when he's ready."

"What have you told him about why you're a single mom?" Andi asked. She couldn't imagine what her sister's life had been like—alone and pregnant—thousands of miles from home.

Kris shrugged. "I told him I got pregnant when I was in high school and went to live with my father's family in Ireland until he was born."

"Didn't he ever ask about your family?" Jenny asked.

"Yes. I told him that my aunt and two sisters were living in California, but that we'd had a big fight and didn't speak anymore. He was just a baby when we moved to Michigan with the Irish cousins, but he thinks of them as family. We've been back to Moira and Kate's twice to visit. And Moira's son, Danny, came out last summer to stay with us a couple of weeks."

Jenny sighed. "That's just plain cruel, Kristin. I wish I could understand but I don't. I want to, but—"

Andi put a hand on Jenny's arm. "Think about that night when you told us the truth about the twins' paternity. Remember how shocked we were? Not so much that you and Josh used Sam's sperm, but because you didn't tell us right away."

Jenny's fair complexion colored. "Okay. So, sometimes

things happen that you don't want to share. But we're talking almost eleven years, Kristin.''

"Jen, she was trying to do the right thing for Zach. And herself. We make choices then we have to live with them, but I'd like to remind you that recriminations are a luxury you can't afford at the moment. Aren't we supposed to be practicing for a wedding?''

Jenny gave a low wail of panic and dashed inside.

Andi and Kris paused just outside the door.

"I didn't want to hurt you. You seemed so devastated that night,'' Kristin said. "I was afraid that learning I was pregnant would make things even worse between us.''

Andi knew there were aspects of that story she was going to have to share, but this wasn't the time. "It's ancient history, Kris. We need to put this whole thing behind us. There are too many other problems going on to worry about something that happened in high school, right?''

"I guess. I just expected you to be more upset. I thought you hated me.''

Andi's insides felt soft and weepy. "I don't. I never did. And I'm glad you're here. Does this mean you might move back for good?''

Kristin frowned. "I don't know. If people see Zach around, they might put two and two together and come up with…''

"Ty Harrison.'' Suddenly Andi knew it was too late to stop the dominoes from falling.

Last night, when she should have been home to greet her sister and nephew, Andi had been in a miner's cabin making love with the man of her dreams. So Linda McCloskey— grande dame of the Gold Creek Garden Club—had opened the door to Kris and Zach—a boy so obviously Tyler Harrison's progeny that no genetic test would be required when Ty petitioned the court for custody of his son.

CHAPTER TWELVE

"YOU KNOW, the last time I visited this part of California, you were just a toddler," Andrew Newhall told his son.

The words stuck in Jonathan's head as they pulled onto Highway 140. He found them oddly comforting.

"Like I said," his father continued, "the last time I came this way, you were just a little boy. It was early June. Your mother and I had attended a conference of newspaper publishers in San Francisco and decided on the spur of the moment to rent a car and drive home."

"I'm sorry, but I can't remember the trip," Jonathan said. "Did we take other vacations?"

Andrew sighed weightily. "No. That was it. Four days on the road. We spent the first night in the park. I remember that the main lodge—I think it's called the Ahwahnee—was booked and I was upset that we couldn't get a room.

"Your mother laughed it off. She said, 'You're so full of yourself, Andrew Newhall. Do you honestly believe that anyone outside of Bainbridge, Missouri, cares that you're a newspaper publisher?'"

His laugh sounded bittersweet. "Your mother always could put things in perspective. After she died, there wasn't anyone to bring me down a peg, to keep my feet on the ground instead of the self-important pedestal I had a tendency to stand on."

Jonathan was glad they'd decided to make this impromptu trip. He hadn't relished the thought of spending the day in the motel while Andi was busy with wedding details. He drove carefully—the winding road demanded it—but he let his gaze soak up the verdant beauty of the Merced River Canyon. As they rounded a bend, the mountainside brightened in color. A blanket of orange flowers—vibrant brush strokes from an Impressionist painter—captivated his attention.

"Isn't that beautiful?" he asked, taking his foot from the gas.

His father leaned forward to take in the sight, but only for a second. Jonathan felt his gaze turn to him. "Jon, I don't want you to take this the wrong way, but that's the first time I've ever—" he emphasized the word "—heard you extol the beauty of anything."

"Anything?" Jonathan repeated.

Andrew turned in the seat to face him. "Your mother loved things of beauty. She collected seashells and watercolor paintings and her flower gardens were the envy of our neighbors. I think it's what first attracted me to her. She was an art major. I was a third-year journalism student.

"My parents were solid, business-minded middle-class folk. No frills—just hard work, family and country. In that order. Jacqueline...Jacki...was lightness and charm. She didn't necessarily fit well into the Newhall way of doing business, but she added tremendous depth to my life."

He paused. "I only wish she'd lived long enough to give more of herself to you. You ended up with too much of me."

Jonathan didn't know what to say. Fortunately, they'd reached the entrance gate of the park and needed to pay for a day pass. His father impulsively bought an annual pass that would allow him access to all the national parks in the country.

"I'm retired," he explained. "I'm going to start traveling

once the girls are out of school for the summer. We could hit every park between here and Florida when we come back to visit you.''

Jonathan drove ahead. ''Is it settled then?'' he asked with amusement. ''Am I staying in Gold Creek?''

''You'd be a fool to leave,'' his father said, returning his wallet to his hip pocket. ''You're a new man, Jon. With infinite possibilities ahead of you. Right here. Why go anywhere else?''

For argument's sake, Jonathan said, ''Well, this lawyer isn't going to be cheap. I might need to get a job.''

Neither man spoke as they drove beneath a massive rock portal. ''Arch Rock,'' Andrew said after checking the map.

When they came to the turnoff that would take them to the Yosemite Valley sights, Andrew said, ''You know, Jonathan, I had a bit of a brainstorm while you were up at the mine. I made a few calls this morning. I wasn't sure if I should bring it up, but...''

''What?'' Jonathan asked.

''Well, remember how ticked off I was about the poor quality of the local newspaper?'' Jonathan nodded, trying to read the road signs at the same time. He didn't want to miss Bridal Veil Falls. Maybe all this wedding talk was getting to him.

''Are you listening to me?''

''Yes, Dad.''

Andrew made a funny sound. When Jonathan glanced at him, he spotted tears in his father's eyes. ''What's wrong?''

''You called me Dad. You haven't done that in years. It was always Father or Andrew. I like Dad better,'' he said with feeling.

Jonathan felt himself getting emotional, too. Emotion led to headaches, so he changed the subject. ''What were you going to tell me about the newspaper?''

"It's for sale."

A horn honked. Jonathan realized he'd stepped on the brake. Embarrassed, he waved apologetically to the driver behind him and turned into the parking lot at the base of Bridal Veil Falls. He took the first vacant parking place and turned off the engine. "Tell me more."

ANDI HAD TWO CHOICES: she could continue to keep a frozen smile plastered to her face or fake a fainting spell and hide in the bathroom. The second was by far the more appealing choice, but that would have left Kristin alone to field all the nosy, if well-meaning, questions, coming her way.

"Are you going to contact the father, Kristin?" Mary Needham asked. During her tenure as a Gold Creak High bus driver, Mary had ferried the triplets to every sporting event the girls had participated in.

"Legally, I believe you're obligated to inform him unless he's proven unfit or dangerous," Linda McCloskey added.

Both had been part of the original teams of caregivers who'd helped Ida take care of the triplets when the infants had come home from the hospital; both were very free with their opinions.

"*My* father was a danger," Ida Jane said with such volume the whole room went silent. "To Mother's pocketbook. He was a born gambler. Mother told me he even bet on my birth. Whether I would be a boy or a girl."

Andi sniffed the punch. Had someone spiked it?

"Did he win, Auntie?" Kristin asked, no doubt grateful for the diversion.

Ida chortled. "Nope. I cost him a pretty penny. He was sure his firstborn would be a son." She looked thoughtful then added, "Vanity thy name is man."

The shower was being held in the front parlor of the bordello, which normally would have been filled with what

Andi called her five-o'clock rush-hour coffee drinkers. It never failed to amaze her how many people seemed to need a caffeine fix before returning to their families.

This afternoon, however, a big sign on the front door read: CLOSED FRI.–TUE. FOR FAMILY WEDDING. On the coffee bar—between the three-tiered wire basket filled with tiny plastic containers of flavored creamers and the self-serve insulated coffee dispensers—was a mountain of beautifully wrapped gifts.

Although Andi and Kristin were the official sponsors of this gathering, Jenny had taken over the bulk of the arrangements, from the menu—finger sandwiches, salads and quiche—to ordering the cake. She also seemed intent on playing hostess.

She entered the room carrying a tray of multilayered triangles crafted of white bread and meat fillings. Andi moved to her side and took the tray from her hands. "Go and sit down," she said loudly. "You're the guest of honor."

Under her breath, she added, "Let them feast on your blood for a while."

Jenny's smile flickered before she took a seat on the small ruby tufted sofa between Sam's mother, Diane, and her aunt. Ida Jane patted her knee supportively. "Fine turnout, Jenny girl. I wonder if there are this many men coming to Josh's bachelor party."

Diane made a small sound of dismay. Jenny and Andi exchanged looks. Andi would have corrected her aunt. But Jenny smiled at her future mother-in-law as she took Ida's hand and said, "I'm sure the bar will be packed, Auntie. I don't know any man who can turn down free beer and pizza."

The circle of women laughed and nodded in agreement.

As Andi navigated from table to table passing out appetizers, she admired the decorations. Two of Jenny's former colleagues had arrived right after school with a crew of freshman girls to hang the silver, purple and pink streamers and helium-filled balloons.

Kris scuttled toward the door. "I'll get more punch."

Beulah Jensen rocked forward like a pink-vested Weeble, the roly-poly toys Andi and her sisters had played with when they were kids. "Can you tell us who it is?" she asked Andi in a loud whisper.

"It?" Andi echoed.

"The child's father."

If anyone else had asked such a blatantly personal question, Andi might have lost her temper. Instead, she tried to keep her tone civil. "In a big city, no one would question the fact that Kristin is a single mother. In Gold Creek, the fact that she hasn't told anyone who Zach's father is makes it fodder for gossip. Why is that? Don't you find it a little embarrassing that one of the reasons she hasn't brought her child home before this is that she knew people would talk about him, speculate about him and generally make him feel uncomfortable?"

Ida Jane looked at Andi and beamed. "You should listen to my Andrea, ladies. She's a very smart person. Did I ever tell you about the time that she tried to get me to marry old man *Polk?* Darned if I didn't kick myself for years for not listening to her."

Andi blinked. "Mr. Polk? I thought you said he had horse teeth and bad breath."

Ida nodded. "Yep. Big and yellow. Made me shudder. But when he died, they found thirty-five Folgers' coffee cans filled with money under his bed. If I'd have listened to you and bought a little denture cleaner, I'd have been set for life."

Andi was speechless until she saw the familiar glint in

her aunt's eye. Then she burst out laughing. *Why can't she be like this all the time?*

She was still chuckling, when a knock on the door made her change directions. Andi handed the plate of canapés to Beulah. The guests were talking about Zach and Kristin again despite Andi's lecture, but she put the chatter out of her mind when she saw who was standing at her door.

Kristin appeared at her side—a cut-glass pitcher of fruit punch in her hand. "So, that's him. Harley-slash-Jonathan. I've only seen him a couple of times. He's cute."

Andi felt her hackles rise. Kristin had always gotten any boy she'd wanted—even Tyler Harrison. "He's mine."

Kristin froze. Her eyes grew large. Her bottom lip trembled. "I know. I didn't mean anything by that. I…I…"

Andi felt like a heel. She was the one who'd said they should keep the past in the past, and here she was jumping all over her sister like some kind of possessive beast. "I'm sorry, Kris. That was mean. I'm an idiot."

Jonathan knocked again.

Kristin smiled and lightly touched Andi's arm with cool, slightly sticky fingers. "No, you're in love. I understand. Really, I do. It's been a long, long time, but I do remember the feeling."

With that, she headed back to the party. Andi opened the door. "Hi. Are you lost? The men's party is down the road a few blocks."

He looked heartbreakingly handsome—new denim jeans, snakeskin boots and a long-sleeve white shirt. The evening had turned chilly. A perfect excuse to drag him upstairs to her down-filled featherbed where she could ravish him to her heart's content.

"I'm on my way there now. Dad's waiting in the car. Sam told me to bring him along. We just stopped to drop off a gift for Jenny."

Andi couldn't stifle her surprise. "You have a shower present for Jenny?" Silky peignoirs and kitchen gadgets—typical shower gifts—sprang to mind.

He nodded. "Dad and I went to Yosemite today and we took the long way back through Oakhurst. I asked for his advice and this is what he suggested." He reached into the dim recess beside the door and brought out a set of golf clubs. "I have another set in the trunk for Sam," he said proudly.

Andi burst out laughing, but quickly swallowed her giggles when she saw the frown on his face. "Sorry. It's a lovely gift. They look very expensive, but...Jenny doesn't golf."

He looked sheepish. "My father said a couple needs a hobby they can enjoy together. When the twins are older, they might take up golf. In the meantime, I bought a catch net they can set up in the backyard to practice."

Her mouth dropped open. "Wow," she exclaimed. "That's the most original shower gift I've ever heard of."

He pointed to the rental car sitting in the parking lot. "It was Dad's idea. He and his wife play together daily. He says it keeps him young." He leaned closer and added in a soft voice. "At least, he implied they were golfing."

The innuendo was clear. Maybe it was time for Andi to take up golf. "So, what are you doing later?" she asked.

He moved the clubs just inside the door then pulled Andi into the shadows provided by the bay window. "After the bachelor party?" he asked, his lips finding hers.

He tasted of coffee and possibly some kind of liquor—sweet and smoky. "Uh-huh," she mumbled, wanting more.

The kiss vaporized the misgivings that had been collecting in her head all day. She'd sleepwalked through the rehearsal, rehashing in her mind the reasons why she shouldn't get involved with him. Only Kristin's presence and her new nephew's moody glumness—plus, the thought of the shower—had kept her from stewing all afternoon.

She wanted him. That hadn't changed after seven hours of being apart.

"Well," he said, trailing kisses across the bridge of her nose, then dotting each eye, "I'm going back to the motel. To the honeymoon suite," he added with a chuckle. "Because tomorrow morning, I'm meeting with a local Realtor to look at some property that I just found out is for sale."

It took a minute to understand what he was saying. "What? Where? Here in Gold Creek?"

He nodded—a rather smug grin on his lips.

"Are you serious?"

"Yes. It sounds like a good deal. It will be even better if we can talk the owner down a few thousand, but I plan to take it no matter what."

A million questions raced through her head. "Where is this property?"

"Just down the block. On the corner of Third and Fremont."

The map of Gold Creek hadn't changed very much since Andi was a child. She drew the image to mind. The only parcel of land he could possibly mean was—

"The *Ledger?*" she cried. "Oh my God, you're buying the *Ledger?*"

He crossed his arms in a satisfied manner. "I'm going to look it over in the morning. Hopefully the owner will accept my offer."

"Why are you doing this?"

"Dad pointed out that I jumped on my motorcycle and ran away from home because I was upset with him for selling our family's newspaper business. He said this was my chance to put up or shut up—so to speak.

"If I really have my heart set on being a publisher, I can

use the money from the sale of the business to buy the *Gold Creek Ledger.*''

Andi was speechless. Noise from the party—peals of laughter from whatever silly game they were playing—blended with traffic sounds and the croaking of frogs in Gold Creek. But louder than all that was the voice in her head repeating: ''He's staying. He's staying.''

But for how long? And was he buying the paper to prove his father wrong or because he wanted to settle down and make a life for himself? With her? She didn't dare ask.

''I don't know what to say,'' she admitted.

His right shoulder lifted and fell. ''Wish me luck. There's no guarantee the man will sell it to me. And there's always an outside chance I'll be running it from jail.'' She saw a twinkle in his eye.

He dropped one more light but sweet kiss on her lips then turned and ran down the steps. ''Can't miss out on free beer and pizza,'' he said with a laugh. ''I'll call you tomorrow.''

JONATHAN COULDN'T REMEMBER the last bachelor party he'd attended. But he had a pretty good idea about what the celebration was usually like. The image in his head didn't resemble this low-key, good-natured gathering in the least, he decided, looking around the private party room of the Golden Corral restaurant.

Jonathan's father seemed completely at ease whether he was talking with cowboys—like Hank and Petey—or people like the veterinarian, Rich Rumbolt and Jim Rohr, Jonathan's attorney. He'd also spent a lot of time with Sam's stepfather, who was an avid golfer.

As he nursed his beer, Jonathan pictured the look on Andi's face when he'd told her about the newspaper. He might be rushing things—businesswise and relationship-wise—but Andrew and JJ Newhall were men of action. Both believed in jumping on an opportunity when it presented itself. The question remained, was the new Jonathan up to the challenge?

"This deal has serendipity written all over it," Andrew had told Jonathan when they sat down face-to-face over lunch. "And I wouldn't have even heard about it if my friend from Sacramento hadn't reported the rumor."

Jonathan had made a few calculations. "What about the price? Too high, don't you think?"

"Hell, yes. The guy's asking way too much for his blue sky," Andrew had said of the owner's asking price. Blue sky was the term for patron goodwill and loyal customer base. "True, he's got a monopoly in this town, but if he doesn't treat us fairly, we'll threaten to start a new paper. Give him a little competition. And believe me, when the good folks of Gold Creek see how a paper *should* be run, they'll drop their *Ledger* subscriptions and come over to us."

They'd crunched numbers on a place mat during lunch. Too excited about the business possibilities to do justice to their tour of Yosemite, they'd cut the trip short and returned to Gold Creek through Wawona, using the park's southern exit. They'd stopped in Oakhurst, where Jonathan had bought the golf clubs.

Sam and his friends had cheered with high-fives all around the table when Jonathan presented him with the gift. Sam had seemed truly touched when Jon repeated the explanation. And Andrew had added his personal testimonial, which got everyone—even Hank—bragging about top golf scores.

"So are you and Andi friends?" Sam asked, joining Jonathan. Hank and the ranch hands were at the bar, getting refills. Several other guests had moved to the pool tables.

Andrew and Jim Rohr were deep in conversation at the far end of the table.

"Yes," Jonathan answered. "It's a good idea, don't you think? To be friends with the woman you love."

Sam didn't even blink at the announcement. "It's the only way," he said with conviction. "Especially if you plan to marry her."

Jonathan approved of Sam's protective nature. He thought about Andi's Daddy List. Sam surely would have made the cut, but would *he?* The old Jonathan wouldn't have stood a chance. Self-absorbed, egotistical, driven.

Thank God I didn't meet her before my accident.

Sam looked at Jonathan over his glass of beer and asked, "How's Andi taking it now that you're Jonathan instead of Harley?"

Jonathan pictured their morning and night in each other's arms. "She's adjusting. It might take awhile to convince her I'm going to stick around. But, hopefully, if things go well in the morning..."

At Sam's questioning look, Jonathan explained about the *Ledger.*

"Well, good for you," Sam said, clapping a hand on Jonathan's shoulder. "What time is your meeting? You're not going to be late for the wedding, are you?"

Jonathan drew a blank. "You mean the reception? Dad and I thought we'd drop in later."

Sam shook his head. "I guess Andrew didn't tell you. I want you both to join us at eleven. For the ceremony. In fact, you're delivering my ring."

"I beg your pardon?"

He held up his left hand. "I slammed my hand in a gate yesterday. The fingers are still swollen. I'll be damned if I'm going through all this folderol without a ring to show for it. The local jeweler is resizing it for me.

"Things are going to be pretty hectic in the morning, so I thought you might pick it up for me. And besides, I'd like my future brother-in-law at my wedding."

The words gave Jonathan a small thrill. "Do you know something I don't?"

Sam chuckled. "I know she loves you."

Really? Before he could ask for proof to back up that assertion, Donnie Grimaldo joined them.

Sam slapped him on the back. "'Bout time you got here."

"I've been busy. Following up on a lead on the Gunderson case." Donnie set his cup of coffee on the table before him.

"Any luck?" Jonathan asked.

Donnie made a so-so motion.

Sam and Jonathan exchanged a look. Sam's smile was almost smug. "I told you Donnie wouldn't take the easy way out."

"Talking about not taking the easy way, a little bird told me that you're courting Andi Sullivan." Donnie gave the old-fashioned word an appropriately derisive inflection. "Is it true?"

Jonathan looked across the table. Sam already knew the truth. If Andi was right about the speed of gossip, maybe everyone knew how he felt about her. "Yes," he said. "Is there a problem with that?"

The officer's right cheek quivered. "Not as far as I'm concerned, but she *is* a friend. I wouldn't want to see her get hurt."

Jonathan reacted defensively. "Even *you* don't believe I killed Lars, I'd never hurt—"

Donnie cut him off. "There are all kinds of hurt. And Andi is fragile. Everybody thinks Kristin is the delicate one.

She looks it, but she's got a will of iron. Believe me," he added on a harsh note.

"Andi, on the other hand, is like a caterpillar. Soft and easily squished. And if you squish a caterpillar, you miss out on the beauty of the butterfly it was meant to be."

Jonathan never would have guessed that a poet resided beneath the gruff exterior of this member of law enforcement.

Sam nodded. "I didn't meet the triplets until they were in high school, but I remember hearing about Andi's Daddy List. It touched my heart. What a neat little kid she must have been—bound and determined to find a father for her family. I hope Lara has inherited some of her aunt's spunk."

"I'm surprised she didn't set her sights on you," Jonathan said.

Sam smiled sagely. "I was a source of frustration for her. She liked me, and I think she really wanted me in the family, but she couldn't figure out how to make that happen. I was too young for Ida and too old for her or her sisters. At the time," he quickly added.

Donnie slugged his shoulder the way good friends can. "You're still too old for Jenny. Once you kick the bucket, I'm going to marry her and inherit your vast wealth."

Sam guffawed. "And our ten children."

Jonathan laughed, too. He knew instinctively he'd never shared this kind of camaraderie. Even the few friendships he could remember were superficial compared to this brotherly affection.

Out of the corner of his eye, he saw his father stand. "I guess we're leaving. Sam, I'd be honored to deliver your ring in the morning."

Donnie suddenly lifted his hand. A key dangled from his index finger. "I thought you might want to get your bike out of impound in the morning. We ran it for clues. Nothing.''

"Really? You're letting me pick it up?"

"It's costing you eleven dollars a day storage fees. Might as well haul it to a garage so someone can fix it. It's gonna need a little work.''

Jonathan accepted the key after a slight hesitation.

He noticed the two men's look of curiosity. "Andi believes I'm some kind of footloose nomad.''

Donnie shrugged. "You don't need a bike to leave. Just the will.''

Again, Jonathan was struck by Donnie's complexity. There was more to the man's story, but Jonathan didn't have time to explore it. He rose and was about to step away, when he felt something change in the atmosphere. Voices dropped. The whole bar seemed to tense.

"Well, look who's back in town," Donnie said, his gaze never leaving the newcomer standing at the end of the bar.

Even Sam looked perturbed. "Jenny isn't going to be happy.''

"What?" Jonathan asked. "I mean, who?''

Sam took a healthy swig of beer then plopped his glass down soundly. "That, my friend, is Tyler Harrison. The man who broke up the Sullivan triplets.''

JONATHAN WANTED to hear about the role this man had played in Andi's life, so he joined Donnie and Sam when they approached the dark-haired slender man.

Harrison watched them approach with narrowed eyes— the same shape and color as Kristin's son's. Now Jonathan understood what Andi had meant when she'd said things were going to get messy.

"Tyler," Donnie said. "Long time, no see. What brings you back to Gold Creek?" Donnie set his cup down on the bar and leaned on one elbow. The casual pose belied the tension Jonathan sensed.

"Just a quick visit," the man replied. "My mother requested it."

Sam put out his hand. "Sam O'Neal. We never really met. I own—"

"I know who you are," Harrison said. One corner of his mouth curled slightly. "Mother sends me a subscription to the *Ledger* every Christmas."

The chill in his voice was almost enough to make Jonathan shiver. Before he could add any sort of greeting, the bartender handed Sam a portable phone. "It's your bride-to-be."

Harrison finished the last of his beer and set the mug down with a solid thunk. His dark eyes glittered. "Ah, yes. Jenny Perfect is getting married." He looked at Donnie, then Jonathan. "The Sullivan sisters strike again."

Donnie's arm came up, hand curled into a fist, but before he could move forward, Sam stepped in front of him. He handed the phone to the bartender. He gave Tyler Harrison a brief glance, then ushered Donnie and Jonathan toward their table.

"Now's not the time. Lara's running a fever. Probably just teething, but Jenny wants to go home."

At Sam's signal, his friends gathered around the table. He explained that he was needed back at the ranch. He thanked them all for coming and mentioned a limitless tab at the bar, but Jonathan sensed the party was pretty much over.

Donnie disappeared before Jonathan could pry any details about Harrison out of him. Andrew, who seemed anxious to leave, appeared with their coats. "Are you ready, son? I'm bushed."

Jonathan nodded.

As they reached the door, a hand settled on his shoulder.

Jonathan turned. "I meant to tell you," Rich Rumbolt, the veterinarian, said. "Your dog is doing great. He could go home tomorrow, but with all the excitement—the wedding and Kristin's son and all—maybe you'd prefer to leave him at the clinic." Obviously the news about Zach had spread. "All kids love dogs, but Sarge needs to rest."

An image of a young boy tossing a ball for a small brown and white dog with floppy ears and a toothy grin entered Jonathan's mind, and just as suddenly a pressure built behind his eyes. He put his hand to his head and groaned. "Damn."

His father thanked the man. "Jon will call your office in the morning. He's had a long day. I think the elevation has given him a headache."

It took both men to help Jonathan to the car. His father drove. "Maybe we should stop at the hospital..."

"No. Pills in pocket." He found his pills and swallowed two without water.

A few minutes later, Andrew helped Jonathan into their suite. The pullout bed had been made and Jonathan fell onto it gratefully.

"Son, are you sure you don't want to see a doctor?"

"No," Jonathan said. The pulsing beat was lessening. "Weird. My usual kind of headache, but I wasn't thinking about the past. Not my past, anyway. Andi's. And then the dog."

Andrew made a short, gasping sound. Jonathan partially opened one eye. "What?"

"The dog. Andi. The wreck. Your mind has probably gotten them all mixed up."

Jonathan would have shaken his head but he didn't want to risk it. "What are you talking about?"

His father clicked on the bedside lamp then turned off

the overhead light. He brought Jonathan a glass of water and sat in the chair across from him.

"Do you remember Snoop?"

"Who?" The pain intensified like a wave crashing in his head.

"Your dog, Snoop. He was a beagle puppy. Your mother bought him for your tenth birthday."

An image came into his mind. The same one he'd seen earlier. "Mom said it would be plagiarism to copy Charles Schultz, so we dropped the Y when we named him. She and I went to the kennel to pick him out right after he was born. And she took me there after school to visit every day until he was old enough to come home with us."

His father's face showed sympathy and understanding.

"He died, didn't he?" Jonathan asked, but the answer was there in his mind. Behind the wall of pain.

"Yes, son. He was in the car with you. When it rolled over."

A blinding flash of insight made him sit up straight. "No Dad. Mom and Snoop didn't die," he said as the truth hit him. "They *left*."

"I don't understand."

Memories long stifled crossed the transom between hemispheres. He saw the scene as clearly as if he were standing outside his ten-year-old body. "I was knocked unconscious. But when I woke up, the paramedics had me on the ground beside the car. I could see Mom sitting, sort of slumped over the steering wheel. There was a trickle of blood on her forehead, but she didn't look dead. She looked asleep. And Snoop had been in the back seat. I didn't see him at all.

"They put me in an ambulance, and I assumed Mom was coming after me, but later at the hospital, you told me 'She's gone, son. And Snoop, too.'"

Andrew closed his eyes as if in pain. "Oh, Jon. I'm so

sorry. I didn't handle Jacki's death well. I was in too much pain. And shock. I was so angry.''

"At the funeral, the casket was closed."

Andrew nodded. "My family didn't believe in open caskets. Jacki's family was all gone, so I didn't fight it. I couldn't bear to look at her and I figured you were too young to see a dead body and understand."

Jonathan felt the medication working. His pain was easing. His shoulders began to release the tension they'd been holding. "You buried Snoop in the backyard before I came home from the hospital, didn't you?"

Andrew reached out, but his hand fell to his lap. "I didn't want you to suffer more."

Neither man spoke for several minutes, then Andrew said, "Jon, people didn't talk about *closure* back then. I'd never heard of survivor's guilt or abandonment issues. But I've done some reading on both subjects, and I think that your mother's death and the way I handled things probably played a big role in how you lived your life. The choice of career. Always on the move. Restless. Homeless. Maybe at some level you figured that you'd cheated death and if you stayed in one place too long, it would find you. Or possibly you decided the best way to avoid being abandoned again was to always leave first."

Jonathan closed his eyes—willing the last of his tension to dissipate. He needed time and distance to examine his father's theory. "Sounds plausible," he said, hoping Andrew would leave. "Tired now."

His father rose and walked to the side of the bed. "I'm not surprised. This is just a guess, but I don't think you got much sleep last night." His tone was teasing, but not unkind.

Jonathan would have protested, but he lacked the ability to be coy. "How can you tell?"

"Because I know you, Jon, even though we have grown apart over the years. This is the first time I've ever seen you let yourself become this vulnerable. And that, son, is love."

Jonathan rolled to his side, calling up the memory of Andi in his arms. He cradled the extra pillow to his chest. "You're right. Now all I have to do is convince her."

Andrew squeezed his shoulder supportively. "Not a problem. Remind me to tell you how I persuaded Gwen to take a chance on a man old enough to be her fath…uncle."

Jonathan heard a soft snicker. He would have smiled, too, but before he could muster the muscles, the world disappeared from view, taking him with it.

CHAPTER THIRTEEN

"WHAT A GREAT DAY for a wedding," Jonathan said as he left his motel room. He leaned on the second-floor railing and looked around. The air was crisp with dew; the clouds from the storm were nothing but a memory. The sky was so bright a blue it almost hurt his eyes.

"And we've got a lot to accomplish in a short time," his father said, joining him. Andrew had just gotten off the phone with his wife and daughters.

Jonathan had overheard bits and pieces of the conversation, and it was obvious his father missed his family. He took a breath, filling his lungs with clean, fresh air. "Dad, don't take this the wrong way, but why don't you go home?"

Andrew froze, his hand on the doorknob. "Excuse me?"

Jonathan cleared the distance between them. "I'm a big boy, Dad. You don't have to stay for my sake. Your family needs you."

The older man's shoulders visibly relaxed. "For a minute there, you sounded like the old Jonathan." Andrew's face flushed. "Not that there was anything wrong with the way you used to be, but—"

"I was an arrogant jerk."

"You were an intensely focused professional with no time for nonsense. You were serious. I used to worry that you'd have a stroke before you were forty. But you did some truly fine work, Jon. You can always be proud of that.''

Jonathan smiled. ''I can't remember the exact wording, but isn't there a saying that no man on his deathbed regrets not spending more time at the office?'' His father chortled. ''It took amnesia for me to understand that, Dad. You retired early for a reason—to be with your wife and daughters. You don't have to hold my hand.''

Andrew closed the door. ''That's not what I'm doing. I'm going with you because I want to be there to see my son fulfill his destiny.''

The words hung in the air a minute. Jonathan recalled hearing the phrase another time. Spoken with grave disappointment. He didn't have a clear image of the circumstances, but he understood that this transaction was important to them both. ''Then, let's go buy a newspaper.''

Andrew nodded and they walked side by side to the car. ''But, I might take you up on that offer to leave for home once we have the negotiations sealed,'' he said. ''I am kinda missing my girls. Will you give my regrets to Sam and Jenny?''

Jonathan got in and unlocked his father's door. ''Of course. And you'll see them again. When you come back for my wedding.''

Andrew looked startled. ''When will that be?''

Jonathan started the car. ''I have no idea. I haven't even asked her, but I have an engagement ring that's just sitting idle,'' he said, keeping his tone light. He'd awakened in the middle of the night with a yearning so intense he'd thought he was suffering from another headache. It took a few minutes to figure out that he missed Andi. He needed her by his side, and he planned to rectify the situation as soon as possible.

As they pulled out of the parking lot, Andrew said, ''Um,

son, I don't want to give advice where it's not wanted, but about that ring in your pocket…''

Jonathan had placed the ring in the motel room's safe and had needed to get the key from his father earlier to retrieve it. ''What about it?''

''Well…my wife made it very clear when I proposed that she wasn't interested in wearing another woman's hand-me-down, if you get my drift. Maybe Andi is different. Maybe she'd be content with the ring you bought for Miranda, but I wouldn't risk it if I were you.''

''I was only kidding about using that ring. I want something extra special for Andi. When I'm at the jeweler's this morning picking up Sam's ring, I'll look around.''

Andrew smiled broadly. ''There's another possibility.'' Jonathan glanced at him and saw a twinkle in his father's eyes. ''We'll discuss it before I leave.''

Jonathan felt a profound sense of accord. Whatever differences they'd had in the past—and it sounded as though theirs had been a tumultuous relationship—they'd forged a new path. One they could travel as friends.

''CAN I TAKE your picture, ladies?'' Lois Murdock asked.

''Not if you want to live to see the actual ceremony,'' Andi groused. The mousse Jenny had lent her was stiff and sticky. Her hair looked as if she'd just poked her finger in an electrical outlet.

Lois wasn't easily put off. She was a transplant from the Bay Area; her husband had taken a huge cut in pay to manage the new auto parts store in Gold Creek. A decision, she'd told Andi, they'd made in order to raise their daughters in a small town.

''Oh, honey, trust me. These candid shots are the ones your sister will treasure the most. Now, scrunch together, girls. You all look so cute in your skivvies.''

Andi glanced down as her sisters obediently crowded on either side of her. The bathroom counter behind them looked like a scene from a Vegas showgirl's dressing room. And in bras, panties and silky slips, she and her sisters could probably have gone onstage.

"Say, 'Weddings,'" the woman said, holding a large black camera to her eye.

Andi faked a smile. She just wanted this to be over. And the actual ceremony was less than an hour off. She wanted to talk to Jonathan and find out how his meeting had gone. She wanted to hear from Donnie about how the murder investigation was going. Mostly, she didn't want to put on the dress her sister had picked out for her to wear.

"I'm going to track down those adorable babies now," the photographer said. "I'll be back when you're dressed."

Andi sighed with relief. She perused the jumbled mess of makeup on the counter. "Is there any mascara? That's the stuff that makes your lashes darker, right?"

Jenny made a loud groaning sound. "I'm going to dry my hair. You help her, Kris." She gave Andi a sour look. "I had no idea you were so femininely challenged."

Andi stuck her tongue out at Jenny's back as she left the room. "So I'm not into makeup. I can load an M–16."

Kristin giggled. "Now, there's a trick that will come in handy around here."

She pawed through the mess, producing a slim cylinder that resembled a pen. After unscrewing the lid, she pulled forth a wand with a tiny brush on the end. "Yeah," Andi said. "I have one of those. Somewhere."

"Well, if you've had it longer than six months, throw it out. They go bad."

The reference to use-by dates made Andi remember her concern about Lars's supply of condoms. Her cheeks warmed.

"What?" Kris asked.

"I was thinking about Jonathan. I'd hoped to hear something from him by now. His meeting was an hour ago."

Kristin hesitated. "Why don't you let me apply your eye shadow then you do the mascara? I haven't done anyone else's makeup since high school. Remember how we'd take three hours to get ready for a dance?"

Andi snorted. "You and Jenny, maybe. I'd be in the playroom, listening to you."

Kris selected a small plastic rectangle and flipped open the lid. "You'd let us dress you up, too." Andi closed her eyes so Kris could apply the color. "When you wanted to impress a boy. Like when you went to the winter formal with Tyler," she said.

Andi couldn't keep from flinching. Tyler was a sore subject—one they had avoided for nearly eleven years.

"Can we talk about the night of our party, Andi?"

"No," she said vehemently. Andi couldn't discuss it, not without admitting her own guilt in the matter.

"I need to, Andi. I need to make you understand how sorry I am that it happened."

Well, here goes nothing. "I won't talk about it if you insist on apologizing," she said.

"Why?"

"Yeah, why shouldn't she apologize?" Jenny asked, joining them. "Kristin slept with your boyfriend. I think apologies are long overdue."

Andi took a deep breath. "Do we really have to do this *today?* It's your wedding, Jen. Wouldn't you rather wait—"

"Andrea, you're stalling. I can always tell when you've got a guilty conscience. Spill it."

Andi looked at the mirror to avoid facing either of her sisters. "I broke up with Ty shortly after the party started," she said with a resigned sigh. "He'd been drinking, and I decided he wasn't my type."

In the mirror she saw her sisters look at each other. "No way," Jenny exclaimed. "I distinctly remember you carrying on about how Kristin stole your boyfriend. The potential love of your life."

Andi used her arm to push aside the makeup and hopped up to sit on the counter. "Okay. Confession time. Just remember that we're sisters and all of this garbage happened a long time ago. We were young and stupid and we bought into the idea that boys were the answer to every question."

"You mean they're not?" Jenny said jokingly. "Tucker will be so sad to learn that."

Andi smiled briefly, then said, "The night of our party I was in a snit. I liked Ty a lot. But he didn't seem to care about anything or anybody, except his stupid motorcycle. So I decided to break up with him. To see his reaction."

She rolled her eyes. "Big mistake. Turned out he couldn't care less. And, believe me, that didn't do anything for my ego.

"Then, not five minutes later, I find out that Kristin's driven off with him in Rosemarie." She looked at her sisters. "It hurt that he didn't want me, but when he went off with Kris, I felt both of them had betrayed me."

When nobody spoke, Andi continued. "Besides, it wasn't as if Kris *knew* we'd broken up. I asked her—later, after the police brought her home—what Tyler had said about me. And she said, 'We didn't talk about you, Andi.'" Andi was aware that her voice sounded like a seventeen-year-old girl's. "Remember?"

Kristin shook her head. "The only thing I remember about that night was wanting to get as far away from the party as possible," she said. "I was mad at Donnie. Heartbroken, actually. He'd broken up with me and I'd heard he was dating Sandy Grossman. She'd always been after him. Ty was convenient. He had a bottle. We went to the dam. I doubt we said more than six words to each other.''

Jenny looked toward the hallway. "Well, you may not have spoken much, but your *actions* had a long-lasting consequence. A consequence who inherited his father's eyes and the same monumental chip on his shoulder."

Andi added, "And sooner or later people are going to notice the resemblance."

"If they haven't already," Jenny said under her breath. "I wasn't going to say anything about this until after the ceremony, but Sam told me they saw Tyler at the Golden Corral last night. He's back in town."

Kristin got a panicky look on her face. "Zach and I should leave. I knew this would happen, but I thought I'd have time to prepare. To make plans. To—"

Andi hopped off the counter and blocked the door. "Kris, you can't hide forever. It isn't fair to Zach. Or Ida. Or you."

"Or us," Jenny said, trying for a little humor. "We're here for you, Kristin. We always have been—even if we got a little screwed up for a while."

Jenny put her arms around both Andi and Kristin. "We've cleared the air. We've discovered—here's a news flash for 'Glory's World'—the Sullivan sisters aren't perfect. Now, can we get on with my wedding?"

Andi felt as though a weight had been removed from her shoulders. For nearly eleven years she'd blamed herself for Kristin's estrangement. Now she knew that while her anger might have made things worse, there'd been more to her sister's story than Andi had known.

After they hastily completed their makeup, the sisters moved into Jenny's room to dress. The photographer snapped them in various stages of undress. Diane, Sam's mother, joined them for a couple of pictures of her zipping up the back of Jenny's dress, then she hurried back to help Greta with Lara and Tucker.

At seven months, the twins were chubby, happy babies who could roll over and make fabulous spit bubbles. Tucker was trying his best to crawl. Andi could hardly be around them without wanting one of her own.

Knowing she couldn't put it off any longer, Andi picked up the bridesmaid dress. She struggled to keep the layers of gauzy material from choking her as she pulled it over her head. "I need some help," she said.

Kristin went to her aid. Within seconds the tea-length dress of pale sage with an over-dress of sheer nylon imprinted with a muted design of leaves and flowers hugged her trim body. Kris wore the same dress in peach. "That's pretty. Look, Jen, isn't she beautiful?"

Andi felt a blush coming on.

"Jonathan won't be able to keep his eyes off her," Jenny said. "Last night at the party, he told Sam he loved her."

Andi almost dropped the hairbrush she'd picked up. "I beg your pardon? Jonathan told Sam about his feelings for me?"

Jenny, who was hunting for her shoes, looked over her shoulder. "Yes. Men talk, Andi. They say they don't but they gossip just like women."

"He sounds pretty serious," Kristin said. "Does this mean we might have a second wedding this year?"

Andi sat down on the bed. "I love him, guys, but I'm afraid," she said in a small voice.

"Fearless Andi Sullivan?" Kris asked. "Impossible."

"Oh, honey," Jenny said, joining her on the bed. "We're all afraid. I'm getting married in thirty minutes, and after that, the whole town of Gold Creek is showing up on my doorstep for a party. You think I'm not terrified?"

Kristin knelt in front of her. "And I have to tell my son's

father that he *is* a father. Surprise, surprise. Tell me what you've got to fear that beats that?''

Andi felt a swift arc of pain. ''I know this doesn't make sense, but I've managed to fall in love with a man who's turned out to be somebody else.'' Her sisters waited expectantly. ''So do I now assume that I'm in love with the new Harley...I mean, Jonathan?''

The thought tickled her funny bone, and she started to laugh. When tears hit, Jenny pinched her upper arm. Hard. ''Snap out of it, Andrea. You can't control everything. Love has its own agenda. We're just along for the ride.''

Andi's stuttering laughter came under control. ''But I always *thought* I could, Jen. First, I tried to find a father for us. When Ida turned down all my daddy candidates, I started looking for a guy who could be everything to each of us. But if such a guy exists he's probably an alien.''

Kristin smiled sympathetically. ''I know what you mean. Every time I meet a new guy, I think, 'Husband material, maybe, but will he make a good dad for Zach?''' She sighed. ''I guess we're not as lucky as Jen. She fell in love with the right guy. Twice.''

Jenny looked down, as if uncomfortable with her sister's comment. ''Actually,'' she said, ''Josh and I were great friends, and I loved him, but I think at least part of what I felt for him was habit. He was my safety net. With Josh around I never had to risk that part of me that was afraid to paint, to write, to express myself.''

''Wow,'' Kristin said. ''And with Sam?''

''It's just the opposite. Sam challenges me to become the person I want to be. He never lets me settle for easy. I love him more than I thought possible. And I can't wait to marry him, but I'm afraid, too. What if I'm not good enough? Look at all the baggage in my life.''

Andi shook her head in amazement. Who would have

guessed Jenny—who always seemed so self-possessed and in control—felt the same way she did?

"Do you remember when we were eight? The pact we made?" Andi asked.

Kristin made a circling motion with her thumb against her baby finger. "You mean with the kitchen knife and mingled blood?"

Jenny's eyes suddenly lit up. "Of course. How did the chant go? Something about life and wind and—"

"Wait. Wait. We need a knife," Kristin said, leaping to her feet.

A minute later she returned with a fingernail file. "Sorry," she said sheepishly. "There must be a zillion people downstairs. The entire Garden Club is fixing food for the reception. I didn't want to go into the kitchen."

They looked at each other then silently agreed to proceed. "Who started?" Andi asked.

"Me." Jenny cleared her throat and said, "Fearless as the night wind…"

"Strong as the mighty oak," Andi recalled on cue.

"Gentle as a mother's touch," Kris intoned.

"The best shall love forever," they said in harmony.

Kristin handed the file to Andi, who looked at it then tossed it over her shoulder. "We're adults now. I think our brains can handle symbolism without us bleeding all over our wedding outfits."

Laughing, the Sullivan triplets pressed their fingers together. Three spokes in a wheel of life, love and sisterhood.

JONATHAN HAD BEEN AFRAID he'd arrive late for the ceremony. His meeting with the Realtor had taken longer than he'd expected, and then he'd needed to pick up a rental car, since his father was returning his car at the Fresno airport.

He quickly parked and raced to the area where several

four-wheel-drive all-terrain vehicles were parked to ferry guests to the hilltop where the nuptials were going to be held. "Am I late?" he asked Hank.

The foreman—who looked dapper in a western suit coat and obviously new jeans—shook his head. "Nope. The women are still in the house, which is a good thing because one of the reins on that fancy carriage that Sam borrowed broke. We had to scramble to improvise."

Jonathan looked toward the log house. In the circular driveway an old-fashioned surrey with four white horses waited. "Wow," he exclaimed. "Is that for Jenny and her sisters?"

"And Ida Jane and Sam's mother and Greta and the twins," Hank said. "You can either take one of these." He nodded at the beribboned ATVs. "Or a horse. There's half a dozen saddled."

"Why so many?"

"They're for the party afterward. Sam always gives the townsfolk a chance to do some trail rides for them that wants to play cowboy."

Jonathan assessed his clothing, glad that he'd taken the time to change out of his city clothes into black jeans, his new boots and a pale blue shirt. A tie hadn't felt right, but it was in the pocket of his western-style jacket, just in case. Along with the ring Sam had asked him to pick up.

"I'll take Jughead," he said. "I've kinda missed him."

Hank nodded as if that made perfect sense. "Then, I'll see you up top."

Jonathan wasn't certain how it would feel to be back in the saddle. That aspect of his life had faded some as the memories of his former life returned, but Jughead, his old friend and Hank's favorite mount, seemed to remember him. Once atop the roan gelding, Jonathan heaved a sigh of pleasure.

"Hey, cowboy, where ya' goin'?" a female voice asked.

Jonathan pulled back on the reins. Andi stood about ten feet from the corral, a tentative look on her face. His first impulse was to sweep her into his arms and carry her off to the most private spot he could find. Instead, he made a clicking sound and walked Jughead closer.

"Well, Andi Sullivan, don't you look breathtaking."

Her cheeks colored prettily. Her hair was curled; the dress she wore was perfect for her, clinging provocatively at all the right places, yet demure and delicate. Her legs looked tan and sleek, and the strappy shoes she wore made him shift in the saddle.

"I don't look like a silly bridesmaid?"

He shook his head, making sure she saw the truth in his eyes. "You're the most beautiful woman I've ever seen. Want a ride?"

She laughed. "Oh, sure, that'll work. Jenny would kill me if I messed up her perfect wedding."

Jonathan urged his horse a step closer. "I know how to ride. I'll get you there in one piece," he promised.

He could tell she was tempted, but at that moment her sister—a vision in ivory lace—called out, "Andrea, get your butt in this carriage. Now."

Andi looked up at him and grinned. "See? I told you. She's dangerous. But—" she ran her tongue over the glossy shine on her bottom lip "—I could use a ride back."

Jonathan's heart turned over at the promise he read in her eyes. "You've got it."

With that she turned and strolled away. She nearly lost her footing once when the high heels threatened to trip her up, but she recovered and joined her family in the gaily festooned coach.

Jonathan could have ridden escort, but decided he needed

a moment in private with the groom, so he gave Jughead his head and they tore up the hillside.

Five minutes later, he tied Jughead with the other horses—several of which he recognized—at the base of the knoll where purple and white ribbons fluttered like butterflies in the surrounding oaks. A bower of greenery and flowers framed a backdrop of blue sky. Jonathan wondered if he'd ever seen a more inspired setting.

"Quite an affair, wouldn't you say?" a familiar voice asked.

James Rohr joined him as they walked toward a group of men standing to one side of the arched trellis. "Where's Andrew?" Rohr asked.

"He got homesick," Jonathan said.

The other man chuckled. "If I had a beautiful young wife waiting for me, I'd be in a hurry to leave, too."

Jonathan tried to picture Gwen, his stepmother. He'd studied the photograph in his wallet, which his father said was two years old, but no solid recollection of the woman or his young stepsisters came to mind. "The girls have changed so much since that photo," Andrew had told him. "I left in such a hurry I forgot to bring pictures, but we'll e-mail you some digital shots as soon as you're up and running."

In business. I'm the new owner of the Gold Creek Ledger. *Or will be when escrow closes.*

As if reading his mind, the older man asked, "How did your meeting go this morning? I offered to come along, but Andrew said he didn't want any witnesses if he took unfair advantage of the man."

Jonathan laughed. Somehow that sounded more like something he might have said. Of course, his father had admitted that Jon came by his arrogance naturally. Andrew had also said that Jonathan's mother had saved him from a life devoid of color and romance. Jonathan was hoping Andi would rescue him the same way.

"It's a done deal, as we say in the mountains," he told the lawyer. "The papers are signed, anyway. There's still a matter of title searches and termite inspections and whatever, but I should be able to take over in thirty days."

Rohr shook his hand. "Congratulations. Hopefully, we'll have this legal matter cleared up before that."

Jonathan frowned. He couldn't forget that he was out of jail on bond and he still had a murder charge against him. He wondered how the citizens of Gold Creek would take a publisher who was on trial for his life. Jon and his father had discussed putting the paper in Andrew's name in case the trial dragged on, but in the end, Jonathan decided he would take his chances with the justice system. He was an innocent man. That was good enough for him. And for Andi, he hoped. Because he planned to ask her to marry him. The sooner, the better.

"Jonathan," a voice hailed.

"The groom calls," he said. "I think he's looking for a ring."

Rohr held out his hand, palm up. "Since I'm one of his attendants, I'll take it."

Jonathan fished in the pocket of his jeans and dropped an emerald-cut, two-carat diamond into the man's hand. The ring sparkled like a dewdrop at dawn. "It's beautiful, but I don't think it will fit Sam's finger," the attorney said, grinning.

"Whoops. Wrong ring." Jonathan quickly switched the diamond for a slim gold band, which he'd noticed was inscribed with two sets of initials and the date.

Before repocketing the engagement ring, he held it to the light. "This was my mother's. She died when I was ten. Dad told me he chose to bury her with her wedding band only because he knew Mother would have wanted me to give this to my lady love.'' Jonathan felt a prickle of tears in his sinuses. He was grateful for his dark glasses, but fortunately no headache followed.

''My guess, that would be Andi,'' the attorney said.

Jonathan smiled then tucked the ring deep in his pocket. ''You know what's odd? Dad told me that when he first got the call about my arrest, he went to his safe and took out Mother's ring. His wife packed for him and made the travel arrangements, but Dad said all he could do was weep.''

He recalled their final conversation before his father left for the airport.

''I wish I could picture Mom wearing this,'' Jonathan had said after Andrew gave him the ring.

''It was a long time ago, son. But you should know that she designed it herself. Spent hours with the jeweler to get it just right. She said the leaves signified transition, because in nature nothing stays the same, and the diamond symbolized duration, because true love never dies.''

The sound of horses walking in tandem broke his train of thought. James touched his sleeve. ''We'd better join the others. Sam promised this would be short and sweet.''

Two dozen people moved from outlying areas—some standing in small groups beneath the shade of the oak trees, others observing the view from the precipice—and gathered in a semicircle, leaving room for the bride and her attendants to approach.

After the surrey came to a stop, designated ushers helped the ladies from it. First was Ida Jane, looking regal in pale lavender. Greta Willits, who was joined by her husband a few seconds later, escorted the older woman to the summit. Next, the mother of the groom stepped out. She walked to a place of honor on Donnie Grimaldo's arm. Then came

Andi and Kristin, each carrying a baby. Last, the bride descended.

From somewhere nearby, a guitar played. Jonathan watched Andi and Kristin walk toward the altar. The uneven ground required them to move slowly—especially with the squirming bundles they carried.

Lara was in a white pinafore with a pink dress beneath, white tights and patent-leather shoes with tiny bows; Tucker wore tan shorts with a dressy shirt and matching vest. On his feet were socks only. Jonathan recalled Hank saying Tucker hated shoes.

The twins seemed a bit awed by the crowd. Lara looked ready to cry, but Andi comforted her with a bowed head and soft word. His heart did a double thump. If she *were* pregnant, they could expect their first child in late November.

An expectant hush fell over the crowd as Jenny approached the knoll. Jonathan looked around. He felt a pleasant sense of surprise to realize he knew nearly every attendee. Many acknowledged his gaze with a friendly nod.

The music swelled. Jenny drew close. She looked radiant. Her tailored, western-style dress of ivory lace made her look regal, but her long auburn hair added a carefree touch that was very much her style. Her hat was adorned with fine netting and fresh flowers, and she carried a nosegay of honeysuckle and pink roses.

Sam, as handsome as a film star in his western tux, waited for her with hand extended, and she went to him with a smile of pure joy on her face. The crowd closed the gap, forming a half circle around them. The judge—the man Jonathan recognized from his arraignment—faced the group.

The vows were simple and heartfelt. A soloist sang a song of love and the promises one heart makes to another.

With his hands folded in front of him, Jonathan turned

his mother's ring so he alone could see it. The diamond twinkled with an inner radiance that somehow made him feel as if she were present.

He closed his eyes, trying to picture her. Although he feared this might produce a headache, what came instead was a whisper on the wind. A soft sigh that held a silent blessing. She'd want him to experience the love she'd known with his father, the joy of holding his own child and sharing precious moments that could never be stolen—even by a fickle hand of fate.

Someone jostled his elbow and Jonathan realized the ceremony was over. He joined the other guests in applause. As Sam and Jenny passed by him, each holding a child, Jonathan had time to whisper, "Way to go."

Sam nodded, his eyes crinkled with humor. "You're next, my friend."

Jonathan hoped.

Then his gaze found the saucy green eyes that made his heart rate soar. Andi's expression as she watched the couple stroll toward their waiting carriage was tender, hopeful and just slightly vulnerable.

He walked to her, acknowledging her sister with a nod. "If you'll excuse us, Kristin, I have a bridesmaid to abduct."

ANDI'S HEART nearly jumped out of her chest when Jonathan appeared in front of her, a look of expectation in his eyes. "I can't go. We have pictures to take," she said, stalling.

"Oh, go with the man," Kristin said, giving her a nudge. "The photographer's going to be here all day. Besides, we missed the first carriage and look at that line." She pointed to the guests milling around, waiting for the vehicles that would take them back to the house.

"My horse awaits, m'lady," Jonathan said with a sweeping bow that made Kristin fake a swoon.

"I can't ride in this dress," Andi complained.

"Sure you can," Jonathan said with a devilish wink. He handed Kristin the bride's bouquet, which Andi had been holding, then bent down and picked her up. "Watch."

His arms felt powerful and comforting. She'd missed him last night, waking often to reach for him. Somehow it didn't seem right that she should fall this hard, this fast.

"I feel like Julia Roberts in *Runaway Bride*," Andi said as he strolled toward the horses.

"Runaway bride-to-be," he said so softly that she might have imagined it.

But if that were so, then why was her heart knocking so loudly she could barely hear herself think?

Hank and a man whose face Andi recognized but whose name she couldn't recall were standing with the animals when Jonathan—and Andi—approached.

Without being asked, Hank untied the big roan Jonathan had been riding earlier and held him apart from the others. "Caught yourself a triplet, huh?" The younger cowboy snickered.

"There's still one left," Jonathan said, winking at Andi.

"Kristin will kill you if she finds out you said that," she hissed, trying to keep from laughing.

Smiling, Jonathan helped Andi into the saddle. Her dress rode up over her thighs, but the stretchy material actually managed to protect her modesty. With an easy effort, he pulled himself up and swung his leg over the horse's rump, riding just behind the saddle.

"That can't be comfy."

He made a face. "You have no idea. But we aren't going far."

"To the barn?"

He chuckled. "Oh, no. Not yet, anyway."

Andi wondered again if this was a mistake. She'd lain awake for hours last night watching the shifting pattern of shadows on the ceiling, hoping for some guidance.

Nothing had happened, of course. No wisdom, no sign from the other side. All she'd gained were matching bags under her eyes, which Kristin had covered with concealer. Andi was on her own here. And she was afraid of blowing it.

Jonathan reached around her to pat his horse's neck. "Let's go, Jughead. Remember, we have a lady with us today."

"Jughead's my buddy," Jonathan told her as the animal started to walk. "I used to exercise him when Sam was away lobbying for wildfire legislation and Hank was busy with day-to-day operations."

She brushed a fleck of pollen off the hem of her skirt. "Where are we going?"

"To the waterfall."

Andi, Jenny and Kris used to go there every spring to sunbathe and go skinny-dipping in the icy water. There was a good chance Josh and one or two of his friends had spied on them, but that had been part of its mystique.

"How do you know about this place?" she asked when they reached the clearing a few minutes later.

"Sam pointed it out one time when we were in the area. He said you and your sisters used to skinny-dip here. My imagination provided weeks of great dreams," he said with an amused chuckle.

He dismounted then helped her from the saddle. The heels of her shoes sank into the soft ground, making her unsteady on her feet. He picked her up again. "Can't let those pretty shoes get dirty," he said, his lips brushing her ear.

Shivers of desire ran through her. Would Jenny kill her

if she spent the day making love to Jonathan instead of rejoining the party? Yes. Besides, trail riders would soon begin trekking past.

Jonathan set her down on a dry flat patch of rock, then spread his jacket on the ground. "We're not staying," he said. "I know you need to be with your family. I just wanted a few minutes alone with you."

Andi was disappointed, but she acknowledged they had no choice. "Okay. Are you going to tell me about the *Ledger?*"

His triumphant smile provided the answer. "You bought it," she exclaimed.

"Signed the papers. It still has to go through escrow. That will take about thirty days."

She didn't know what to say. One side wanted to dance in glee, the other voted for caution.

When she didn't answer, he added, "The paper's just one piece of the picture, Andi. I want to start a new life for myself in Gold Creek, but it won't be complete unless you marry me."

The words she'd waited her whole life to hear. She wanted to shout and laugh, but a familiar vacuum deep inside sucked the joy out of the moment.

"Andi, I love you." He took her hand and placed something in it. Something sparkly. "This was my mother's engagement ring. I'd like you to wear it."

A pressure like a two-ton vise squeezed her chest. She gazed mute upon the most beautiful ring she'd ever seen. She couldn't answer because she couldn't breathe. Little squiggles of grayness crept into her vision.

"Andi," Jonathan called out, his voice growing more distant.

The green grass called out invitingly. She closed her eyes

and let herself sink into the soft haven. Just a moment of escape—to collect her thoughts. That's all she needed.

"Andi. Are you okay?" Jonathan cried, tapping her cheek with chilly fingers. "Andi, honey, tell me you're okay."

She heard fear in his voice. The man she loved was afraid. Afraid *she'd* leave *him*. The irony made her smile.

"You're smiling. That's good. You're coming out of it. Great. I have to tell you, Andrea, I don't have a good feeling about this proposal."

She opened her eyes. "Would you feel better if I said yes?"

Jonathan's eyes narrowed suspiciously. He made a V with his index and middle finger. The beautiful ring twinkled above his first knuckle. "How many fingers am I holding up?"

"Two. Is that really my ring?"

He passed it to her, and she slipped it over her finger, pushing slightly at the knuckle. "It's beautiful. I've never seen anything like it."

He explained the symbolism and she was touched, both by his mother's grace and forethought and by his willingness to share it with her.

"Harley…I mean, Jonathan," she said, blushing at her gaffe. "I've never been proposed to, and this is the most incredibly romantic moment of my life. But, obviously, we have things we need to talk about. Unresolved issues."

He placed his hands on her shoulders and made her face him. "I love you, Andi. I'd marry you tomorrow, if you'd say yes, but I understand if you want to wait awhile." He gave a Harley smile. "Especially since I'm still a murder suspect."

She started to scold him, but his kiss robbed her of breath.

Her head started to spin again. She couldn't believe she'd actually fainted. Maybe she was allergic to makeup.

When he pulled back, he was breathing hard, too. "About the trial, Donnie's working on another angle, and my lawyer thinks the case will be resolved in the next week or two. My point was that I'm well aware of the obstacles in our path. I just want us to face them together."

She looked at the ring. "As an engaged couple?"

"Who...possibly...live together?" he added, his tone hopeful. "In a haunted bordello."

Andi couldn't help but laugh. "That sounds a tad scandalous for Gold Creek."

He looked crushed.

"I like it."

"You do?"

"Yes. I do. And," she added, "I've got several nice rooms you could rent."

His smile disappeared. "I beg your pardon?"

Andi stood up. Her ankles wobbled unsteadily on the damp ground but she managed to keep her balance. "The rent money would go a long way toward some badly needed improvements," she said. "I couldn't possibly bring all of these burdens into a marriage. A crumbling old bordello. An antique business on the verge of bankruptcy. Not to mention all my family problems."

She looked at her glorious new ring. "I'll marry you, but not until we have a few of these things fixed. Marriage is serious business. I plan to do it right."

Jonathan hadn't moved. He was sitting hunched slightly forward, elbows on knees. "Coming?" she asked, offering her hand.

He looked up. "We're engaged?"

She nodded.

"And I can move into the old bordello?"

She nodded, fighting a smile at his befuddled tone.

"But I have to pay rent."

"I need the money."

"For a computer system?"

"New wiring, first. We don't want to burn the place down, right? Although, that *is* an idea." She laughed to make sure he knew she was kidding. "We should probably go. And I don't know about announcing our engagement today. I don't want to steal Jenny's thunder."

His lips tensed. "I don't care whom we tell or when, but you will wear the ring, right?"

"Oh, yes," she said with feeling. "This is mine. And, by the way—" she struggled to keep a straight face "—just because you're renting rooms at the bordello doesn't mean you have to *sleep* in them."

CHAPTER FOURTEEN

ANDI WASN'T SURE what she expected to find when she and Jonathan rode into the paddock area near Sam's barn, but it wasn't Donnie Grimaldo with his gun drawn.

"What on earth is happening?" she cried.

Jonathan made a clicking sound, and Jughead picked up the pace. "I don't know, but I sure as hell hope he isn't looking for me."

Moments later, they dismounted and Andi took off as fast as her high heels would allow. Jonathan passed the reins to a waiting cowboy and hurried after her.

"What's going on?" she asked, taking in the scene. Kristin, who looked as though she'd seen a ghost, was clinging to Jenny, who looked angry. Sam—the usual purveyor of calm—had a cell phone to his ear and paced in a short, tight line a few steps away. A dozen or so people clustered nearby.

Jenny looked at her accusingly. "Where were you? We could have used the marines."

Jonathan put a hand on her shoulder. "She was with me, what's the problem?"

"Tyler Harrison is the problem," Jenny answered. "He just left, but only after Donnie and Mr. Rohr made it clear there would be legal ramifications if he didn't."

Donnie, who had momentarily disappeared, rejoined the group. His gun was nowhere in sight. Andi assumed it was safely locked in his patrol car.

"I apologize," he said, looking embarrassed. "I overreacted."

Kristin looked at him but didn't say anything.

Donnie addressed Andi and Jonathan, the latecomers. "Ty said he dropped by to see if the rumors were true. That Kristin's child looked a lot like him."

Kristin let out a groan and pressed her head against Jenny's shoulder.

Andi went to her. "Let's go to the house, Kris. You don't want to get eye stuff all over Jen's wedding dress, do you?" she asked, trying to lighten the mood. The town had feasted enough on their woes, without adding more gossip to the mill, Andi decided.

"Where's Zach?" she asked, looking around as they walked to the house. In the mowed field to the left of the log home, three colorfully striped tents had been erected. Parked cars lined both sides of the road and people seemed to be everywhere. Music from a Sonora-based Celtic rock group called the Black Irish Band drifted to them.

Noting the constant stream of women—arms laden with food—moving between the kitchen and the tent area, Andi headed for the front door and the privacy of the living room.

"He's playing a computer game in Sam's office," Kris told her. "He didn't hear a thing, thank God, but he's bound to find out. Everyone is talking about it."

Jonathan dashed ahead to open the door.

Kristin happened to look down at that moment and gasped. She grabbed Andi's hand. "OhmyGod. A ring."

Jenny, who'd followed a few steps behind with Sam, sprang forward to see. "Andi," she cried. "You're engaged? For real?"

Jonathan cleared his throat and made an ushering motion. "Maybe we could discuss this inside."

Andi gave him a look of gratitude she hoped he'd understand. "Where's Ida Jane?" she asked.

"Upstairs, taking a nap with the twins," Jenny said. "I think the excitement of the wedding was too much for her. I hope she didn't hear about Tyler showing up—she doesn't need to worry about that on top of everything else."

Sam poked his head into the kitchen and had a word with his housekeeper then led the way to the living room. He walked to a built-in bar. "A drink, anyone? All the champagne is outside waiting for the best man's toast, but we have most everything else here."

Andi and her sisters declined, but James Rohr asked for a scotch. Sam poured three and handed one to both men. "To Jonathan and Andi," Sam said. "Congratulations on your engagement." The men clinked their glasses together before swallowing the liquid. Andi smiled at her brother-in-law, then turned to Kristin.

"Do you have a plan, Kris?"

Her sister's strawberry-blond head shook despondently. "I thought I'd have more time. According to Jenny, Ty hasn't been in town since graduation."

"Don't blame me for—" Jenny started to say, but Jonathan interrupted.

"Excuse me, Jenny. This probably isn't my place, but we should be looking at the future not the past. Since we have a lawyer present—and a cop…" Andi hadn't even noticed Donnie, who hovered near the doorway. "Maybe we could ask them about Kristin's rights in this matter. I mean, did you get a sense that this guy was here to demand custody of his son or what?"

He made a slightly self-deprecating shrug that reminded Andi of Harley. "That is the issue, right? I came in late to this discussion—by about eleven years," he added with a smile.

Everyone sat down, including Donnie, although he stayed as far back as possible. Jim Rohr offered to meet with Kristin on Monday if she would stay in town an extra day. He also told Jonathan, "Deputy Grimaldo may have a lead in your case. With luck we'll wrap that up next week, too."

"What kind of lead?" Andi asked.

"I'm waiting on a report from the forensics lab in Sacramento," Donnie told her. "That's all I can say. But we should know something by Tuesday or Wednesday."

Sam cleared his throat. "I don't think Kristin needs to panic. When Donnie and I were *escorting* Ty back to his car, he mentioned that he was leaving for Japan on business. I got the impression he might be gone for several months, didn't you?" he asked Donnie.

"Yes. And last night at the bar, he said he was in town to see his mother. I don't think this was planned."

Jonathan made a funny sound. He put his hand to his forehead as he did when experiencing a headache, but Andi had the impression that whatever was troubling him wasn't an old memory working its way to the surface.

"Forgive me if this isn't the time or place to bring this up, but…this morning while I was at the Realtor's…" He paused and added, "I've bought the *Ledger,* by the way."

After a second round of congratulations, he returned to his subject. "What I started to say was that earlier this week my father stumbled across some information about a development company moving into the area. Are you aware of this?"

Sam nodded. "I've heard rumors. A few folks have sold, looking for greener pastures, big bucks. What's your point?"

"I just found out who was behind Meridian, Inc. It turns out the CEO is Tyler Harrison."

No one spoke for a minute, then Donnie said, "So, he's bought a few parcels of land. What's the big deal?"

Jonathan shrugged. "It depends on what he plans to do with them. If he has a large enough holding, he could push for whatever redevelopment suits his agenda.

"This might be a coincidence, but the Realtor said someone in the City Planning Department mentioned there's been talk about redefining the boundaries of the business district, as well as a possible ring road for traffic to bypass the town.

"According to the map he showed me, the old bordello—because of its location—would fall directly in the path of this new road."

Andi's stomach flipped over. "The bastard. He tried to buy the bordello, you know. Ida Jane got a letter from Meridian in the mail. But I threw it away. When we wouldn't sell, he tried to get in through the back door."

Jenny's face went stern. "We'll fight him. There's no way he can bulldoze the bordello. It's a historic landmark."

James Rohr leaned forward. "Is it designated as a historic property, Andi? If so, he can't touch it."

All eyes turned her way. The application for historic recognition had been on Ida's desk for two years. It was thick as a book and looked complicated. She'd set it aside and never got back to it. "Not yet," she said woefully. "I've been—"

Jonathan put his arm around her shoulders. "She's been a little busy. But I have a month before I can take over the paper, so I volunteer to look into it. This sounds like a good way to learn more about my community."

Andi couldn't let him take on her job. "But you have enough on your hands—the trial, the Blue Lupine, Sarge..."

He made a negating motion. "Speaking of Sarge," he said, turning to Kristin, "I was wondering if your son might be interested in a dog. With all the construction going on at the bordello right now, I'm afraid Sarge might get run over or something. Do you think Zach might like a pet?''

''I wanted a dog, but Mom said we couldn't afford one,'' a youthful voice said from the doorway.

Kristin paled noticeably.

Jonathan rose and walked to greet Zach. ''Well, you're in luck. This dog comes with a trust fund. He's filthy rich. His previous owner died, but he named Sarge in his will. The dog has money coming out his ears. And he has really big ears,'' Jonathan added playfully, using his hands to illustrate.

Andi saw her nephew almost crack a smile until he looked at his mother.

''We could take him home with us,'' Kristin said. ''If it'll help.''

''Great.'' Jonathan smiled and looked at his watch. ''I saw Rich Rumbolt in the crowd, but he told me his office was open today until three. If we hurry, we could spring Sarge and still make it back in time for cake. What do you say, Zach? Wanna go?''

After a slight hesitation, the boy nodded. Jonathan put his hand out to Andi, ''Coming?''

Her heart was getting that squishy feeling again. She looked at Jenny, ''Do you need me for pictures?''

Jenny looked close to tears, too. ''We won't cut the cake until all of you—including Sarge—get back.''

Andi sprang to her feet, and promptly keeled sideways onto James Rohr's lap. ''Damn shoes,'' she cursed.

She looked at Jonathan who appeared to be stifling a grin. ''I'll be right back,'' she said. ''These ankle busters have got to go.''

Andi ran barefoot upstairs to Jenny's room where they'd dressed just two hours earlier. She couldn't believe how much her world had changed in one day. *A wedding, an engagement, a probable paternity suit, what else could happen?*

An odd shiver passed through her but she ignored it. She and Jonathan were going to live together. They were engaged. Except for Tyler Harrison's potential threat to the bordello, life was finally falling into place.

Her shoes were easy to find—they were the ugliest ones in the room. Flat sandals with two, functional straps. Her feet nearly wept in joy when she eased her toes into them. She spotted a plastic bag and quickly filled it with the clothes she'd worn to the ranch that morning. With any luck she and Jonathan could cut out of the party early.

"Are you running away from home again, Kristin?" a voice asked.

Andi looked up from the messy heap of clothes-strewn bed. "Hi, Auntie," she said, ignoring the mistaken identity. "I thought you were napping."

Ida Jane made a dismissing motion. "Only old women and babies nap. I was thinking."

"Oh. Of course. I should have known," Andi said, grinning. "Would you like me to escort you downstairs? You don't want to miss the party. All your friends are here."

Her aunt looked around as if just realizing where she was. "This isn't home. Where am I?"

Butterflies fluttered in her belly. "We're at the Rocking M, Auntie. For Jenny's wedding. Remember?"

Ida gave her a look of pure disbelief. "What are you talking about? Jenny's wedding was at the bordello. Everybody came. It was the biggest party the town ever saw. You were there."

Andi tried to swallow but her mouth felt full of cotton. "That was when she married Josh. But he died and—"

Before she could finish, Ida let out a high thin wail and started to weep. Andi rushed to her side and put her arm around her aunt's trembling shoulders. "Auntie, it was last summer. You remember, don't you? The babies came," she added, trying to distract her with something positive. "Little Tuck and Lara…"

Suddenly, her aunt moaned, then went limp. Andi struggled to keep her from collapsing on the floor. "Jenny," she cried. "Somebody, help."

Tears erupted from her eyes as she gently eased Ida to the carpet. All her years of first-aid training disappeared from her brain as she stared in horror at the only mother she'd ever known. *No, no, no, you can't die,* she repeated in silent litany. *Ida Jane, please. Don't leave me.*

Jonathan appeared at her side. Sam and Donnie followed. The three men operated like a well-trained team. Thanks to Sam's expert planning, both the paramedics and the fire department were on hand for the party, so within minutes Ida was on a gurney headed for the hospital.

"IT WAS A STROKE."

Jonathan wasn't certain how he'd been elected spokesperson, but in the three hours since Ida Jane's collapse, he'd become primary liaison between the hospital staff and the Sullivan triplets.

Sam had returned to the ranch where Donnie, Hank and Jim Rohr were holding the fort. Everyone had agreed that the party should go on—even if the principal players were elsewhere. Several of Ida's friends had been to the hospital to check on her condition and see if they could help.

Jonathan had been impressed by the way the town had rallied around one of its native daughters.

"The good news is they got her stabilized so fast and were able to administer a drug that helps mitigate the effects of a stroke. They're hopeful she'll be fine."

Andi looked at her sisters. "It was my fault. She was

confused and I tried to straighten her out—like usual...
What difference did it make if she thought you were mar-
rying Josh, not Sam?'' she asked, looking at Jenny. ''Why
do I always do that? I screwed everything up.''

Her sisters said all the right things, but Jonathan could
tell Andi wasn't buying any of them. She blamed herself
and she planned to torture herself for a bit longer.

His opinion was confirmed when he offered to take her
home an hour later. They were in the hospital cafeteria
where Jonathan had insisted she drink a glass of orange
juice.

Kristin had left to check on Zach. Jenny had returned to
the ranch to feed the twins.

''I'll stay,'' Andi said dully. ''It's the least I can do.''

''The nurse said Ida Jane is resting comfortably. There
isn't anything for you to do.''

She shrugged.

''Andi, love, this wasn't your fault. She's nearly eighty-
three. She has high blood pressure. It was an exciting morning. Any of those things could have triggered the stroke.''

''But it happened when she was with me. I'm bad luck,
Jonathan. I have a big mouth and I don't think before I
speak.'' She looked at him, her eyes full of tears. ''You
don't want to marry me.''

''Yes, I do.''

She went on as if he hadn't spoken. ''You can't move
into the bordello.''

''I already have.''

She blinked. ''What?''

''My bags were packed in the trunk of my car. I hadn't
planned to stay in the honeymoon suite without you, so I
asked a couple of the guys I used to work with to move
them to your place.''

''But—''

He covered her hand with his. "I'll go back to the motel if you really want me to, sweetheart, but not tonight. Please. I can't let you go home alone. And you can't stay here. You need me. And I need you. For tonight, anyway. Okay?"

She finally agreed, but Jonathan knew it was only because she was utterly exhausted. He took her home, helped her undress then crawled into bed beside her. It wasn't the way he'd planned to spend his first night at the bordello, but in a way, it helped him get his bearings.

As he lay in her soft bed, Jon thought about the woman he loved. In the shadows that moved across her ceiling, he saw his future. A life with Andi Sullivan as his mate would be as challenging as it would be wonderful. His thoughts turned to what he'd learned about his past. Like Andi, Jonathan Newhall had been a man of action. He'd moved forward with little contemplation of what consequences his actions might bring. According to his father, he'd accomplished a great deal, but what did he have to show for it?

Not a home. Like this wonderful structure was to the people it had given shelter to over the years.

No loving family of his own—although, thankfully, he'd made steps to establish a connection with his younger siblings. With any luck, he might soon be able to provide his sisters with a niece or nephew to visit in California.

But what else did he have? His father had informed him that he'd rented a climate-controlled storage unit in Missouri before leaving on his motorcycle trip. His history was there, and Jonathan finally admitted to himself—right before dawn—that he couldn't go forward until he went back.

He would have asked Andi to accompany him, but she was needed here.

Ida Jane would recover, but she'd require various kinds of therapy, the nurse had said.

Kristin had decided to return to Oregon until the end of the school year. But she'd made up her mind to move back to Gold Creek in June. "It's time to do the right thing," she'd told them as they sat in the waiting room. "Running away doesn't solve anything. It only puts off the inevitable." She'd turned to Andi. "Were you serious about refurbishing and renting out the basement of the bordello? I think it would make an excellent massage clinic."

Even the town needed Andi. If Tyler Harrison—and the company he owned—was intent on changing the face of Gold Creek, he'd have to get past Andi Sullivan first. Jonathan had seen the grim determination in her eyes when she'd vowed to rally the citizens against the outsiders.

Jonathan would help her cause as much as he could once he had his newspaper up and running, but he wouldn't operate the *Ledger* as a one-sided opinion paper. According to Andrew, Jon had a tradition to maintain. Journalistic integrity, his father had told him, was in the Newhall genes.

Yes, Jonathan decided, the big picture looked good. But before they could start building a life together, they each had something to resolve. Andi had to learn to forgive herself and accept that she couldn't run the entire show on her own.

And Jonathan had to leave.

"He's coming back."

Andi heard Jenny, but she didn't look up from the computer keyboard where she was entering inventory codes into the new program she'd installed. "I know."

"Ida Jane is doing great at the rehab center. She'll be back home in a couple of weeks."

Zero-dash-six four nine dash... "I know."

"That low-life drug dealer who killed Lars over the price of dope is being arraigned today.

"Isn't it fantastic the way Donnie kept tracking down every little lead until he nailed the guy? I wonder what would have happened if the stupid jerk had gotten around to washing Lars's hair and blood off the bumper of his truck before Donnie found it. I heard that he claims it was an accident. He said they fought, and Lars hit his head on the truck, but that doesn't excuse him for letting Jonathan take the rap for murder."

"I know."

Andi could hear Jenny moving around the antique store with her dust cloth.

"Kristin called this morning. She said Jim Rohr still hasn't heard anything from Tyler. What the heck is that about? I've been tempted to confront Gloria to see if she knows what kind of game her son is playing, but her column has been conspicuously missing from the *Ledger* the past three weeks. Do you think Jonathan got her fired before he left for Missouri?"

"I don't know."

Jenny made a low growling sound. "If you don't stop answering every question with 'I know' or 'I don't know,' I'm going to hit you."

Andi pressed Control-S to save her work then pushed back from the new computer desk in her fancy, ergonomic chair. The computer, desk and chair had been part of Jonathan's going away present to her.

"This will keep you out of trouble until I get back," he'd told her as he'd hooked up the printer on the second Wednesday after Jenny's wedding. It had taken him a week to secure permission for his trip from the judge, and then he'd stuck around a few days longer to make certain the electrician he'd hired completed the job of rewiring the old bordello.

He'd flat out refused to leave until the work was done

and the new fax and phone lines were installed. "I don't want to get back and find a burnt-out shell of a bordello," he'd said. "And I *will* be back. You know that, right?"

"I know," she'd answered, but at some level her heart was crumbling. Her head believed him. Her sisters believed him. Even Ida Jane believed him.

She'd spent ten days in the hospital and then moved back to the Anberry Rehabilitation Hospital where she'd recuperated after her hip injury. The rehab center was in Atwater, a town in the Central Valley some forty-five minutes away from Gold Creek.

Andi and Jenny took turns making the drive. Today was Friday—Andi's day to visit, but Kristin had called earlier to say that she, Zach and Sarge would stop to see Ida on their way home.

They were lucky. Ida seemed to be making remarkable progress, but Andi knew that some things had changed forever. Ida no longer read the large-print books Andi brought her from the library. She didn't work on crossword puzzles or play solitaire.

Jonathan had given her two simple handheld video games when he'd stopped to see her before his trip. She'd exclaimed over them, but to Andi's knowledge they'd never made it out of their boxes.

Ida had offered Jonathan some travel advice before he left, though. "Don't try to make it over Tioga Pass till June," she'd warned him.

Since that was two months off, Andi had nearly fainted.

"I plan to go the southern route," he'd replied, giving Andi a private wink—as if he'd been able to guess what she was thinking.

Of course, he was coming back, she told herself sternly. He owned a newspaper now. Or would in a few more days. His thirty-day escrow would be up tomorrow. And his gleaming maroon Hog—perfectly restored by a friend of Donnie's who Andi couldn't remember—had been delivered and was sitting in her driveway under a rainproof tarp.

Surely, an itinerant journalist would return for his bike, right? In case he got the urge to indulge in a little wanderlust.

Her sisters insisted she was being stupid. Borrowing trouble, Jenny called it when Andi had confessed her fear.

True, Jonathan called every day. At dawn. "Wake up, Princess Andi. We have a busy day today," he would tease.

But there'd been no call this morning. And Andi was worried. Jonathan had dropped out of sight once before. He'd crashed his bike and lost his memory. He'd taken a new name, met a woman named Andi and started a life wholly different from his old life. What if…

As the thread of panic built in her belly, she took a deep calming breath and looked at her sister, who still had a contentious glare on her face. "Take your best shot. But you'd better remember I'm a ex-marine."

Jenny made a huffing sound that told Andi she wasn't impressed. She tossed down her dust cloth and crossed the room. Except for the chatter coming from the adjacent coffee parlor, where Beulah Jensen was conducting a meeting of the Gold Creek Garden Club, the old bordello was empty.

Beulah had recently defeated Linda McCloskey for the club's presidency. Which had proved a boon for Andi, who had hired Linda on the spot to fill in when Andi was visiting Ida or working on inventory or arranging for a contractor to remodel the basement.

"I lug a pair of twins around every day of the week," Jenny said. "You want to see biceps. I'll show you biceps. But you'd better be prepared to put up yours, baby."

"This sounds interesting," a familiar voice said. "Can I watch?"

Andi's heart almost leaped out of her chest. "Jonathan," she cried just as her sister yelled, "Harley."

Jenny blushed fiercely. "You're back," she said. "I'm leaving." She picked up her purse and dashed for the door. As she passed him, she bestowed a peck on his cheek and in a stage whisper said, "Thank God you're back. She's been impossible to live with."

Andi's knees trembled so badly she had to sit down. Her handsome chair threatened to roll off its hard plastic floor protector, but before that could happen, Jonathan grabbed the molded armrests and pulled her to him. He leaned close enough that she could see the bloodshot condition of his eyes and smell the coffee on his breath. He looked exhausted.

"I missed you," he said.

His eyes may have been tired but his expression—and the depth of emotion in his voice—gave a different message.

"You came back," she said inanely.

"I told you I would. You believed me, didn't you?"

She nodded, her gaze dropping so he wouldn't see the lie. His pullover Henley was pearl gray and bore the logo of a sports team she didn't recognize; it was tucked into worn navy-blue sweatpants. His shoes were broken-in high-top basketball shoes. *Have I ever seen him wear tennies?*

She looked at his face again. He was Jonathan, but something was different. An unwelcome little fear took hold of her. She swallowed to get enough moisture in her mouth to speak. "Is it really you?"

He leaned closer and rested his forehead against hers. "Do you know anyone else who would get up at four in the morning and drive a rental truck straight through from Flagstaff, Arizona—towing a Mercedes, no less—just to get home to you?"

The words helped, but the kiss he gave her sealed the

deal. He was Jonathan. Or Harley. The name didn't matter. It was the man inside that counted.

He straightened and pulled her into his arms to kiss her properly. He tasted the same, too. Heat and sweetness. God, she'd missed him. She'd nearly lost her mind on the long nights since he left. Yes, she understood his reason for leaving. This might be the last chance for a very long time to return for the belongings he'd left in Missouri. Once he took over the paper, he'd have his hands full with a new challenge.

"Look who's back!" a high-pitched voice chortled.

Jonathan looked toward the coffee parlor. "Beulah?"

Andi nodded, grinning. "The Garden Club has contracted to meet here once a month now. And the weekly board meetings are held here, too."

Twelve faces peered at them. "Hi, ladies," Jonathan called, waving cheerfully.

"Is that your fancy car behind that U-Haul?" Mary Needham asked. "Looks like a drug dealer's car."

He made a deprecating gesture. "You're right. It does. But it's a memento from a past life," he said. "And I needed something to replace Rosemarie," he added. "Maybe you ladies could think of a name for it."

That got them talking. They disappeared back into the parlor.

Jonathan took Andi's hand and led her to the bay window, away from curious eyes but with a view of the sleek Mercedes with tinted windows. "I know it looks like a gangster car, and I thought about selling it. But an old buddy of mine, Oshi Kienda, told me that particular model rates very high in safety tests. Especially when a child's car seat is involved."

She looked at him speculatively. "Is that wishful thinking or do you know something I don't know?"

His face fell. "It was a month yesterday since we were at the mine. I guess I was hoping that you might have—"

Andi froze. Had it been a month? Really? She counted in her head, trying to visualize a calendar. Had she missed a period? Could it be possible?

Her jaw dropped open. "I've been a little under the weather the past week or so. I thought it was because you were gone."

He looked momentarily stunned then his expression turned wary. "Don't toy with me, Andi. I've been driving for days. I could snap, just like that." He demonstrated with his fingers.

She started to laugh, then she threw her arms around his neck and kissed him, hard and fast. "I don't know the answer, Jonathan. Life stopped for me when you left."

"Oh, baby," he said softly. "I'm sorry. I shouldn't have gone."

"Did you accomplish what you went for?"

Jonathan thought about her question for a good minute. Did I? He'd visited his mother's grave, but he hadn't been able to draw her image to mind. He'd visited the newspaper office where he'd spent so much of his childhood. Either the new owners had completely revamped the building or his right brain had created a false memory of how it had looked because the place seemed totally different. The experience had left him sad, and he'd returned to his hotel with a bad headache—the first in weeks.

"I guess you could say I did," he told her. "I went through a couple of the boxes as I was loading them into the van. A few of the photographs and CDs seemed to hold memories connected to my past, but mostly they're just possessions that don't mean a thing."

She looked concerned for him. "I'm sorry. You must be disappointed."

"Not really. Some of it—especially the furniture—looks expensive. I didn't want to spend time away from you, so I packed it up and brought it with me. We can go through everything here. Before we sell the more valuable things, I'd like to consult my dad in case they were gifts or belonged to my mother."

"Did anything ring a bell?"

"No, there wasn't a lot of bell ringing, but there was some door closing. I saw my former girlfriend while I was there. I thought she might explain why we broke up."

"What did she tell you?"

"Not much. She didn't have time for chitchat. She married a fellow attorney shortly after we split up. They're expecting their first child in July."

"Oh. Did you remember her?"

Jonathan shook his head. "No. Not even a glimmer." In all honesty, he couldn't imagine what had attracted him to Miranda in the first place. Although beautiful, she lacked Andi's fire and irreverent spirit.

"I'll need your help to go through the boxes."

She nodded seriously. "No problem. We have plenty of storage space upstairs, now that Ida's given me permission to inventory the antiques in the rear bedrooms. I've even sold a few pieces on eBay," she said proudly.

He hugged her again. "Fantastic."

Her success made her glow. "I think we'll actually show a profit this month."

"You're an awesome businesswoman." He kissed her cheekbone, then moved lower to her jaw. God, he'd missed her. He longed to take her upstairs, to kiss away the lingering sadness he read in her eyes. He wanted to make new memories that neither one would forget, but he sensed Andi holding back. Maybe there were still a few ghosts to chase away. "Can you come outside with me?"

"Now?" She consulted her watch. Functional, no nonsense. Like the tan cargo shorts and black, short-sleeve polo shirt she was wearing. Instead of sandals, she wore running shoes with low-cut socks.

"Are you still jogging—excuse me, *running* every day?"

Her cheeks turned pink. "No. Lately, I've been staying in bed so I wouldn't miss your call," she said, her tone indignant. "Except this morning. Why didn't you call?"

He nuzzled her neck until she made the little kitten sounds that drove him mad. "It was too early when I left, and when I stopped for lunch, the line was busy."

"I missed you, Jonathan," she said with feeling. "So much. I was okay during the day when I could keep busy, but at night…it felt like the bordello walls were closing in on me."

He lifted her left hand to his lips and kissed the engagement ring he'd given her. "Come with me."

She nodded, then called out, "Linda? Will you watch the store?" Andi smiled. "Linda's a lifesaver. I've hired her on a regular basis. She works four afternoons a week and fills in at both the antique shop and the coffee parlor as needed."

"Good," he said. Holding her hand as tight as he dared, he led the way to the porch. "Now you'll have time for the important things in life—like your husband." He looked at her as they descended the steps. "What made you decide to hire Linda?"

"Ida Jane. When we moved her to rehab, it was clear I couldn't be in two places at one time. I asked myself what was more important—a business or a great-aunt who may not be around forever."

Jonathan hugged her close. "Perspective is a wonderful tool. According to my photographer friend, Oshi, I used to be a workaholic who seldom slept, rarely ate and drove my co-workers crazy. He called me a droid."

He also said he never turned down a chance to do a story with me, because I was good. Damn good. Jonathan felt a little ache in his temple. He ignored it. He would be good again. As a publisher instead of a reporter.

As they stepped to the pavement he spotted a familiar shape lurking under a tarp. "Hey, I bet that's my bike. How's it look?"

"Fine."

Telling description. "Good. It ought to sell for top dollar."

"You're selling it?"

"Of course." He kissed her temple. "There's a chance you're carrying my baby. Do you think I'd let you ride with a guy who nearly killed himself the last time he drove it?"

She laughed, relief written clearly on her face. "Why'd you have it delivered here? The body shop guy said he could have sold it ten times before he was even done with the work."

"I wanted to see it."

"To say goodbye."

"No. Just to remind myself how lucky I am. If not for that bike, I might not have met you."

"You lost everything because of that bike," she argued.

"No, I gained everything because of it."

She still didn't look convinced. He had one last shot. As they neared the cab of the cargo van, a high-pitched whine made Andi pause. "What's that sound?" She leaned down to look under the chassis. "Loose belt?"

He dangled the key. "It's not running." He hurried to the driver's-side door and opened it. A good share of the seat sprang to life. Two pale blue eyes in a face of white fur blinked and a big pink tongue popped out.

"Jonathan," Andi shrieked. "You've got a puppy."

She sounded happy. She ran to greet the excited little animal.

"It's a boy. I couldn't find a female, like your old Daisy. I looked everywhere. He's one of the reasons I'm a few days late. I had to wait for his shots and whatnot."

"A puppy," she repeated, drawing the wiggling ball of fur into her arms.

"He probably needs a potty break," Jonathan warned. He reached into the side compartment in the door and pulled out a retractable leash, which he clipped to the pup's collar.

"What's his name?"

"Well, he doesn't actually respond to his name, so we could still change it. I've been calling him Harley."

Andi's sudden laugh made the dog turn in her arms and try to climb over her shoulder. Jonathan took him from her and set him on the ground.

Within seconds Harley had squatted and done his duty then ambled off to investigate the area. Andi hugged Jonathan fiercely. "Harley," she repeated in a dreamy voice. "I can't believe it. I thought you were afraid of dogs."

"Oh, please, a little guy like that?" He made a *pffing* sound. "I could take him, no problem."

She chuckled and brushed her lips along his jaw. "I think I'm ready to set a date."

His heart missed a beat. "Really? When?"

Her gaze went to the puppy, then returned. "I want to say tomorrow. The three of us. Tahoe. But," she said, with a sigh. "I'm on the planning committee for Ida Jane's party. We want to celebrate her coming home. Kris and Zach will be coming down from Oregon to help organize things."

She looked disappointed. "Don't worry, love. We'll find the right day for a wedding—or it will find us. Haven't you figured it out yet?"

He kissed the puzzled look from her forehead. ''You were destined to be mine, Andi Sullivan.''

Tears made her eyes a luminous green that reminded Jonathan of something he couldn't quite remember. But it wasn't important, because Andi loved him. She was going to marry him. Together, they'd build a life in Gold Creek— a small town filled with history but facing the challenge of a changing future.

Back when he'd been a successful reporter, Jonathan probably couldn't have envisioned this kind of happiness. He'd lacked the imagination. He'd lost himself—his heart and soul—long before the accident had wiped out his past.

Through Andi's love, he'd recovered his heart, if not his memory. And in the process of loving this very special woman, he'd found the man he was meant to be. A man who wasn't afraid to love. A man who knew the value of a dream.

*   *   *   *   *

Please turn the page for an excerpt from Kristen's story—THE COMEBACK GIRL. This stand-alone, emotionally compelling novel—the final title in Debra Salonen's family saga,

THOSE SULLIVAN SISTERS

—will be available next month.

CHAPTER ONE

"Is SOMETHING WRONG?" Kris tilted her head as she asked Donnie the question.

Yeah. Everything. "Nope. Everything's peachy."

Her lips flattened as if trying not to smile. "Me, too. If you overlook the guillotine hanging above my head."

For some reason, he was tempted to tell her about his dilemma. Maybe Kris could bring some new ideas about how he could have his cake and eat it, too. Plus, she was a single parent—

Before he could open his mouth, her ten-year-old son walked out of the kitchen. Donnie hadn't realized the boy was present. Suddenly grateful that he hadn't spilled his guts, he looked at Kris and said, "Do you have those cards and flyers? I should probably be getting home in case Lucas needs help with his math."

Kris walked directly to a small antique desk with curved legs and a matching chair upholstered in dusky gold silk. The upper part of the desk sported a row of cubbyholes along the back. He recalled seeing the desk in the triplets' study at the bordello. The room where he and Kris made love for the first time—on a bed of beanbag chairs.

He could still remember how nervous they'd been that Sunday afternoon when her aunt and sisters were at the movies in Oakhurst. He'd told his mother he was going fishing.

"Did you used to date my mom?" a youthful voice

asked. The tone held enough hostility that at first Donnie was afraid the boy had read his mind.

"Yes," Donnie answered.

Another question hung in the air. But Donnie knew Zach would never ask it. To do so would have left him too vulnerable. Exposed to ridicule and hurt.

"I was a year ahead of your mother in school. She was a cheerleader, and I played football. We went together for a couple of years. Right, Kris?"

She nodded, but looked too surprised to speak.

"Then I went off to college, and your mother discovered I wasn't the only fish in the sea." He tried to keep his tone light, but the look on Zach's handsome, troubled face made him feel like a jerk. The boy deserved the truth, but he wasn't sure how much Kristin had told him or wanted him to know.

"You broke up and she got together with my...dad?"

Donnie wasn't sure why Zach chose to include him in this discussion, but he nodded, and looked to Kris for guidance.

"Are you sure it's not *you?* That you didn't knock her up and for some reason she's not telling you?"

The question hit Donnie hard. *If only...*

"Zach," Kristin said sharply. "That's enough. I explained what happened and who your father is."

"Yeah, but you obviously slept around. You could be wrong," her son returned nastily.

Before either adult could respond, the boy shot from the room. The very walls of the house shook when he slammed his door.

Kristin looked stunned.

Donnie reacted without thinking. He walked to her and pulled her into his arms. A heartbeat later she burst into tears. Her arms linked behind him and she held on tight.

Donnie lowered his chin and breathed in the smell of her frothy curls. So sweet, so...

He opened his eyes, marshaling his thoughts. He knew better than to go down that road. He could surely comfort an old friend without losing his head.

Kristin seemed to regain her composure at the same moment. She stepped back and dug in the pocket of her sweatshirt for a tissue. "Thanks," she mumbled. "That was very nice of you. And generous. He's been acting out a lot lately, but that's the first time he attacked a stranger."

"It comes with the territory. I'm a cop."

She cocked her head thoughtfully. "You've grown into a really good man, haven't you?"

Her praise offered a comforting balm. It didn't take away his disappointment about the way things were working out with his dream job, but it helped. "I do okay—for a local yokel."

She blinked. "What's that mean?"

Donnie sighed. "Nothing. Sorry."

He turned to leave, but she stopped him. "Tell me. I cried on your shoulder, aren't you entitled to do the same?"

"No. Really. It's nothing. Once in a while I start sniveling about never making it out of this town. Just takes a good swift kick of reality to make me remember how good I've got it."

She picked up a small gray box that had gotten pushed behind a stack of magazines. "Here are my cards," she said. "Sounds like you're having second thoughts about your career, Donnie. I don't believe it. You've always wanted to be a deputy."

"I love my job, but there are times I feel as though I'm wasting my skills here. Not that I think I'm God's gift to law enforcement, but I wouldn't mind trying a few new avenues while I have the chance."

She opened the box and set the top on the counter. "So, why not put in for a transfer? I bet the CHP would jump at the chance to have an officer with your experience. Or the FBI."

She made it sound so simple. Without intending to, he blurted out, "Actually, I've been accepted into the Federal Air Marshal program. I still have to go through the training and pass the physical, but with my background that shouldn't be a problem."

She dropped the box and spun around. "Donnie," she exclaimed, her face alight with joy. "That's fantastic. Congratulations." She gave him a quick hug then blushed as if regretting her impulsive act.

His response—equally inappropriate—died the moment he recalled his ex-wife's news. "Yeah. The only problem is, I can't accept the offer."

"Why not?"

He snickered softly. "Because my ex is going to Africa and my mom has to help take care of her sister in Texas, which means there's no one to take care of Lucas." He couldn't prevent the bitterness he felt from seeping into his tone.

"Oh, Donnie, I'm so sorry."

He looked away. He didn't need sympathy. Or pity. He needed a housekeeper who could take over completely while he was away. Or, even, better—a wife.

HARLEQUIN *Super* ROMANCE®

*presents a compelling family drama—
an exciting new trilogy
by popular author Debra Salonen*

THOSE SULLIVAN SISTERS

**Jenny, Andrea and Kristin Sullivan are much more
than sisters—*they're triplets!* Growing up as one of
a threesome meant life was never lonely...or dull.**

**Now they're adults—with separate lives, loves,
dreams and secrets. But underneath everything that
keeps them apart is the bond that holds them together.**

MY HUSBAND, MY BABIES
(Jenny's story)
available December 2002

WITHOUT A PAST
(Andi's story)
available January 2003

THE COMEBACK GIRL
(Kristin's story)
available February 2003

HARLEQUIN®
Makes any time special ®

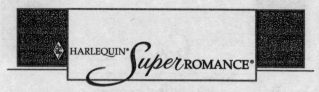

**Welcome to Koomera Crossing,
a town hidden deep in the Australian Outback.
Let renowned romance novelist Margaret Way take
you there. Let her introduce you to the people of
Koomera Crossing. Let her tell you their secrets....**

In **Sarah's Baby** meet Dr. Sarah Dempsey and
Kyall McQueen. And then there's the town's
matriarch, Ruth McQueen, who played a role
in Sarah's disappearance from her grandson
Kyall's life—and who now dreads Sarah's
return to Koomera Crossing.

Sarah's Baby is available in February
wherever Harlequin books are sold.
And watch for the next Koomera Crossing story,
coming from Harlequin Romance in October.

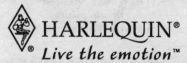

Visit us at www.eHarlequin.com

HARLEQUIN SUPERROMANCE®

If you enjoyed what you just read,
then we've got an offer you can't resist!

Take 2 bestselling love stories FREE!
Plus get a FREE surprise gift!

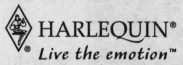